Motif for Murder

**Center Point
Large Print**

**This Large Print Book carries the
Seal of Approval of N.A.V.H.**

Motif for Murder

LAURA CHILDS

CENTER POINT PUBLISHING
THORNDIKE, MAINE

This Center Point Large Print edition
is published in the year 2007 by arrangement with
The Berkley Publishing Group, a division of
Penguin Group (USA) Inc.

Copyright © 2006 by Gerry Schmitt & Associates, Inc.

The text of this Large Print edition is unabridged. In other
aspects, this book may vary from the original edition. Printed in
Thailand. Set in 16-point Times New Roman type.

ISBN: 1-58547-888-1
ISBN 13: 978-1-58547-888-0

Library of Congress Cataloging-in-Publication Data

Childs, Laura.
    Motif for murder / Laura Childs.--Center Point large print ed.
        p. cm.
    ISBN-13: 978-1-58547-888-0 (lib. bdg. : alk. paper)
        1. Women detectives--Louisiana--New Orleans--Fiction. 2. New Orleans (La.)--Fiction.
    3. Separated people--Fiction. 4. Kidnapping victims--Fiction. 5. Scrapbooks--Fiction.
    6. Large type books. I. Title.

PS3603.H56M68 2007
813'.6--dc22

2006021248

*This book is dedicated to the people
of New Orleans and the surrounding Gulf Coast.
Courageous, indomitable, and resilient,
you are an inspiration to us all.*

1/07

Acknowledgments

Thank-yous go to agent Sam Pinkus, husband Bob, sister Jennie, and dogs Elmo and Madison. Many thanks to all the scrapbook magazines, scrapbook websites, scrapbook shops, and stamping stores for kindly promoting my books.

Chapter 1

MORNING sunlight peeked though heavy draperies as the man lying beside Carmela stirred gently. Easing one eye open, she gazed at the bare shoulder of her husband, Shamus Meechum.

Sunday, Carmela thought. *Lovely Sunday. My shop is closed, the bank is closed, and we have the whole day stretching ahead of us. How glorious.*

She planted gentle butterfly kisses on Shamus's shoulder and the back of his neck, then snuggled in close to him. And just as she felt herself melting in anticipation of Shamus's strong embrace, he stretched languidly and eased himself out of bed.

"You're getting up *now?*" Carmela asked, sounding more than a little disappointed. Her oval face tilted up at him, her blue-gray eyes, almost the exact shade of the Gulf of Mexico, stared at him curiously.

"Lots to do today, babe," Shamus replied in an up-and-at-'em tone. Wriggling into a nubby white cotton robe he'd pilfered from the San Francisco Four Seasons, he flashed his trademark boyish grin at Carmela. "But first I'm going to cook breakfast." Shamus glanced at himself in the mirror, seeming infinitely pleased with his pronouncement, as though he'd just announced that he intended to scale Mount Everest.

Carmela winced. On the rare occasions Shamus had ventured into the kitchen, he'd proved to be extremely messy. So the notion of wiping egg albumin off of every visible surface wasn't particularly appealing to her.

"Let me," offered Carmela, knowing they were perilously low on Mr. Clean. "You don't really—"

But Shamus held up a hand in a stern, statesmanlike grand gesture. "Please," he said. "Consider this my special treat. I want you to just lay here and relax. Really enjoy yourself." Moving swiftly across the bedroom, Shamus pulled open the honey-colored velvet draperies with a flourish, bringing a spill of sunlight into their elegant French Provincial bedroom and revealing the spectacular vista of their backyard.

Lulled by the idea of lounging in bed, Carmela gazed out at the magnolias and tumble of bougainvilleas. And a smile flickered across her face. She was finally back where she belonged, she decided. Back in her home in the lovely Garden District of New Orleans with her husband Shamus. They'd just gone through two rotten, miserable years where they'd been estranged from each other. When she'd pretty much given up any hope of reconnecting with him. But now the bad times were over. They'd weathered Hurricane Katrina, drawn strength from the volunteer work they'd done in the community, and now they were magically, wonderfully a couple again. Acting like giddy newlyweds. Whispering sweet endearments, giving each other tender kisses. All the arguments, recriminations, and terrible fights seemingly forgotten in the process.

"Cheese omelet, toasted brioche, and champagne

mimosas. How does that sound?" asked Shamus, coming out of the bathroom. He was tall, six feet two, with a sinewy body, lazy smile, and flashing brown eyes. Oh, and the accent. Softer and gentler than most, indicative of his upbringing in Baton Rouge.

"Your menu sounds delicious," said Carmela, luxuriating under the silk covers, deciding to just lie back and let her husband attempt his culinary masterpiece. And damn the mess.

"C'mere you critters," said Shamus. He leaned down and scooped up their two dogs, boosted them onto the bed. "Be sweet and keep your momma company," he told them as he headed downstairs.

"Hey Boo, hey Poobah," said Carmela as the dogs bounded toward her across mounds of covers. Boo was a girly-girl Shar-Pei, fawn-colored, generously wrinkled, with a curly teapot tail. She had a gazillion pedigrees and a sweet, demure manner. Poobah was a scruffy brown-and-white mutt with a partially ripped-off ear that Shamus had found on the streets of the French Quarter. They loved both dogs fiercely.

Carmela propped a pillow behind her back and sighed. She was hoping they could all spend time together today. Either lazing around here at home or taking a walk through the Garden District. It was mid-April, already warm, with the humidity starting to build. And their undauntable city of New Orleans was a virtual kaleidoscope of pink, purple, red, and butter-yellow blossoms and blooms.

Reaching to adjust Poobah's collar, which was for-

11

ever twisting off, Carmela paused. She'd heard something downstairs. Like maybe the refrigerator door slamming, then something being dropped.

Carmela gazed at Boo, the real watchdog of the two. Boo's tiny triangle ears had suddenly pitched forward.

"You heard it, too, didn't you, girl?"

Carmela listened again, feeling a twinge of worry. *That didn't sound good at all. In fact, it sounded like . . .*

Crash!

. . . breaking glass. Oh my.

Carmela grimaced, hoping against hope it wasn't the Baccarat crystal stemware. The Baccarat pieces had been a wedding present from one of Shamus's wealthy relatives. And at ninety-five bucks a pop per champagne flute, they were awfully pricey to replace. Her scrapbook shop, Memory Mine, was still humming along and proving to be fairly profitable. But not ninety-five-dollars-a-flute profitable.

"Shamus?" Carmela called out. She waited. Heard nothing. The dogs, however, were suddenly flying off the bed and racing down the staircase, yipping and barking their fool heads off every step of the way.

"Hey, guys," said Carmela, reluctantly crawling out of bed and pulling on her robe. "It's not that big a deal, okay? I'll come down and clean up."

In fact, Carmela decided, *maybe I better hustle my tush downstairs and take charge of breakfast. But in a nice way. No more power struggles between Shamus and me. From now on everything's going to be fifty-fifty. Very simpatico.*

Another loud *slam* convinced Carmela it was time to intercede.

What was that? she wondered. *The toaster exploding? The coffeemaker backfiring?*

Combing her fingers through her short blond hair, she gave it a quick pouf. A couple weeks ago, Shamus had put a metal pan filled with black beans in the microwave, set the timer for eight minutes, and darn near caused an explosion that rivaled a nuclear chain reaction. In fact, she'd been downright amazed at the firepower of beans.

"I'm coming," Carmela called out, wishing she really could have stayed in bed longer. That she and Shamus had stayed in bed *together.*

Out on the landing now, Carmela scurried across the whisper-soft Aubusson carpet, then padded down the winding staircase. This house she lived in, her house now, never failed to impress her. Gorgeous bordering on splendiferous, it boasted twenty-six rooms, parquet floors, hand-carved mahogany woodwork, and crystal chandeliers. Little ol' working-class Carmela Bertrand from Metairie was now living in absolute splendor in the heart of New Orleans's Garden District. And wasn't that just a kick in the ass?

Halfway down the staircase, a strangled, high-pitched scream rose from the kitchen, halting Carmela in her tracks. It was, she was fairly sure, the cry of a dog in pain.

Boo? Poobah? Somebody cut their paw?

Carmela flew down the rest of the stairs, her anxiety

easing slightly when a cacophony of barking started up again. But then the noise built into serious, get-away-from-my-house type barking.

What the . . . ?

Fingers of fear plucked at Carmela's heart as she ran the length of the dining room like an obstacle course. Dodging high-backed Chippendale chairs, she picked up traction on the silk carpet, flew around the wine cart with its four dozen bottles of Shamus's favorite vintage reserve Bordeaux and Burgundies, then spun around the buffet, coming too close and cracking her hip on a protruding corner. Without hesitating, Carmela plunged forward as the barking grew louder and more frenzied.

Pushing through the swinging door, Carmela raced into a kitchen that looked like a twister had cut a swath through it. Broken eggs and coffee grounds had spilled on a floor littered with shattered glasses and dishware. On the kitchen counter pans were over-turned and the knife rack tipped over, gleaming stain-less steel blades spilled everywhere.

Knives? What just happened here?

"Shamus?" Carmela called loudly, a little angrily, over the racket of the dogs. "Are you okay?"

Boo's furry muzzle was pulled into an unattractive, wolflike snarl. The hair on the back of Poobah's neck stood straight up, and his normally curly tail was extended out and down in a gesture of defiance.

"Shush," Carmela told both dogs, trying to soothe them. "Quiet down." Reluctantly, they complied as

Carmela bent down to reassure them.

The quiet of the house seemed to mock her. The *drip, drip* of milk from the overturned milk carton on the counter. The steady ticking of the dining room clock.

"Shamus," Carmela called out again, this time a little more tentatively. "You're scaring me."

Nothing.

And then, like a muffled shotgun burst, a *slam* echoed just beyond the back door.

Nerves on edge, pulse racing, Carmela leapt across shards of broken glass to pull open the back door. And there, backed up to her house, was a black car. A Cadillac Eldorado. Someone—and this was only a fleeting impression—had just slammed the trunk closed and was scrambling into the passenger seat. A man wearing a dark jacket, blue jeans, and a pair of dirty sneakers.

And as the car suddenly roared to life and lurched forward, spinning its wheels, tearing the hell out of their carefully manicured lawn, Carmela was absolutely certain she heard a faint pounding coming from inside the car's trunk! And an all-too-familiar voice shrieking her name in desperation!

"Shamus!" she screamed back, her voice piercing the Sunday morning quiet like the death knell of a dying animal. Then, like a runner in a footrace, Carmela launched herself after the car, bare feet pounding furiously across the turf, robe flying open. "Shamus!" she screamed again.

15

But the car had already bumped across the lawn and hit the narrow back alley. Then the Caddy lurched left, picked up speed, and disappeared from sight.

Putting a hand to her fluttering heart, even as her head spun in bewilderment, Carmela's knees began to wobble so badly she was forced to sit down hard on the still-wet grass. Seconds later, hot tears coursed down her cheeks.

"Kidnapped," she moaned. "I think my poor Shamus has just been kidnapped!"

And then, like a mantra suddenly turning itself over and over in her brain, Carmela whispered to herself, *It's because of the bank. Because of the bank. Because Shamus's family owns Crescent City Bank.*

Rousing herself to her feet, racing back into her house, Carmela dug frantically in the wicker hamper, searching for her gardening clothes. Those were the closest, the handiest. Carmela found a pair of khaki slacks and one of Shamus's shirts on a hook, shrugged into them, not worrying how she looked. Grabbing for the wall phone, Carmela punched in 911 as she pushed her feet into a pair of rubber thongs.

"Emergency operator," said a female voice on the other end of the line.

"My husband!" screamed Carmela. "Somebody took my husband! Kidnapped him, I think!"

"Calm down," said the operator. "Is he there with you now?"

"No!" screamed Carmela. "I just *told* you he wasn't! Send a squad car. Send *two* squad cars. Set up a road-

16

block around the Garden District. The car was . . ." Carmela fought for clarity "I think a black Cadillac. One of those, uh . . . an Eldorado."

"Did you get the license plate number?" asked the operator.

"No!" said Carmela. "I didn't get it!"

She pounded her fist against the wall. *Damn.* Shamus had told her something like this could happen, but she'd never in a million years believed him. In fact, she'd barely listened to him when he talked about what to do.

Carmela dropped the receiver, and it clunked against the wall as the operator continued to ask questions in her maddening, efficient manner.

He always said his uncle Henry or his sister, Glory Meechum, would be the most logical target, thought Carmela. She pondered this for a fleeting moment. *But instead they took Shamus.*

Carmela glanced about fearfully, suddenly wondering if the kidnappers might come back for her.

No, think about . . . think about . . . Uncle Henry! she suddenly decided. Uncle Henry lived just across the alley and then three houses down. He'd know what to do.

Carmela pounded back outside and across the backyard, the dogs following on her heels. She dodged a Chinese fan palm, jumped a small mimosa bush, ran through a freshly mulched rose bed, feeling herself sink in a good four or five inches. Then she was in the narrow cobblestone alley, heading toward Uncle

Henry's house, the dogs close at her heels as if this was all good sport.

"Uncle Henry!" Carmela called as she dashed up his back stairway, pulled open the screen door, and found herself in his spotless bachelor's kitchen. She paused, breathing hard.

"Uncle Henry?" she called again.

Carmela padded through the kitchen, into the hallway. The dogs, suddenly quiet, followed her, leaving little mulch-bed footprints. Glancing right into the cozy breakfast nook, Carmela saw only Eduardo, Uncle Henry's aging macaw, snoozing on his perch in the sun. She peered left into the large formal dining room. Twenty-two cushioned chairs stood like sentinels around his heroic oak table. No Uncle Henry there either. Fighting a rising feeling of panic, Carmela walked slowly down the center hallway as a half-dozen portraits of Meechum relatives stared down at her with trademark disapproval.

Carmela finally found Uncle Henry in his library. He was sprawled in his tufted leather chair, a leather-bound book clutched in one hand, and a bullet through his forehead.

Chapter 2

CARMELA reacted before she thought. She grabbed the book from Uncle Henry's hands, praying no blood had been shed on it. Not seeing any, she closed the book with a dull thud, startling herself in the quiet. Uncle Henry loved his books and treated them better than most people treated their children; in fact, they were his children. Room after room in his grand home had floor-to-ceiling shelves, displaying his priceless collection.

Carmela set the book atop a stack of books that rested on a small table a few feet away from the chair. Then she started to back away from Uncle Henry, afraid she might disturb the crime scene. *Stay back,* she warned herself. *Don't touch anything.*

But it was too late. Her stepping back acted as an invitation for Boo and Poobah to come forward and greet Uncle Henry. They bounded onto his lap in anticipation of an ear scratch, then suddenly hesitated as their paws touched him.

Instinctively, both dogs knew something was wrong, and their excitement died fast. Their bodies tensed, the muscles in their necks strained as they stretched their wet noses toward Uncle Henry. Nostrils flared with each inhalation as they smelled the mixture of blood and gunpowder. Silently, they dropped to the floor.

And Carmela watched in horror as the dog's actions caused Uncle Henry's body to tilt to one side. She reached forward, but stopped, worried that she and the dogs might have already destroyed important forensic evidence.

Uncle Henry's body continued to tip until his head rested against the side of the high-backed chair. A red streak now smeared the back cushion. Afraid this change of position would cause Uncle Henry to fall out of the chair completely, Carmela decided to try to gently sit him back upright.

Reaching out to grab him, Carmela noticed another book tucked in the space between the seat cushion and the chair. She grabbed that book, tossed it onto Uncle Henry's nearby desk. Then she guided his still-warm body back into its original position. But as she released him, Uncle Henry's body began to list in the other direction. Carmela's hands shot out to stop him, but gravity was working against her.

This can't be happening, she thought to herself. Then she stopped her meddling and crept away. "Got to call nine-one-one again," she said out loud. "And they're going to think I'm utterly crazy."

Backtracking into the kitchen, a terrible thought struck Carmela. *Maybe the killer is still inside this house!*

Which caused Carmela to race out the back door and summon the dogs to follow her. "Come on Boo, Poobah, we need to get back home." She jogged down the alley behind the houses, then paused in the center of her backyard garden, listening, her senses seemingly heightened.

Water trickled from the fountain, wind rustled the wisteria, and the sound of distant sirens filtered through lush vegetation. The assault of the flowers' colors and the various shades of green made her head spin. Overcome with fear for Shamus and grief for Uncle Henry, Carmela didn't know what to do. She felt as though she were spinning like a pinwheel, sparks flying everywhere.

"Definitely got to call nine-one-one again," Carmela told herself firmly as the dogs began to howl in tune with the sirens. The kitchen door stood open as she dashed in. Her feet crunched atop glass, and the toe of her thong kicked a knife, sending it skittering across the tiled floor. The phone still hung from the wall, beeping a constant drone. Pressing the hook down, the dial tone returned, and Carmela redialed 911.

"Nine-one-one emergency dispatch. What is the nature of your emergency?" The same woman's voice returned.

"I want to report a murder!" Carmela's voice carried a shrill tone that she absolutely hated, but panic had taken hold, and her respiration was becoming severely compromised.

"Ma'am," the operator warned, "you'd better calm down before you hyperventilate."

"I'm trying," Carmela managed to choke out. "But he's been shot!" She put a hand to her heart, felt it beating like a timpani drum.

"Who's been shot?" asked the operator. "Your husband? I thought you said he was abducted? Did they shoot him, as well?"

"No, no, now it's Uncle Henry," moaned Carmela. "Uncle Henry's been shot."

"And your husband . . . ?" The operator left the question hanging in the air.

"Still gone . . . abducted, as far as I know," said Carmela in a rapid-fire manner. "After I talked to you I ran over to Uncle Henry's house for help, and I found him shot!"

"Breathe, ma'am, breathe," instructed the operator. "Have the officers arrived on the scene yet?"

Carmela cocked her head toward the back door. The dogs were howling louder, and the sirens were definitely closer.

"I think they're almost here," Carmela told her.

"Very good," said the operator, trying to maintain her calm, efficient tone. "Please stay on the line until they get there. I certainly don't want you finding another body."

"That makes two of us," gasped Carmela.

"And I'm dispatching an ambulance to Uncle Henry's house. What is that address please?"

"It's . . . it's . . ." Carmela couldn't remember. "It's across the alley and three houses down."

"East or west of your home, ma'am?" asked the operator.

"East or west? Uh . . ." Carmela's mind was in a turmoil. All rational thought and knowledge seemed to have abandoned her. "Left," she stammered. "You have to turn left to get there."

"Okay, ma'am, I think I can figure that out."

"Hurry!" urged Carmela.

"I'm working on it, ma'am."

Rubber squealed and engines roared loudly in the back alley. "Thank goodness, the police are just arriving," cried Carmela as she started to hang up the phone.

On the way to the hook, the dispatcher's voice instructed her. "Please stay on the line until—"

But Carmela slammed the phone down and rushed out the back door.

"Boo. Poobah. Hush." She wanted to lock the dogs in the house, but with the mess on the floor, she was afraid they'd injure themselves. Besides, what if an important clue had been left in *this* struggle?

Two police cruisers careened to a stop in the alley, sirens blaring, blue and red roof rack lights pulsing like mad. The doors on the vehicles flew open, and three officers emerged, two men and one woman. Carmela hurried to meet them as the dogs continued their tirade.

"Shush," she waved her hands at Boo and Poobah. "They're here to help." Carmela ran a hand through her hair, trying to smooth her tangles, knowing she probably looked like a wild woman. Then she took a deep breath and said, "Thank goodness you're here."

Officer Henri Reynolds respectfully removed his sunglasses and cap. "You're the lady who called nine-one-one?" he asked. Manners oozed out of the Southern gentlemen like sweat on a hot summer day.

Carmela wasn't sure what to tell him first, but reason and logic won out. "My husband was kidnapped," she started. "Someone driving a black Eldorado. You know, a Cadillac." She stopped to snatch a breath, fought to hold back tears. "You need to hurry and catch them. They went that way!" Carmela pointed down the alley and paused when she saw the back of Uncle Henry's house. Decided she'd deal with that issue once everything had been done for Shamus first. Carmela swallowed hard. Uncle Henry could wait a little longer.

"How long ago did all of this happen?" the female officer asked from behind mirrored sunglasses. Her nose was pointed, and her small teeth worried her bottom lip. Her badge said T. Barker. She had pulled out a black spiral notebook and was making quick jottings.

"I think it was . . ." Carmela paused, trying to add up the time it took her to run to Uncle Henry's house and back, along with evidence tampering and moving items around in the crime scene. "About five, ten minutes," she said.

Officer Reynolds tried to take control, but Officer Barker wouldn't release her hold. "Did you see which way the car turned at the end of the block?"

"Uh, no—" Carmela started.

"Did you get the license plate?" Officer Barker continued.

"No, but—"

"Did you see *any* identifiable markings on the car at all? Dents, decals, whatever?" Barker turned to her partner, Officer Beltram. He looked like he'd just stepped out of high school. His pale complexion had an angry red rash where he had shaved. "At least she got the color of the car," said Barker. She pointed toward the front seat, and her young partner slid back in, started to hammer keys on the console computer. Barker turned back to Carmela, "Are you sure it was an Eldorado?"

Carmela was stunned. Wasn't this woman supposed to protect and serve? If she didn't know better, she'd think she was getting slapped. Now Carmela's mouth hung open as she looked from one face to the other. She blinked and said, "Don't you think you should set up some sort of roadblock or send out an all-points bulletin?"

"We're working on that, ma'am," said Officer Reynolds, shooting a frown at Barker.

Carmela continued to blink back hot tears. "Shamus was thrown into the trunk, so please don't shoot at the car," she begged them. "You could accidentally hit him." She felt tears beginning to pool in her eyes again but refused to let this rather brusque female officer trigger a tearful response. She knew she needed to keep her senses at the forefront right now, not her emotions.

There was a mumbled conversation between Barker and her partner, then she straightened up. "You're Mrs. Shamus Meechum?" Officer Barker's voice had suddenly changed from snappish to deep concern.

"Yes," said Carmela. "Shamus Allan Meechum is my husband."

"The Crescent City Bank Meechums?" asked Reynolds, studying her more intently now.

"That's right," said Carmela. "And this is our house." Carmela swung an arm wide as though she were displaying her home for a magazine photo shoot. "Someone broke in, smashed up the kitchen, and jammed my husband into the trunk of a car that is speeding farther and farther away as we stand here doing absolutely nothing."

"Don't worry ma'am, we know exactly what we're doing," snapped Officer Barker. Her newfound concern surprised Carmela as Barker gave a quick nod, then spun on her heel and jumped back in her squad car. "Officer Reynolds will take your report," she called out. "We'll canvass the neighborhood and radio this in immediately." She fastened her seat belt, and the car backed up, spinning its tires in the process. Then the cruiser sped down the alley and disappeared from sight.

"Ma'am," Officer Reynolds said as he moved closer to Carmela.

Boo and Poobah had been sitting at Carmela's feet during this strange interview but, with movement from the remaining policeman, started woofing again.

"That's okay; he's here to help us," Carmela told them, kneeling down to calm the dogs.

"I'm gonna go in now and take a look around," said Reynolds. "You say that the struggle took place in the kitchen?"

"Terrible struggle," said Carmela.

"You touch anything?" he asked.

"I used the phone and ran through the kitchen with the dogs," said Carmela. "But I didn't touch anything else. At least I *think* I didn't." *Of course, there's poor*

26

Uncle Henry over there that I still haven't told you about.

Donning purple latex gloves, the officer entered the house, Carmela tight on his heels. "I'm going to bring in the crime scene unit to fingerprint and photograph the entire scene," said Reynolds. "But, can you tell me, is anything out of place? Has anything gone missing?"

"You mean besides my husband?" Standing in the doorway, Carmela's eyes darted about the kitchen. The place was trashed. It was difficult to focus on what had been there and what might be missing.

"I've only recently moved back in, so I'm not sure," she mumbled.

"How do you know your husband was kidnapped?" asked Reynolds. "Was a ransom note left? Did you receive any phone—?"

But Officer Reynolds was cut short as Carmela's cell phone suddenly shrilled.

Carmela grabbed her cell phone off the counter and flipped it open. "Hello?" her voice cracked.

"Why, *cher,*" a woman's voice purred. "What ever are you doing answering the phone before noon on a Sunday? I thought you were reconciling with Shamus. You can't be reconciling if you're on the phone," scolded Ava Grieux. Ava was Carmela's best friend and proprietor of the Juju Voodoo Shop, a tiny shop in the French Quarter that specialized in candles, amulets, herbal charms, and other souvenirs. Tourists flocked to Ava's shop, always eager to experience the

27

"mystical" side of New Orleans.

"Ava!" Her friend's name exploded out of Carmela's mouth as all the emotions she'd been holding in check escaped. Tears rolled down her cheeks, tiny hiccups served as punctuation.

"What's wrong?" asked a suddenly concerned Ava. "Are you all right?" Anger seasoned Ava's next words. "If Shamus has hurt you, I'll find a voodoo priest to cast a spell on him so fast his skin will blister and things will start to drop off. He'll wish he never—"

"Ava, Ava, stop," begged Carmela. "Shamus has been kidnapped!"

Ava was incredulous. "What? What are you talking about?"

Carmela sniffed and wiped the back of her hand across her eyes and then under her nose. So much for being a Southern belle. She glanced back at Officer Reynolds, but he hadn't noticed her actions. Carmela turned her back to him and lowered her voice. "Shamus has been kidnapped. He was cooking break-fast for me when someone broke into the house. They grabbed him and threw him into the trunk of their car. And that's not even the worst of it! Poor Uncle Henry—"

"I'll be right over," promised Ava.

"Wait, Ava. Ava?" Carmela cried into the phone, but no one was there. She turned around to the police officer to tell him about Uncle Henry, and was startled to see Detective Edgar Babcock standing near the kitchen table. Tall and lanky with ginger-colored hair cropped short against his scalp, Babcock was attractive in a cop sort of way. He always seemed to dress extremely well, and today his dark blue linen blazer and khaki slacks were no exception.

Carmela watched as his intense blue eyes quickly took in the crime scene then landed on her.

"Hello," was all he said.

"Hi," she said back, her voice shaky. Carmela had met Edgar Babcock two years ago when she'd gotten peripherally involved in an art forgery case. She knew he was intelligent, cagey, and just a little bit sassy. At one time he had also had major hots for Ava.

Carmela wasn't surprised to see Edgar Babcock working the scene; she was just amazed at how quickly he'd arrived to step into his role.

"You said someone broke into your house?" Detective Babcock's voice was soothing, encouraging.

Carmela nodded. "I heard things crashing and glass breaking, so I thought—"

"You thought what? Better run downstairs to see what Shamus was breaking? What kind of a mess he was creating?"

"I didn't want to have to clean the kitchen after him, so I thought I would take over, but—"

"But—?" Babcock prompted her to speed the story along.

"When I ran into the kitchen, it was empty," said Carmela. "Of course, it was a disaster area, but—"

"Shamus wasn't here."

"Stop finishing my sentences," Carmela said.

"Then hurry this up," Babcock told her, not unkindly.

"I see you're as patient as always," said Carmela. Slightly rattled, she continued. "Anyway, I ran out the back door and saw a man slamming the trunk of an Eldorado. He jumped in and drove away, and then I heard Shamus yelling from inside."

"What did he yell?" Babcock asked her.

She stared straight at him. "Carmela," she said in a small voice. "He yelled out my name."

"That's all?" asked Babcock.

"What else was he supposed to yell?" snapped Carmela. "The Tulane Green Wave cheer?"

Detective Babcock continued to gaze at her mildly.

"Anyway," continued Carmela, her tone slightly more temperate now, "I barely heard him. The engine revved, and then the car peeled out."

"What did you do then?" pressed Babcock.

"Threw on some clothes and called nine-one-one." Carmela motioned to what she was wearing and pointed to the phone. "I tried to go get help, but—" She stopped as Babcock suddenly held up a hand and walked to the back door. He twisted the lever on the French door, then leaned down to examine the frame and doorknob.

"Doesn't look like it's been forced," said Babcock.

Officer Reynolds came over to look. "There's some pretty bad scratches," he pointed out. "Looks like someone might have put a pry bar to this door."

"Those are from the dogs," offered Carmela.

30

Edgar Babcock shrugged. "Maybe we'll be able to lift a few fingerprints." He punched in numbers on his cell phone, had a mumbled conversation. When he hung up, Babcock nodded to Reynolds. "Lab techs are on their way; make sure they dust here first."

"Absolutely," said Officer Reynolds.

Detective Babcock turned his attention back to Carmela once again. "I'm sure since Shamus worked at the bank and has a somewhat . . ." Babcock searched for the right word ". . . let's say *colorful* past, his fingerprints are probably on file. Do you know if yours are?"

Carmela thought hard, but before she could answer, the dogs started barking excitedly. She peered into the backyard for the cause of the commotion.

Ava. Her friend was strutting purposefully across the yard while Boo and Poobah pranced around her, happily begging for attention.

"My lord," said Babcock, exhaling.

Carmela glanced at the detective, slightly peeved that his hard-edged focus had crumbled so quickly. Obviously, the man was still slightly smitten.

Ava, as usual, was a vision to behold. This fine morning Ava was wearing formfitting white Capri pants, a hot-pink shirt tied at the waist, classic black sunglasses, and high-heeled stiletto sandals. Her rich brown hair, pulled back with a white headband, flowed enticingly behind her. She looked like a Hitchcock heroine who'd just stepped off a movie set.

"Stay down, little darlings," Ava chirped to the dogs. "I love you, too, but your mama needs me more." A wicker picnic basket dangled from one arm and appeared to throw Ava off balance as she wove around Boo and Poobah.

"I can't believe she can walk in those high heels and carry something that cumbersome," said Babcock as they stepped outside to meet her and he watched the beauty queen hobble toward them.

"Detective Babcock, here so soon and dressed to kill," drawled Ava as she tipped her sunglasses up and fixed luminous brown eyes on Edgar Babcock.

At the word *kill,* Carmela flinched. *I still need to tell them about Uncle Henry. But everyone keeps inter-rupting me and—*

"My poor *cher,* how are you holding up?" asked Ava as she put an arm around Carmela and hugged her tightly. "I knew you wouldn't have any necessities, so I grabbed a couple cups of café au lait and some blue-berry muffins." She stared deadpan at Babcock. "There might be enough for you, too, if you're lucky."

"Ava—" began Carmela.

But Ava held up a hand. "Now before you say a single word, *cher,* I need to ask you something very important. Are you absolutely *positive* Shamus was kidnapped? Because the unmitigated louse did run out on you once before."

"He was, Ava," said Carmela. "There was a terrible commotion. And poor Uncle—"

A bloodcurdling scream suddenly echoed from

down the alley. Followed by a second more drawn-out scream.

Ava's eyes went wide. "Good heavens," she exclaimed. "Could someone around here be slaughtering a pig?"

"Shamus! Murder! Shamus! Murder!" came a harpy's unearthly shriek.

The back door smacked open as Officer Reynolds came rushing out of the house to see what the commotion was all about. "You okay, Mrs. Meechum?" he called to Carmela.

Carmela made a wry face. "Not really. In fact, I'm afraid the situation just went from bad to worse. That woman you see barreling toward us is Glory Meechum, Shamus's sister. And I'm pretty sure she just discovered what I haven't been able to tell you about yet."

Chapter 3

YOU'RE just telling me *now?*" screamed Edgar Babcock. "How can you *forget* to tell the police there's a dead body over here!" He shook his head, pointed randomly toward the alley, and watched in horror as a very large woman in a splotchy, floral print dress attempted to run and scream her head off at the same time.

Glory Meechum gasped for breath between each word and after every step. "Shamus! *Clump clump.*

Help me! *Clump clump.* Murrrrderrrr!" The silk hand-kerchief Glory clutched in her hand flapped wildly as her chunky arms pumped. If she could move her feet as fast as she thrashed her arms about, she probably could have run a marathon. Or at least qualified in time trials.

"I've been *trying* to tell you about Uncle Henry," said Carmela to a sputtering Babcock. "Now Glory's found his body and is freaking out completely. And she's going to come even more unglued when she finds out Shamus is missing!" Carmela took two steps back. "I'm also not going to be the one to tell her about Shamus. Glory absolutely despises me. In fact, she'll probably blame *me* for her brother's disappearance." Carmela brushed at her eyes as tears leaked out.

"She thinks Shamus is here?" Babcock pulled latex gloves off his hands with a loud *snap.* "She doesn't know yet?"

"Of course not," said Carmela. "I've only had time to call nine-one-one. Twice. Nobody else. And visit with you," she added sarcastically.

Ava viewed the matter in a more practical manner. "*Cher,* you might want to get behind the detective for protection," she told Carmela as they watched Glory lumber toward them. "I'm not too confident in her stopping power." Ava's slender body was a perfect hourglass. Glory looked like a Pyrex baking dish, round and deep.

Boo and Poobah, excited by Glory's ungodly screams, raced forward to meet her as she crossed the yard. Barking and nipping at her heels, the dogs reveled in their newfound sport.

Which gave Glory another reason to freak out. "They're attacking me!" she shrieked.

"They remember you," Ava muttered under her breath.

"This isn't the best time to let loose that wicked humor of yours," Carmela warned Ava. Though she tried to avoid Glory as much as possible, Carmela knew she'd probably need the woman's support. And maybe her money.

Careening across the grass, Glory crashed smack-dab into Detective Babcock's outstretched arms. Glory hit so hard she rocked Babcock back on his heels and set his teeth to chattering as she continued to cry and wave her arms about. But he had at least succeeded in keeping her from rushing into the house.

Between blubbery, gasping breaths, Glory turned hard eyes on Carmela and screamed, "I hope your dogs had their rabies shots! One bit me on the ankle."

"Like she could actually feel anything through all that padding," Ava muttered.

Babcock put his hands on Glory's shoulders and shook her firmly, trying to bring her to her senses. "Calm down. Catch your breath." He kept his commands short and to the point.

"But I have to see Shamus." Glory's ample bosom heaved, and her breath hissed like a steam engine. "Uncle Henry's been shot! Murdered! Call an ambulance! Call nine-one-one! Call out the National

Guard!" She took another deep breath, fighting to gain some slight composure, and glared at Carmela. "Carmela, don't just stand there like a ninny. *Do something!*"

"I've already called nine-one-one," Carmela said simply, trying not to contribute to Glory's amped-up anxiety.

"Then why are you over *here?*" Glory turned her thick neck and faced Babcock. Her gaze switched to Officer Reynolds. "Shouldn't you people be over *there?*" She started to point toward Uncle Henry's house, then stopped, suspicion suddenly crawling across her doughy face. "Where's Shamus?" she asked sharply. Glory's eyes drilled into Carmela. "What did you do to him?"

"I didn't do anything," Carmela said, looking distraught. Suddenly, the thought of Shamus bouncing around in the dark in someone's car trunk was too much to bear.

Glory batted her chubby arms at Detective Babcock. "Unhand me this minute," she ordered. "I have to find Shamus. Get out of my way." She gave him another smack.

"Ma'am," Babcock told her firmly, "I can't let you enter this crime scene."

"But the crime scene is . . .." Glory motioned toward Uncle Henry's house . . . "over there." She swung her head back toward Shamus's house. "You're telling me this is . . . too?"

Carmela nodded.

Glory's eyes took on the feverish glow of a wonked-out pinball machine, then they rolled slowly back into her head as she started to collapse.

Babcock and Reynolds had a difficult time handling her dead weight as they lowered her to the sidewalk.

"She must have thought Shamus was shot, too," said Carmela.

Ava stepped closer to Glory. She made a halfhearted attempt to fan her, then gave a slight shrug. "Or maybe Glory was worried about bloodstains on the carpets."

Carmela stared at the unconscious woman. She almost felt sorry for Glory. The operative word being *almost*.

Another siren split the air, then its shrill shriek changed to a slow *whoop whoop*. It was the ambulance pulling up in front of Uncle Henry's house.

"You two take care of her," Babcock pointed to Officer Reynolds and Ava, until I send the ambulance guys over. "And you . . ." he stared at Carmela . . . "are coming with me."

"Sure," said Carmela. "Okay."

"You didn't touch anything over there, did you?" asked Babcock as they set off across the back lawn.

Carmela chose not to answer.

CARMELA AND DETECTIVE EDGAR BABCOCK STOOD in the darkened library, staring at Uncle Henry. The two EMTs from the ambulance stood behind them at a respectful, ten-foot distance.

"This is exactly how you found him?" asked Babcock. Carmela winced. "Not . . . exactly."

"What?" said Babcock. Then louder, "What?"

"He wasn't quite as slumped as he is now," said Carmela. "And he was holding a book."

"You took it out of his hands?" asked Babcock.

Carmela made a motion toward the side table. "I set it on the table over there."

"And why did you do that?" asked Babcock.

Why did I? wondered Carmela. *Probably because I was in shock, I wasn't thinking straight.* "I suppose because I didn't want any blood to get on it," she told Detective Babcock. "I thought it might be a valuable book and important to him."

"And what else did you do?" prompted Babcock. "I know you did something else. I can feel it."

With this comment, Carmela grimaced. "I sort of moved him," Carmela admitted. "Gently, of course."

"You moved him," repeated Babcock. "Why?" He held up a hand. "This is going to be good, isn't it?"

"Well, first Boo and Poobah jumped into Uncle Henry's lap," began Carmela.

"The dogs?" gasped Babcock, rolling his eyes. "Oh, Lord."

"They were so happy to see Uncle Henry, but as soon as they touched him, they somehow . . . uh . . . knew he was . . . uh . . . ." Her throat felt suddenly dry and constricted. "I tried to stop them, but they . . . um . . . sort of knocked Uncle Henry off balance."

Babcock closed his eyes and shook his head.

"Uncle Henry would have toppled out of the chair if I hadn't stopped him," explained Carmela. "He tilted one way and then I overcompensated and he went the other way." She knew it sounded lame, but it was the honest truth.

"So you tampered with the crime scene," said Babcock. It was a statement, not a question.

"Not on purpose," said Carmela. "I just didn't want him to fall and . . . um . . . hurt himself." She was sure she heard a faint snicker from one of the EMTs behind her.

"You didn't want a dead man to hurt himself," said Babcock. "Okay, now I've heard everything." He pulled out his cell phone, punched in a number. "Now I gotta get a *second* crime scene unit out here," he told Carmela. "And you guys . . ." he gestured to the EMTs . . . "you go across the alley and make yourselves useful. There's a woman who fainted over there. Help her. Give her some oxygen or some smelling salts or whatever it is you people do."

As the EMTs took off, Babcock focused his intensity on Carmela again. "Who else has access to this house?" he asked.

Carmela bit at her lip. "Glory, me, Shamus. And Mrs. Jardell, the housekeeper," Carmela told him.

Babcock looked around. The house was obviously empty. "Where is she?" he asked.

"Don't know," said Carmela. "Day off?"

"Listen carefully," said Detective Babcock. "I want you to go back to your house and wait for me. Don't do anything, don't touch anything, don't make any calls, okay?"

Carmela nodded. "No calls. They're probably going to ban me from ever calling nine-one-one again anyway." She hesitated. "But what about Shamus? Shouldn't he come first? I mean . . . he's . . . um . . . he's still alive." *Lord, I pray he is.*

"You're positive your husband was kidnapped?" asked Babcock.

Carmela nodded. "Yes, of course."

"Because your friend said—"

"I know she did," said Carmela. "But that was different. Shamus left because the two of us had problems. This time someone took him against his will. For real."

Babcock nodded, trying to juggle everything. "Okay, okay, I'm on that, too, okay?"

Carmela fought back tears. "Okay."

WITH A HEAVY HEART, CARMELA RETRACED HER steps across the alley and into her backyard. Officer Reynolds was nowhere to be seen, but Ava was sitting in a lawn chair, chatting with the ambulance techs and halfheartedly fanning Glory, who was still stretched out cold on the sidewalk. An oxygen mask had been clamped over Glory's face, a blanket placed under her head. Like miniature sphinxes, Boo and Poobah sat on either side of her, keeping watch.

"She okay?" asked Carmela.

Ava nodded. "Bobby here listened to her heart and

40

pronounced her strong as an ox."

Bobby, who could barely take his eyes off Ava, bobbed his head in agreement. "She'll probably come to in another minute or so. Sucking a few O's will really help."

"Glory's been making little snorts and grunts, so I'm sure she's almost back to normal," said Ava.

Carmela wiggled her fingers at Ava, indicating she wanted her friend to join her over by the rose arbor. They strolled over together, Carmela looking serious and a little defeated.

"Detective Babcock thinks I had something to do with Uncle Henry's death," Carmela told Ava.

Ava raised her sunglasses to the crown of her head, then her carefully waxed brows formed an arch over flashing eyes. "Of course he doesn't think that, darlin'. He knows you just ran over there to get help." Ava put a hand to Carmela's cheek and touched it gently. "After everything that's happened this morning, I can't believe you're not passed out on the sidewalk like Glory. I know I would be."

"Oh, Ava, what am I going to do about Shamus?" asked Carmela. "Some wackos kidnapped him right out of our house . . . and who knows what they're going to do with him!"

"I know that, honey, but the police are johnny on this case," said Ava. "Heck, I bet there's a chance that old boy will be home in time for supper tonight."

"I don't know," worried Carmela. "They shot Uncle Henry . . ."

"We can't think about that now," said Ava hurriedly. "We have to have positive thoughts about Shamus. I know I've never been completely positive about him before, but this time I'm really going to try."

"If there's a ransom demand," continued Carmela, "I don't have any money." She shrugged. "The scrapbook store is operating in the black, of course, but I'm far from well-off. New businesses take time to get established—"

"Hush," said Ava. "These kidnappers aren't *stupid*. Since they took Shamus they must know his *family* is rich." She looked around. "You live in the Garden District, people assume you're rich."

"Money isn't everything," said Carmela.

"It isn't to people like us, the ones who never really had any," said Ava. "But once you have it, you hang on tight. Like Glory over there." Ava stopped suddenly and gazed at the house. "Can you hear the phone from out here?"

"Why do you—? Oh." A terrified look came across Carmela's face. "You mean what if someone actually *calls* with a ransom demand?" Carmela put a hand to her heart again. It was a horrifying thought. But it could happen. In fact, the more she let her mind get accustomed to the idea, the more she hoped it *would* happen. Then she'd at least have an inkling of what she was up against. "Maybe I should get the cordless phone from Shamus's study," said Carmela. She glanced around helplessly. "I seem to have lost my cell phone."

Ava reached into her purse and pulled out her cell phone. "Here, call the house and see if we can hear it ring. That way you'll know."

Carmela took the phone tentatively. She quickly pressed the number in. The cell phone beeped and nothing happened for a second. Then the cell phone started to ring in her ear. Both women leaned toward the house, straining to hear the phone. Nothing.

"What the hell just happened here?" demanded an angry voice.

Startled, both women jumped.

Glory had pulled herself to a sitting position and was staring at them, looking for all the world like an angry Easter Island statue.

"Feeling better?" asked one of the ambulance crew. He struggled to put a blood pressure cuff around Glory's arm, but she batted him away.

Carmela walked over to Glory and knelt down beside her. "Are you okay?"

"Who hit me?" demanded Glory. She tugged at the floral-patterned dress that had ridden up above her pudgy knees and tried to smooth it down.

"You fainted," said Ava cheerfully.

"Wha . . . ?" said Glory, wiping her hands together and glaring at everyone around her. The two ambulance guys moved off to a safe distance. Their patient was fine. Better than fine.

"Fainted?" repeated Glory as though she was testing out a new language.

"Right after you found Uncle Henry," prompted

Carmela. She'd decided the best thing to do was be completely straight with Glory.

But Glory's angry expression crumpled upon hearing Carmela's words. "Uncle Henry," she whispered. "Dead." Her eyes widened, and she gazed up at Carmela. "And Shamus . . . ?"

Carmela bit her lower lip. "Kidnapped," she finally said.

That seemed to touch a nerve. Glory's confused face once again clouded over with anger. "That's ridiculous," she snapped. "Who would want to kidnap Shamus?"

"Kidnappers," said Ava disdainfully. "Duh."

Glory struggled to her feet with a succession of deep grunts, swatting away Carmela and Ava's hands as they reached out to help her. "So what else haven't you told me?" she demanded. "Is the house in shambles? Will our family be on the evening news?" Glory narrowed her eyes and ground her teeth together. "Oh, the shame." She brought the back of her hand to her forehead and appeared ready to faint again. But this time neither Carmela, Ava, nor the emergency techs moved in to help her. All were afraid of being swatted at again.

"Can I get you a glass of cold water?" asked Carmela, forcing a look of concern on her face. "Cool washcloth for your brow?" *A baseball bat to knock you out again?*

"Feeling better?" asked Detective Babcock, as he strode up behind them.

44

Everyone turned toward him as he walked up. Even Boo and Poobah, who seemed to be enjoying this dramatic scene immensely.

"The crime scene guys are over there now," Babcock told the EMTs. "Then you can go in and do your thing." They moved off as Glory continued her rumblings.

"Are you in charge here?" Glory demanded.

Babcock glanced at Carmela. "I suppose you could call it that."

"I want immediate action," said Glory. "If this is, in fact, a legitimate kidnapping, it happened because the Meechums are a prominent Louisiana banking family. So we need to contact the governor, the state police, and the state banking board."

"I just got off the phone with the state police," said Babcock. "They're already working with us. We'll run prints against what's in our local database as well as AFIS. If we get a hit, we'll cross-check with DMV on Eldorados." He glanced at the torn-up lawn. "And we'll get photos of those tire treads, too."

"Thank you," breathed Carmela. Finally, some forward progress concerning Shamus's disappearance.

Glory continued to tick off her list. "I'll need to call my attorney and my board of directors. And I don't want a single word of Shamus's disappearance leaked to anyone, especially the press. We have business deals pending that could be adversely affected."

Carmela was shocked. "You don't want to put this on the news?" she asked. "Don't we *want* help from the public? Don't we *need* help?"

Glory suddenly whirled in Carmela's direction. "I think you've done enough," she thundered. "Shamus left you once before, and I wouldn't blame him for doing it a second time."

"Now just a minute," said Babcock. "This is a legitimate—"

But Glory was out for bear. "In fact, Carmela, I want you out of here . . . off the property! I'll give you five minutes to pack your bags and leave."

"What?" said Carmela, shocked. "You're kicking me out?" Glory's words hit her like a punch in the stomach. How much could she take? First Shamus, then Uncle Henry, now this. "You can't be serious," stammered Carmela. "I live here—"

"This is *my* house," thundered Glory. "Shamus is my brother, and Uncle Henry is—"

"Your uncle," finished Ava. "I think you made your point. You own it all. Big freaking whoop."

"You think this is funny?" asked Glory, a hard mask settling across her broad face. She lowered her head like a bull about to charge and dropped her voice to a menacing tone. "You're nothing but a trollop, Ava Grieux. And Carmela is and always will be a disgrace to my family. Carmela, you now have *four* minutes to pack your bags and get out. And be sure to take those mangy animals with you!"

Chapter 4

F AMILY, don't ya just love 'em," said Ava, as she slammed the trunk on her little blue Honda. "Well, thank goodness we have two cars to schlep all your stuff."

"Too bad one of them isn't a minivan," answered Carmela. Her car wasn't much bigger than Ava's. A Mercedes convertible that Shamus had bought for her a while back. Everything she thought she'd need or want, including two squirming dogs, was squeezed in tight. "Oh man," worried Carmela, "if I so much as hit a pothole, everything's going to come popping out like a jack-in-the-box."

Under the watchful eye of Detective Babcock, Carmela and Ava had run upstairs and scooped up as much of Carmela's clothes and cosmetics as they could carry. He had been helpful and sympathetic, even suggesting that Carmela would probably be safer back in her old apartment in the French Quarter. It was located in a courtyard with limited access and across from Ava's voodoo shop.

That her old apartment hadn't been rented yet, hadn't even been completely *emptied out,* seemed like an ominous portent to Carmela. As though the last few months with Shamus had been some sort of wild dream, and now it had all come crashing to a halt.

Babcock had also assured Carmela that her main phone number, the one listed in the directory, would be rolled to her apartment as well as to her cell phone, and that the police would be monitoring each and every call.

It was far from a perfect situation, Carmela decided, but it was the best they could manage for now. And since Glory controlled all the money in the family, Carmela knew she'd have to work with her, such as it was.

"Okay," said Ava, taking a final inventory. "We've got clothes, hair dryer, hot rollers, makeup, dogs, dog beds, dog toys, and canisters of dog food. All we need now is a little old lady to throw on the roof, and we'll look like the Joad family in *Grapes of Wrath*."

"We've got Glory's wrath," said Carmela.

"You got that right," replied Ava.

"Oh rats," said Carmela, frowning and putting a hand to her mouth. "I just remembered Eduardo."

"Who the hell is Eduardo?" asked Ava. "Please tell me you didn't pick up *another* stray dog."

"He's Uncle Henry's parrot," explained Carmela. "Who knows what'll happen to him if I just leave him." She shook her head. "I don't think Glory's gonna step in and take care of him. And Uncle Henry loved that grizzled old bird."

They pulled their cars around the block and parked in front of Uncle Henry's house. With two police cruisers pulled halfway up on the lawn, and the crime scene van there, too, a good-sized group of gawkers had gathered. As Carmela and Ava walked up the front sidewalk, a TV van with a satellite dish on its roof eased down the normally quiet, tree-lined street.

"This is developing into quite a spectacle," said Ava.

"At least *this* crime will make the news," said Carmela, as she knocked on the door.

One of the crime scene guys came to the door but kept the screen closed. "Go away," he told them brusquely. "Crime scene."

"You gotta let us in," said Ava.

"What?" he asked. "Are you relatives or something? Neighbors?" His shadow moved behind the screen door and a tangled web of black-and-yellow crime scene tape.

"Relative," Carmela told him. "Henry Meechum is . . . was . . . my husband's uncle."

The screen door swung open to reveal a tall, dark-haired man in a navy-and-white nylon police jacket with the name Diego embroidered over the front pocket. "Sorry for your trouble ma'am," he said. "But I can't let you in."

"She came for the bird," explained Ava. Lounging in the doorway, Ava rotated a shoulder and let a warm smile spread across her intriguing face. "Eduardo."

"Oh, him," said Diego, his soft brown eyes suddenly glued to Ava's every move.

"The bird's still here?" asked Carmela.

"Yup. Thought I was going to have to call animal welfare to come get him. I guess it's lucky you ladies showed up after all."

"So I can come in?" asked Carmela.

"Yes," said Diego. "But only you, and you must be very careful."

49

"I'll wait here," said Ava.

"I'll wait with you," said Diego.

"YOU GOT YOUR CELL PHONE WITH YOU?" ASKED Ava, enviously eyeing Carmela's blue Marc Jacobs handbag.

Carmela dropped a load of clothes on the bed in her apartment and dug in her bag. She had finally located the little silver phone. "Camera phone," she said, holding it up. It was the last thing Shamus had given her. He loved techy little items and had been delighted that she liked the iPod he gave her for her birthday. So the camera phone had come next.

Ava grabbed a poufy silk pillow off the chaise lounge and flapped it in the air. "Everything's so dusty in here," she remarked. "And a little musty, too," she added, sniffing the air.

"Nobody's been in here for a couple months," said Carmela. "Not since we aired the place out after the hurricane and then used it as 'photo central.'"

In the weeks following Hurricane Katrina, many of Carmela's customers had been left with envelopes and albums filled with water-damaged photos. And once some order had been restored in New Orleans, they had descended upon Carmela, asking for her advice and help. Knowing that photos are memories, and memories are truly precious, Carmela immediately converted her old apartment to a place where they could dry out and salvage as much as possible of her customers' waterlogged photos.

Dropping an armload of clothes, Carmela glanced around her old apartment. It felt funny to be back but oddly comforting, too. This was the place where she'd won her independence after Shamus had walked out of their marriage. This was where she'd regained her strength, her self-reliance, and her fortitude.

When she and Shamus had finally made peace with each other, she'd brought those traits back to their marriage. So their relationship of late had been a lot more balanced, a lot more give-and-take. But now . . .

Carmela bit her lip as tears prickled her eyes.

"They'll find him, honey, don't you worry," Ava assured Carmela upon seeing that her friend was in distress again. "Whoever snatched Shamus doesn't really want *him*, they want his family's money. Try to look at this whole thing as a dangerous, very bizarre business deal."

"You think so?" asked Carmela.

"Of course," said Ava. "You'll get a phone call tonight, mark my words. Then Glory will crab about putting up the money, but she'll eventually do it. And this whole nightmare scenario will come to an end. Except for the part about Glory, of course. That old bag will still be around . . ."

"And I'll be indebted to her forever," said Carmela.

"Shit happens," said Ava. "Especially in New Orleans." She pursed her lips, blew out, and stared at the cage containing the parrot. He was sitting on his perch, looking sleepy again. "You sure you want to take care of this little guy?" she asked. "He jabbered in my ear the whole way over here. Reminds me of my aunt Laureena. Kind of a crazy old gal, ran a little café where she served the best peach pie in the whole world. 'Course, Aunt Laureena never did get married." Ava paused again. "Hope *that* doesn't run in the family."

"You know, Ava," said Carmela, "I can finish up here. You've given up most of your Sunday for me already."

"No problem, *cher*. That's what friends are for. Besides, I want to help."

"Don't you have a date tonight?" asked Carmela.

"I wouldn't feel right going out tonight when you're worried sick about Shamus—" began Ava.

"I think that's exactly what you should do," said Carmela. "Besides, I've got to walk the dogs, run to Riley's and get groceries, and finish hanging up my clothes."

"You're sure you don't mind?" asked Ava.

"Not at all," said Carmela. "Besides, I think I'm still in a state of shock, and I need a little alone time to process things."

Ava nodded. "Run everything through the old microprocessor. Okay, but I'll be home early. When you see my light pop on, be sure to call, okay? Even if it's just to say hi."

"Count on it," said Carmela.

AMAZINGLY, HANDLING ROUTINE CHORES *DID* SERVE to calm Carmela down. She walked Boo and Poobah down Dauphine Street, keeping her cell phone with her the whole time in case the kidnappers chose to call. At the end of the block she saw that Bonnet's Cheese Shop was open, so she peered in the front door. The owner, Elroy Bonnet, a fat Cajun who probably had an over-the-top cholesterol count from sampling his own wares, beckoned her in.

"I've got the dogs," she told him.

He waved her in anyway. "Ain't nobody going to mind them," Bonnet told her happily. "Because there ain't nobody here. I was just about to close up."

So there were tastings all around. A tiny wedge of Brie for Boo, a thin slice of Colby for Poobah. Carmela bought a pound of cheddar, a half pound of Muenster, and a nice round of Camembert. Camembert was Shamus's favorite cheese. She figured just having it around might be a sort of psychic inducement for his safe return.

When she finished walking the dogs, Carmela drove down to Riley's Market where she bought three bags of groceries as well as a GooGoo Cluster, which she ate on the way home. Chocolate was a dandy holistic remedy, she decided.

Two hours later, Carmela's clothes were hung up, she had fresh sheets on the bed, and the dogs were fed. Now she was in the kitchen chopping carrots, onions, and celery, dicing potatoes, and slicing chicken breasts. In no time at all she had a pot of her favorite Chicken Gumbo Ya-Ya simmering on the stove.

Everything feels normal, Carmela thought to herself,

except for the fact that my husband was kidnapped this morning, and his uncle was murdered. How bizarre is that? Oh, and his crazy sister doesn't want a single word to leak out about anything.

The *briiiing* of the phone startled her. Maybe this was the ransom call!

"Hello?" said Carmela. Her throat was suddenly dry and constricted, her voice tentative.

"Mrs. Meechum," said Detective Babcock, "I'm just calling to check in with you."

"What's going on, Detective?" asked Carmela, suddenly all business. "Talk to me."

"Not a whole lot to report," said Babcock. "We haven't located the housekeeper yet, but we've been engaged in an unfortunate bit of wrangling with your sister-in-law's attorney."

"About . . . ?" said Carmela.

"Releasing information to the TV stations. She's still adamantly opposed to it."

"I thought you said you could get around that," said Carmela. When he'd gone upstairs with her and Ava, Babcock had pretty much assured them that he could maneuver around Glory.

"Now the attorneys are in the act," said Babcock, as if that explained everything.

"Can we somehow supercede Glory's wishes?" asked Carmela. "After all, I'm Shamus's *wife.*"

"Our lawyers are recommending that we wait and get a court order from a friendly judge first thing tomorrow morning," replied Babcock.

Carmela glanced at the antique wooden clock sitting on the bookshelf alongside her collection of vintage children's books. It seemed to mock her, to remind her that time was indeed ticking away.

"Okay," she said finally. "Do I need a lawyer to jump in the act, too?" She knew a few lawyers but didn't have a half-dozen high-powered ones locked on retainer like Glory did.

"Let's wait until tomorrow," suggested Babcock. "Maybe this will all sort out on its own."

"The police are still monitoring my calls?" asked Carmela.

"Absolutely," said Babcock. "You hear something, we hear something."

"Okay," said Carmela, feeling tired and defeated and dejected. "Bye."

CARMELA LAY IN BED, DOWN COMFORTER PULLED UP to her chin, dogs snoozing at her feet. She tried to relax, tried to systematically will every muscle and fiber, from the tips of her toes to the top of her head, to unkink and sink into deep relaxation. But it was difficult. Because even though her body was giving grudging cooperation, her mind wasn't. It raced unpleasantly, giving her a speeded-up, hyper feeling.

Quiet, she told herself. *Just let go and relax.*

There, now she felt a little better. The buzzing in her mind seemed to be subsiding. Good thing she'd taken those yoga classes with Ava. Learned how to make that mind-body connection.

She was just drifting off to sleep when . . .

Briiiing.

What was that? Carmela rolled onto her side, then pulled herself upright, trying to think, struggling to focus.

Briiiiing.

Telephone, she told herself. Panicking, she fumbled on the nightstand, heart thumping in her chest. She turned on a lamp and grabbed for her phone. Hitting the Answer button, Carmela put the phone to her ear, heard nothing but a dull hum. She lowered it, convinced she'd stabbed the wrong button. Then her panic turned to horror as, pixel by pixel, an image began to fill the tiny screen.

It was Shamus. Dressed in jeans and a blue work shirt, tied to a wooden chair. His eyes stared straight ahead at her, and there was a wide strip of silver tape across his mouth.

Stunned and trembling, Carmela fumbled at the tiny buttons, praying she remembered how to work the functions.

She did. She managed to save the image, just as the screen went blank.

Chapter 5

"ARE you serious?" asked Baby. "Kidnapped?" Her blue eyes widened in complete surprise as Carmela disclosed her terrible secret to the small group of friends that were gathered this Monday morning at her scrapbook shop, Memory Mine. "Honey," pressed Baby, "shouldn't you be huddling with the FBI or something? Giving a statement to the police?"

"Why did you even come in today?" asked Gabby, Carmela's youthful but very capable assistant. Twenty-three years old and very pretty, Gabby had dark hair and even darker eyes. Today she looked very Junior League in a pink tweed jacket and light gray slacks.

"I didn't have anything else to do," replied Carmela.

Everyone had been stunned by the report of Uncle Henry's murder, of course. That had made the TV news. And was probably the main reason they were all here this morning. But this new revelation about Shamus rocked them to the core.

"You should be at home," admonished Tandy. Skinny as a rail with hyperthyroidal eyes, Tandy was a big believer that folks should retreat to the home front in times of trouble.

"Why?" asked Carmela. "Make it easier for the kidnappers to call with their ransom demands?"

Tandy winced. "I didn't mean *that*. I just thought you'd be more . . ."

"Comfortable," finished Baby. She was pixie blond, fiftyish, and still gorgeous, fidgeting with a huge eighteen-karat gold link bracelet that looped around her tiny wrist. "You certainly don't want to hang around here, listening to our problems."

"Oh, but I do," Carmela told them. "You are all exactly what I need and want today. True friends who can help impart a sense of normalcy to a very nasty situation."

"I suppose I can understand that," agreed Baby. They were a team, after all. A scrapbooking group that got together almost daily to share creative ideas, discuss family problems, and celebrate personal triumphs.

Carmela gazed around Memory Mine. This scrapbook shop that she'd conceived and created on her own was her baby, her pride and joy. It had survived Hurricane Katrina and even served as a place of solace for fellow French Quarter business owners who hadn't been so lucky. They'd huddled there, held hands, prayed together, made plans and promises to forge ahead.

After weeks of helping neighbors clean up, Carmela had sorted through her own stock of scrapbook paper and albums that had gotten soggy, seemingly by osmosis. And with great determination, she had stocked new merchandise, sent out newsletters and promotional e-mails, had helped salvage countless water- and mildew-damaged photos for her customers. And, slowly, Memory Mine had emerged better than ever. The little scrapbook shop represented Carmela's creative vision. And, today of all days, it allowed her to draw strength from just being there.

"The police are on top of all this?" asked Tandy. "Because there's an awful lot to work on. *Two* crimes, goodness me."

"Absolutely they're on it," said Carmela. Detective

Babcock had called her last night after she'd received the photo image. She'd immediately e-mailed a copy of the image to him. And he'd checked in with her first thing this morning. Just as she was brewing a pot of strong chicory coffee, gazing at herself in the mirror, and wondering if she should chop her hair short again. The way Shamus liked it.

They were "working on things," Babcock had told her. They'd been able to trace the phone connection and picture to a resending service in the Bahamas, but that was as far as they'd gotten. Carmela had thanked him politely, even though his words had sounded cphemeral and slightly lame. Like when you told someone the check was in the mail— but it wasn't.

Now Carmela knew she had to either keep busy or go completely insane. Which is why she'd decided to come in today and oversee her business.

"What are you working on?" Carmela asked Baby and Tandy. They were huddled at the large back table that had been dubbed "craft central."

"Oh, honey," said Baby, "you don't really want to know."

"But I really do," said Carmela. "Truly."

"Well," said Baby. "Tandy's doing a scrapbook page on a zydeco concert, and I'm doing a paper memory quilt."

"What is a paper memory quilt anyway?" asked Tandy, peering over at the dozens of pages spread out around Baby.

"A big project," sighed Baby. "I'm going to make a

gazillion scrapbook pages and then glue and sew them together into one big quilt."

Tandy peered over her bright red half-glasses. "For what purpose?"

"We're having a family reunion this summer," explained Baby. "So I'm going to do a scrapbook page devoted to each member of our family. Then when they're put together into my so-called quilt, I'll use it as a tablecloth. Of course I'll put a sheet of clear plastic over it for safekeeping."

"How many relatives do you have?" asked Gabby.

"A lot," laughed Baby. "And it isn't easy coming up with different motifs for each one of them. Some are easy, of course, like my cousin Lester. He works for the forest service, so his scrapbook page will be recycled paper with lots of rubber stamp impressions of leaves and dragonflies."

"That's a great idea," said Carmela. Even though she was edgy and her limbs felt wooden, she wanted to join in.

"Do you think so?" asked Baby. "Then what about Uncle Hugo? He's retired and doesn't do anything."

"What are his hobbies?" asked Carmela.

Baby shrugged. "He watches a lot of baseball."

"And we just happen to have tons of twelve-by-twelve-inch paper decorated with baseball designs," said Carmela. "Team logos, pinstripes, baseballs, you name it."

"Great," said Baby. "Now what about my dear old momma?"

60

"Isn't she a baker?" asked Gabby, getting into the spirit. "How about creating a collage with photos of food and copies of her handwritten recipes?"

"You know what else?" said Carmela. "Before you stitch or glue your pages together, you should use the color copier to reduce each page by sixty or seventy percent. Then you can use those smaller images for the front of your reunion invitations."

"Those are great ideas," said Tandy. "But how about cranking out a couple ideas for me? Usually I'm busy scrapbooking my grandkids. But this concert page is a little more out in left field."

Carmela studied what Tandy had so far. A sheet of paper covered in musical notes, three photos, a couple charms, and a concert ticket. Carmela switched Tandy to a different sheet of paper that featured a colorful, slightly funky playbill format and let her fit in an additional photo.

"You know," said Carmela. "You should probably use deacidification spray on that ticket." It was always a good idea to neutralize acids, especially when including tickets that were often printed on cheaper paper.

"Okay," said Tandy. "What else?"

"And those little charms?" asked Carmela. Tandy had a handful of charms. A moon, a tiny violin, and some small coins. "How were you going to affix them?"

"Thread?" said Tandy.

"Think about sealing wax," said Carmela. "It'll lend

a few arty spots of color and really hold them tight."

"You have some here?" asked Tandy.

Carmela nodded to a huge wall unit that displayed an array of scissors, punches, rubber stamps, pens, color chalk, fibers, and more. "Lots of it," she said.

WHEN LUNCHTIME ROLLED AROUND, CARMELA WAS feeling less like the walking wounded and a little more like herself. Although each time the phone shrilled, everyone sitting at the back table, anticipating a ransom request, just about jumped out of their skin. Yet, there was not a single word from the kidnappers or the police. Was no news good news? Carmela would have to wait and see.

"I'm running down to the French Quarter Deli for salads," said Gabby. "What do you want, Carmela?"

"Nothing, thanks," said Carmela. She was bent over a catalog, writing out an order for specialty papers. Mulberry paper was big these days; so was corrugate, Indian batik paper, Japanese Asamashi, and translucent Kinwashi paper. Gabby was going to be starting up her Paper Moon classes again in a few weeks, so it was probably smart to restock now.

"Honey, you have to eat something," called Baby. "Get her a turkey salad," she instructed Gabby. "She could use the protein, and the tryptophan will help calm her down."

BABY AND TANDY LEFT RIGHT AFTER LUNCH, SHOWering Carmela with kisses, hugs, and admonishments to call them no matter what the news was, no matter what the time might be. And then, for some reason unknown to the great gods of retail, Carmela and Gabby were constantly busy. It seemed like absolutely everyone stopped by for scrapbook supplies. They sold military-themed emblems and papers, silk ribbon and charms, rub-on titles and quotes, die-cut frames, and dozens of packs of rub-on transfer images.

One woman, just back from a trip to Lafayette, Louisiana, the unofficial capital of French Louisiana, had taken some wonderful color photos of the Cathedral of St. John the Evangelist and its ten-story domed tower. She was wondering how best to showcase the historic church, and Carmela came up with some elegant paper with gold fleur-de-lis designs as well as some marvelous architectural-themed stencils that featured church doors, rose windows, and elaborate archways.

Later in the afternoon, as things slowed to a dull roar, Carmela began thinking about Uncle Henry. She supposed there would be a funeral later this week. Probably Thursday or Friday? The time and date would be up to Glory, of course. But Carmela wanted to contribute something, too.

Maybe I can design the program, she thought to herself. She was aware that, more and more, programs were being handed out at funerals these days. Little folded booklets that sometimes gave a brief biography of the departed, listed the music and official speakers, and often included inspirational quotes or short poems.

Carmela pawed through her personal stash of paper, mostly single sample sheets she'd gotten from suppliers. At the bottom of the stack she found a purplish-gray colored paper with a faded leaf background that might work. It was elegant, subdued, not too feminine. Perfect if she could order another hundred sheets fast. Or better yet, she could create a master sheet and then color copy the hundred or so that would probably be needed. That would work just fine.

For typography she'd need some press type in an elegant, rounded script. The visual could be a photo image of Uncle Henry ghosted over with a piece of vellum. She wasn't sure if she'd use photo corners to give it dimension or add some other elements, but she knew she had the germ of an idea going. More than a germ, in fact.

"Carmela," said Gabby, "I'm taking off now."

Carmela straightened up and looked around. It was late afternoon and almost dark out. She was shocked that the day had gone by so fast. Grateful, too. She'd had a few moments when she thought she might jump out of her skin but, for the most part, working at Memory Mine had kept her relatively grounded.

"You gonna be okay?" Gabby asked. Gabby was married to Stuart Mercer-Morris, the king of the Toyota dealers, so she had someone to go home to tonight. Even though Stuart maintained the chauvinist attitude that Gabby should stay home, paint watercolors, and plan intimate little dinners for his friends and clients.

"I'll be fine," Carmela told her. "I'm going to putter around here for another fifteen minutes, and then I'll head home. Well, to my apartment anyway," stammered Carmela.

Sympathy written on her face, Gabby came over and patted Carmela's shoulder. "I know," she said. "I know. And if you feel like staying home tomorrow, please feel free."

"Thanks," said Carmela, "but I'll probably end up back here."

"Take care," said Gabby as she slung a well-worn Coach bag over her shoulder.

Locking the front door behind Gabby, Carmela gazed out the front window. Her shop was located on Governor Nicholls Street, almost in the heart of the French Quarter. This was a great location that seemed to attract locals as well as tourists. Of course, her artful window displays helped, too. Right now she had a selection of journals and scrapbook albums set up in the front window. But she'd been noodling around an idea to replace them with a display of handmade cards and fun tag art.

As Carmela stared across the street at the green awnings and wrought-iron gates of Glisande's Courtyard Restaurant, mesmerized by the twinkle of tiny white lights in the palm trees, her cell phone suddenly shrilled.

Good Lord, she thought, as she scrambled for her

phone. *I can't miss this one! This could be it!*

"Hello?" she said, trying to sound confident.

"Carmela," said a voice. It was low, male, with a flat Cajun accent. "I have something you want."

"Excuse me?" said Carmela.

"Or don't you want him back?" came the voice, slightly teasing now. "I hear he hasn't always been such a good boy."

Teeth clenched, Carmela said, "Is Shamus all right? Let me talk to him."

"I can't do that right now. He's at . . . what you might call a different locale."

"What do you want?" asked Carmela. Detective Edgar Babcock had instructed her to remain calm, ask the kidnappers what their demands were. As if she didn't have a pretty good idea already.

"Money," said the voice. "Lots of it."

"How much?" asked Carmela. *Stay calm,* she told herself. *Don't betray an ounce of fear. Pretend this is just a business transaction. Try to keep a cool, analytical head.*

"Five million," came the voice again.

"I don't have that kind of money," said Carmela. She looked down, saw that her fingers were white from gripping the tiny phone.

"Talk to your kinfolks, I hear they got *lots* of money. More than they deserve."

"It's going to take some time to get that much cash together," said Carmela.

"Tomorrow," said the voice. "We want the cash

66

tomorrow. Smaller bills, unmarked, none of that exploding dye shit. Then you get your husband back."

"How do I know Shamus is okay?" asked Carmela. She was going to say *"still alive"* but decided she didn't want to plant that negative thought in the kidnappers' minds. "What guarantee do I have?"

"We sent you a photo last night," said the voice. "To insure sweet dreams."

"Not good enough," snapped Carmela. She was tired of this sicko taking verbal jabs at her. Now she was going to push back, make a few demands of her own. "I want a photo of Shamus and a note written in his own hand," she told the caller.

"Don't try to play hardball with me, lady," hissed the voice. *"I'm* the one in charge."

"Those are my terms," said Carmela, her heart in her mouth. "A note written in Shamus's own hand." She was well aware that her call was being monitored. Detective Babcock would probably think she was reckless and insane. Who knows? Maybe she was.

"Wait a minute," commanded the voice.

Then Carmela was left to wait and pray as a mumbled exchange took place between the caller and, she presumed, the other kidnappers.

"Awright," said the caller. "But if this deal doesn't come off perfectly, Shamus Meechum gets one shot to the head." There was a buzz and a click, and then he was gone.

Legs shaking, hands trembling, Carmela stumbled

to the front counter and collapsed on the stool behind it.

Too risky, too risky, she told herself. *I should have just gone along with them.* She stared at the phone in her hands, pushed the Call End button, then was stunned when it rang again. She put the phone to her ear, fearful it was the kidnappers calling again, changing their minds.

Detective Babcock wasted no time. "That was incredibly stupid," he told her. "Just what exactly were you trying to prove?"

"What if Shamus is dead?" Carmela asked him.

"You can't ever think that way," he admonished. "You have to stay optimistic."

"I am," said Carmela. "Which is why I asked for a photo and a note."

Babcock was having none of it. "It was a stupid request. You're putting your husband in grave danger."

"No, he's *already* in grave danger," said Carmela. "I was just trying to buy an insurance policy." She could hear Edgar Babcock mumbling cuss words to himself, but she cut him off by asking, "Did you trace the call? Do you know where they called from?" *Enough fault-finding with me. What are you doing?*

"We're working on it," snapped Babcock. There was a *clunk* and then a whispered conversation, similar to the one the kidnappers had just had. "What we're gonna do is stake out your apartment tonight," he told her. "Put a couple of our guys on the street, just in case. Are you still at your shop?"

"You know I am," said Carmela. "You've probably got somebody peering out from behind the azaleas across the street. Or dangling from the wrought-iron balcony."

"We don't," said Babcock, "but please don't leave for another ten minutes. We're going to send someone over to follow you. A security detail."

"Sure," said Carmela, suddenly feeling over-whelmed with despair and exhaustion. "Whatever."

The quaint, gaslit streets of the French Quarter were humming with activity as Carmela made her way home. People wandered along, window-shopping, admiring the estate jewelry, antique silver, and bone china displayed by the many antique shops. Others dodged in and out of souvenir shops, buying Mardi Gras beads and boxes of sugary pralines to take home. And always, clutches of people weaving in and out of rowdy music clubs.

Glancing overhead, Carmela saw strands of yellow and red Mardi Gras beads ensnared in overhead power lines. Hurricane Katrina had come and gone, swamping the lower part of the French Quarter. Then Mardi Gras, though a scaled-down version, had come and gone as well. And the French Quarter, that same ninety square blocks that had been laid out by a French engineer in 1718, had survived. Through wars, fire, pestilence, more fire, and flooding, the French Quarter carried on with bustling grace and insouciant dignity.

Carmela ventured a surreptitious glance back at more than one of the figures who were making their way through the narrow streets of the French Quarter. But if she had a police tail, she never spotted it.

Chapter 6

JUST as Carmela was peeking at the two small New York strip steaks that were browning under the broiler, Ava knocked on the door. Her special cadence. A single knock, a pause, then three quick knocks.

"You're just in time for supper," said Carmela, letting her in.

"That was the general plan," said Ava. She marched over to the kitchen table and dumped an armload of saint candles onto it. These tall, glass votive lights, wrapped with colorful paper depictions of saints, were a staple in Ava's shop. And Ava fervently believed that when lighted and placed in a special area of the home, her candles would bring about good luck and peaceful resolutions.

"Now," demanded Ava, pushing back a handful of curly auburn hair, "tell me more about this strange phone call you received."

Carmela had called Ava right after she hung up with Babcock. Told her everything. There wasn't much more to tell, but she filled her friend in as best she could.

"What did your caller sound like?" asked Ava. She sat down on a kitchen chair and pulled her long legs under her. Wearing blue jeans and a tight paisley T-shirt, Ava looked like she was in her early twenties instead of her late twenties.

"Cajun accent," said Carmela.

"That narrows it down only slightly," said Ava, pursing her lips and making a face. Western Louisiana, around Lafayette, Breaux Bridge, and New Iberia was Cajun country. Thousands of folks who lived out there spoke with a Cajun or at least a partial Cajun accent.

"He also sounded nasty and dangerous," said Carmela, setting plates, knives, and forks on the table. Her hands were trembling, but she knew she had to keep busy.

"I can't believe you asked for an actual note from Shamus," said Ava, watching Carmela carefully.

"You think I screwed up?" asked Carmela. "Because Detective Babcock sure thinks so."

"No," said Ava slowly. "I think you showed a lot of gumption. The fact that you didn't get all crybaby hysterical tells these scummy kidnappers that they're dealing with a tough-minded, rational person."

"Unlike Glory," said Carmela.

"Jeez," said Ava. "You think Glory's gonna pony up that five million dollars?"

"Babcock is going to deal with her on that," said Carmela. "But, yeah, I definitely think she will. Glory loves her baby brother Shamus. Which means she'll do absolutely anything for him. Including part with money."

"Still," said Ava. "Five million. It's gonna kill her."

"Yes, it will," said Carmela, reaching for an oven mitt. "So at least there's some upside to all of this."

CARMELA TOYED WITH HER STEAK WHILE AVA ATE ravenously.

"This is so good," she rhapsodized. "And this Beer and Brown Sugar Sauce is to die for. You are a truly wondrous cook."

"You don't have to scrape your plate, Ava, there's more sauce if you want it." Carmela got up from the table and went to check the pan. "Lots more."

Ava held up a hand. "One more forkful and I shall commit a major *faux pas* and burp."

Carmela smiled. "Well, we wouldn't want that, would we. Besides, there's cheesecake."

"From Riley's?"

Carmela nodded.

"Chocolate chip cheesecake?"

"Your favorite," said Carmela.

"Bliss," sighed a contented Ava as she leaned down, dug around in her oversized leather handbag, and pulled out a copy of *Celebrity Gossip Magazine*. Ava was a major fan of anything that smacked of celebrity. She watched all the TV gossip shows, devoured the magazines.

"Who do you think has the biggest gay fan base?" asked Ava as she thumbed through the glossy pages. "Streisand, Cher, or Madonna?"

"Not sure," said Carmela, dumping dishes into the sink.

"Take a guess," urged Ava.

"Um . . . Streisand."

"Gotta be," said Ava. She flipped through a few more pages. "Jeez, look at this plunging gold metallic dress. Gotta have the ta-tas to pull that one off." She flipped a few more pages. "Okay, what couple's gonna have the next high-profile divorce?"

Carmela turned and stared at her.

"Oops, sorry," said Ava. "Didn't mean to bring up the *d* word."

CARMELA AND AVA WERE JUST FINISHING THEIR cheesecake, debating the merits of a second glass of Shiraz, when a single sharp *rap* sounded on the front door. Then there was a faint scratching sound.

"You expecting somebody?" asked Ava. She tried to sound casual but was suddenly jittery. Boo and Poobah had both padded briskly over to the front door. Low, protesting growls rumbled in their throats.

"What the—?" began Ava.

Carmela put a finger to her lips, then scurried over to the wall switch and doused the lights. Taking a deep breath, she pulled back the curtains and peered out into the dimly lit courtyard.

The fountain was burbling away, the bright pink bougainvilleas were spilling out of their ceramic pots. A magnolia tree, dripping with Spanish moss, cast a few sketchy shadows in the moonlight. But that was it. There were no lurking figures, no maniacal kidnappers who had suddenly materialized to torment them.

And no signs of a security detail either.

"Nobody there," said Carmela, puzzled.

"*Somebody* rapped on the door," said Ava. "We're not just hearing things. And we didn't drink near enough of that wine yet to just imagine things."

Together, both women pulled the door open gingerly and peered out. At knee level, two quivering canine noses peeped out, too.

"Still nothing," said Carmela. The picturesque courtyard really was empty.

Feeling bold, Ava stepped outside and looked around. Just as she was about to close the door, she said "Whoa," in a tone that clearly indicated surprise and awe.

"What?" asked Carmela.

Ava pointed to a small white square tacked in the center of the planked wooden door. "That," said Ava. "Looks like somebody took you seriously after all."

Carmela peered carefully at the small white square.

Held in place with a small silver pushpin was a Polaroid photo of Shamus.

Carmela quickly snatched the photo from the door and hustled the dogs in. Then both women dashed inside, slammed the door shut, and threw the dead bolt.

Carmela flicked on the lights and stared at the photo clutched in her hands.

"How's he look?" asked Ava, crowding in to get a look. Then her face clouded. "Oh dear . . . ."

The photo was dark and grainy. Shamus had obviously been dragged outside so the photographer, if he could even be called that, had been able to make use of the last dying rays of the sun. Shamus was standing, tied to a scrawny tree in front of a large pile of dilapidated wood. This time he was blindfolded.

"Oh my Lord," said Carmela, horrified. "Look how he's all slumped over. He looks so beaten and defeated."

"Turn it over," urged Ava. "See if anything's written there."

There was. The number *"$5,000,000"* was scrawled at the top, plus the words *"Tuesday noon, St. Louis Cemetery No. 1, Carmela comes alone."*

Under it was a note in Shamus's own handwriting.

> A note to
> verify that
> everything's ok. Pay
> ransom and bring me home.
> Yours, Shamus

"That's his handwriting?" asked Ava.

"Absolutely," said Carmela. She'd instantly recognized Shamus's hurried scrawl.

"Holy shit," said Ava, awed by what she saw. "The kidnappers actually listened to you!"

"But that's not the half of it," said Carmela. "Look what else Shamus did!"

Ava peered at the note again. "What? It's sad and creepy." She stared quizzically at Carmela, who seemed suddenly hopeful. "Am I missing something?"

"Shamus knows that we sometimes create scrapbook pages with name acronyms!" said Carmela excitedly.

"Explain please," said Ava. She was not understanding Carmela at all.

"Tandy did one just the other day," Carmela told her. "For her grandson, Toby. She spelled the word *Toby* vertically down her scrapbook page in capital letters. Then she made sentences using each of those letters as the first letter."

"Huh?" said Ava. "Like a cryptoquip or something?"

"The capital *T* in the first sentence said 'To my Grandson.' The capital *O* in the next one said, 'Our dear little boy.'"

"I get it, I get it," breathed Ava. "So what did Shamus spell out?" she asked, searching down the note.

"Avery," said Carmela.

"Avery?" said Ava. "You mean like where you keep birds? No, wait, that's aviary."

"Avery must mean Avery Island," said Carmela. "They must be holding Shamus somewhere out near Avery Island." Avery Island was a three-hour drive out west in the middle of Cajun country. It was the home of McIlhenny Tabasco sauce as well as a wildlife refuge, active salt mine, and large azalea garden.

"Wow," said Ava, suddenly impressed. "A real live

clue. Shamus is a lot smarter than I thought he was."

Carmela stood there for a moment, eyes narrowed, one hand rubbing the side of her face. Finally she said, "We have to go look for him."

"Wrong," said Ava, shaking her head vehemently. "We've got to call the police and tell Glory to pry open her bank vault."

"The police will want to do this by the book," said Carmela. "They'll want to make the exchange tomorrow noon, just like the note says."

"So that's good," said Ava, nodding.

"Listen," said Carmela. "These guys already *murdered* Uncle Henry. They went to Uncle Henry's house asking for or looking for something, and when they couldn't get it, they shot him and then came across the alley and took Shamus. Don't you see? Whoever these people are, they're desperate and utterly ruthless!"

"Then you better get Detective Babcock on the phone this instant and tell him about this 'Avery' clue," insisted Ava. "Besides, I thought your apartment was supposed to be staked out. Why didn't the police see whoever put the note on your door? Why are they not tripping over themselves right now to help us?"

Carmela thought about that for a moment. "Because whoever stuck that note on the door probably snuck through your store," said Carmela. "He didn't just boldly march through the archway leading in from the street."

Ava frowned. Her shop was open late tonight. And Carmela was probably correct in her assumption. If Tyrell, Ava's assistant, had been busy with a couple customers, anyone could have sashayed past the amulets, candles, and voodoo dolls and exited via her back door. From there, it was just a few steps across the dark courtyard.

"Besides," continued Carmela, "if the police do head out to Avery Island and go cowboying in, Shamus could get killed in the crossfire."

"What if *we* go cowboying in and get our butts shot off?" said Ava.

"Okay, here's another fly in the ointment," said Carmela. "What if we tell Babcock about the Avery location, and he doesn't send anyone at all? What if the police decide to just sit tight and hope tomorrow's exchange goes off without a hitch? But here's the real pisser," said Carmela. "What if the kidnappers just try to grab the money and run tomorrow? What if Shamus doesn't even figure into their equation?" Carmela was really wound up now. "I mean, the kidnappers could put a bullet in Shamus's head and dump him in a swamp. There are *thousands* of acres of desolate swampland out there!" She shook her head. "No, we've got to go out to Avery Island and look for him now."

"That's a very terrifying and insane idea," argued Ava. "First of all, we don't even have a bead on Shamus's exact location. Avery Island is a huge area. Shamus could be stashed just about anywhere."

"Let's look at the first picture from the camera phone again," said Carmela, fumbling in her purse. "Maybe we can make some kind of connection, figure something out."

"You want us to drive out to Avery Island tonight," said Ava. She was staring at Carmela, her lovely brown eyes glowing with a fervent gleam. "Just pick up and go."

Carmela stared back at her friend. "Yes. Yes, I do. I have a gut feeling about this."

Ava crossed herself, then lit a match and touched the flame to two of her colorful saint candles. "Maybe we should petition the saints," she said.

Carmela stopped arguing and stared at the flickering candles. "Which saints are those?" she asked.

"I just grabbed a couple from the group we have on sale right now. These particular two are St. Valentine, patron saint of lovers, and St. Vitus, patron saint of comedians."

"Close enough," said Carmela. She paused, watching the flames dance. "So . . . what's it going to be? We gonna go out there?"

"You know, *cher,*" said Ava, "I don't like the way you're thinking."

"How can you say that?" asked Carmela. *"I'm* thinking the way *you're* usually thinking."

"That's what scares me," said Ava.

Chapter 7

BUGS splatted the windshield of Carmela's Mercedes as they barreled out State Highway 90 through Des Allemandes and Houma, then headed northwest through Morgan City and Franklin. The land stretched out flat on either side of them, swampy and boggy, with occasional stands of gum, ash, willow, and live oak. There was very little traffic save the droning eighteen wheelers that plowed past them, buffeting them in their powerful wake.

Earlier, when Carmela and Ava had casually driven out of the French Quarter, they'd pretended they were going to Bon Tiempe restaurant for dinner. This restaurant, set in a rehabbed mansion in the Faubourg Marigny district adjacent to the Quarter, had the perfect ill-lit parking lot tucked away behind its hulking form. Once Carmela had determined no one was directly on their tail, she'd bounced the car down a rutted alley, made a few twisting, snaking turns through the Bywater District, then headed through a drive-through daiquiri stand for good measure. Now they were well into the heart of Cajun country.

Just before the turn-off to New Iberia, Carmela headed south toward Avery Island. Ava was on her fourth frozen daiquiri and feeling no pain.

Then they were bumping along a country road that snaked through tall cane fields until they finally hit a cypress forest, the edge of bayou country. Now dense

80

foliage closed in on them, making a dark night seem even darker.

Just this side of Avery Island they hit a narrow wooden bridge.

"It's a toll bridge," said Ava, rolling down her window and sticking her head out to read the sign. "But nobody's here, so just go on across."

They rolled across the bridge then, another hundred yards in, came to a metal gate.

"Crap," said Carmela. She was afraid they'd come all this way for nothing.

But Ava jumped out and scurried toward the gate. She fiddled with the latch for a minute, then swung it open. "Not locked," she called as Carmela drove through. She left the gate wide open as she climbed back into the car. "Turn off your headlights," she told Carmela. "And go slow."

They crept past the McIlhenny Tabasco pepper sauce factory. Tourists visited the old factory daily, so it wasn't the kind of place where Shamus might be held captive.

"You see any place where Shamus could be locked up?" asked Carmela. She'd rolled her window down, too, so she could look and listen. But all she heard was the rustle of wind through palm fronds and the call of night birds.

Ava shook her head. "Nope." She pointed to a wooden sign that read *Jungle Gardens*. "Maybe there's something down that way."

Turning down the lane they were soon engulfed in a

veritable jungle of foliage and flowers. Trumpet creeper and wisteria looped down, giant banana leaves brushed against their car.

"This is amazing," said Ava. "It feels almost prehistoric. You ever been out here before?"

Carmela nodded. "Once. My daddy brought me when I was little. Before he got killed on the river. He was part Cajun, you know. And part Norwegian, too." She let the warm memory of a loving father wash over her for a moment. "He always referred to himself as a Cawegian."

"You learned some of the language?" asked Ava, fascinated.

"A little," said Carmela. "Like *fais do do* is a dance or party, and *babiller* is to scold, and *tooloulou* is a fiddler crab." She slapped an arm. "And *moustique* is mosquito."

"What do you think?" asked Ava, as they crept along the road.

"He's not here," said Carmela, braking the car. "There's no way he could be here. Tourists come here . . ." She peered about speculatively. "Just too many people."

"Maybe he's in the *area*," offered Ava. "I mean, didn't you say they tossed Shamus in the trunk? Let's think about this. How did Shamus know where he actually was when he sent you the 'Avery' clue?"

"Don't know," said Carmela. "Maybe he punched out a taillight or something, peeped out, and caught a snatch of a sign."

"Okay," said Ava. "That's logical. But it means Shamus is not necessarily *at* Avery Island. He's somewhere *around* here."

"This is a huge area," said Carmela, looking glum. "We can't just drive around calling his name like he's a lost puppy or something."

"Shit," said Ava. "We've come this far, I hate to give up now."

Carmela pulled the Polaroid out of her handbag and cradled it gently in her hands. Then she turned on the dome light and studied it. "What else do you see in this photo, Ava?"

Ava peered at it carefully. "A mess."

"Yeah," said Carmela, "but what kind of mess?"

Ava wrinkled her nose. "Kind of swamp ratty."

"Exactly my thoughts."

"So?" said Ava. "That still doesn't tell us a thing. *Everything's* a little swamp ratty out here."

Carmela tapped the photo with her index finger. "Look at this," she said. "What does it look like to you?"

Ava studied it again. "I don't know. Looks like a wooden fence or something. Maybe a shed that's falling down. Or maybe . . ." Ava squinted, cocked her head. "Is it a boat? Up on some kind of platform for repair?"

"That's what I was thinking," said Carmela slowly.

"So what is *this* thing?" asked Ava, pointing at a soft, round-looking blob.

"Dunno," said Carmela. She stared at the dark

Polaroid, willing it to come into sharper focus, reveal more detail. She had an idea in the back of her mind but couldn't pull it up. It swam to the surface, circled maddeningly, then, dove down again. "Boat," she said suddenly. "With shrimp nets."

"Holy shit," said an excited Ava. "That might be it. Shrimp nets. Some asshole has an old shrimp boat in his backyard. An asshole who lives somewhere around here!"

They backtracked across the bridge and drove up Highway 329, hit State Highway 90 for about a quarter of a mile going west, then turned left down County Road 14 and wound their way deeper into bayou country. The night was cool now, a lopsided orange moon shone down amid a glimmer of stars.

"You know where you're going?" asked Ava as they skimmed along at a good sixty-five miles an hour.

"Haven't a clue," said Carmela. "But I somehow *feel* we're getting closer."

"Female intuition," said Ava. "I surely do put more stock in it than astrology or any of that *feng shui* stuff."

"Or your saint candles?" asked Carmela.

"*Those* work," said Ava.

After twenty minutes of twists and turns they saw pinpricks of light up ahead. A town.

"Thank God," said Ava. "At least we're some-where."

"But where?" asked Carmela. She put her foot on the brake, slowed as they passed a small wooden sign.

84

"Delcambre," she said. "We're in Delcambre."

"I've heard of it," said Ava.

Delcambre was a small, compact town that had the good fortune of being located on Bayou Carlin. With a small amount of navigating, this waterway led savvy fishermen and shrimpers directly into the Gulf of Mexico. In the days following Hurricane Katrina, many of these same fisherman had motored small boats over to New Orleans and pulled off some heroic rescues.

"A fishing village," said Carmela. She slowed and pulled to the side of the road. "And look over there. A dock. With shrimp boats."

"Well, I'll be," said Ava. "Now what?"

"Are you hungry?" Carmela asked.

"I could eat something," said Ava.

Carmela eased the car back into the road. "Then let's find us a shrimp joint."

BAYOU BOZ'S FISH CAFÉ HAD A PINK NEON SHRIMP sign that flashed and buzzed, trophy-sized mounted fish, black-and-white photos depicting hurricane damage, and a collection of rusted saxophones hanging on their painted green walls. They also had a battered wooden bar with bottles that reflected like a kaleidoscope in a cracked mirror, a miniature dance floor, and a row of scuffed-up booths.

Carmela and Ava took a seat in one of the booths.

"Feels like neighborhood," remarked Ava. Bayou Boz's had that comfortable, easy feel of folks dropping by several times a week. A place where the wait-resses called you by your first name and you never had to dress up.

"Help you ladies?" asked the waitress. She was a woman on the far side of forty with big hair, dangly earrings, and a sharply pressed pink blouse embroidered with the name Bobbie.

"Fried catfish and a bottle of Acadian Amber," said Ava. "All this drivin' around's made me hungry again."

Carmela studied the menu. It was extensive and had a variety of traditional fare such as gumbo, alligator, po'boys, and crawfish. "Maybe a bowl of your shrimp gumbo and a glass of iced tea," said Carmela.

"Good choice," said Bobbie. She wrote everything down carefully, then bobbed her head. "Comin' right up."

Ava looked around. "You think I can smoke in here?" She pulled a pack of cigarettes from her purse.

"Let's put it this way," said Carmela. "I think it's been done before."

"So . . . what are you thinking?" asked Ava. "That these guys are shrimpers? That maybe they sell their catch to this restaurant?"

"Maybe," said Carmela. "You never know."

"From the looks of things," said Ava, "there are lots of shrimpers down in these parts. Lots of back roads and bayous, too."

"Like finding a needle in a haystack," said Carmela. Though her words sounded dour, she was still feeling somehow hopeful. After all, they'd come this far . . .

When their food came they dug in with relish.

"This is fine catfish," remarked Ava. "How's your gumbo?"

"First rate," said Carmela, reaching for another slice of cornbread that had come along as a side dish. "I didn't realize I was still hungry."

"Stress does that to you," said Ava. "Revs up the appetite. That's why I'm so doggone fat." Ava reached down and patted her flat stomach. "I'm always under stress."

"Nothing bothers you," said Carmela, "except not having a date on Saturday night. And you don't have an ounce of fat on your bones. You happen to be skinny and drop-dead gorgeous. In case you haven't noticed, all beautiful women are skinny. It's a very unfair package deal."

When Bobbie brought their check, Carmela put two twenties on the table.

"I'll get your change," said Bobbie.

"Keep it," said Carmela.

Bobbie's eyes widened. "Thank you, ma'am. We don't get a lot of what you'd call seriously good tippers down here. Much obliged."

"A question, though," said Carmela.

Bobbie hovered at their booth. "Sure."

"We're looking for some guys from around here," said Carmela. "Guys who might have been shrimpers at one time, but might not be now."

"You know their names?" asked Bobbie. "Because if . . ."

"We don't know their names," said Carmela. "But it's really important we talk to these guys."

Bobbie studied her carefully. "Guys who *used* to be shrimpers."

"Something like that," said Carmela. "And the thing of it is, these are not nice guys."

"You've had some sort of problem with 'em?" asked Bobbie.

"You might say they *caused* a problem," said Ava.

Bobbie hesitated for a few moments. Then, in a much lower tone of voice said, "If you have what Dr. Phil might call *serious issues* with a couple guys from around here, I'd say you might be lookin' for the Obelia brothers."

"The Obelia brothers," said Carmela. "They come in here much?"

Bobbie pointed to the cracked mirror behind the bar. "Not since they did that."

"Ah . . . they are trouble," said Ava.

Bobbie rolled her eyes. "One of 'em did two to six in Phelps." Phelps was a correctional center, a prison, in DeQuincy.

"An ex-con," breathed Carmela.

Bobbie put a hand on her hip. "There's three brothers in all. I think one or more might work at the oil refinery out by Lake Charles now."

"You know their address?" asked Carmela.

"Last I heard they lived down Hubble Road." Bobbie pointed to a scarred black wall phone with a skinny directory dangling from a chain. "You could check on the exact address."

"Thanks," said Carmela. "I'll do that."

"Be careful," said Bobbie. She hesitated, a small line insinuating itself between her plucked brows.

"What?" asked Carmela.

"There's another pair of guys that are always in some kind of trouble, too."

"Who's that?" said Ava.

"Buford and Rusty Gallier."

"They come in here, too?" asked Ava.

Bobbie shook her head. "No, but my daughter went to school with one. The youngest one, Rusty. He was a mean bully from what I heard. Dropped out his sophomore year."

"And they're shrimpers?" asked Carmela.

"I don't know what they are," said Bobbie. "Maybe trappers, swamp rats, poachers, dope dealers. Do a little bit of everything."

"Thank you," said Carmela. "That really helps." *Shamus, I'm coming,* she thought to herself. *Gonna find you if it kills me.*

"THE OBELIA BROTHERS ARE OUT ON HUBBLE ROAD," said Ava. She was clutching a piece of paper on which they'd scribbled the two addresses. Now the trick was going to be *finding* those two addresses. They'd gotten directions from Bobbie and the bartender on finding Hubble Road, but now they were turned around.

"Damn," said Carmela, putting her car into a sharp turn. "Another dead end." Every road seemed to be dead-ending at a dike or makeshift boat launch.

"Go back toward the town, *cher,* and we'll start again," said Ava.

"Right," said Carmela. She was beginning to feel frustrated and wondered if they shouldn't just bag the whole thing.

No, I can't do that, she told herself. *I just can't.*

Back at the main drag, they studied the directions, managed to make all the correct turns and, ten minutes later, found themselves bumping along Hubble Road.

"Success," breathed Carmela.

"I'd have a better feeling if this road was paved," said Ava. They were jouncing around like crazy, hitting potholes left and right. "How far out is this place supposed to be?"

"Couple miles, I think," said Carmela.

"It seems darker out here," said Ava. "And scarier."

"Bayous are like that," said Carmela. "Very scary, but places of great beauty, too."

They drove in silence for a while and then Ava said, "Shut off your headlights."

Carmela reached forward and hit the switch, eased her foot off the gas. Now they were coasting in darkness. "You see something?"

"Yeah."

"Lights?"

"Pretty sure," said Ava.

Carmela let the car come to a rolling stop. Now she could see flickers of light through the trees, too.

"Well?" said Ava.

"Pop open the glove box, will you?" said Carmela.

"What?" asked Ava as she complied. "You got a gun?"

Carmela grabbed a tiny flashlight and a plastic bag, jammed both into her pockets. "Let's go."

"We're just gonna go creeping around?" asked Ava. "I mean, don't we need a plan?"

"This *is* the plan," said Carmela. She stepped out of her car, shut the door gently. Then she started moving slowly, quietly, down a rutted driveway toward a house she still couldn't quite make out. Five seconds later she could feel Ava behind her.

"Spooky," whispered Ava as they stepped gingerly toward the house.

Now the house was coming into view. A small cabin, one story, built about three feet off the ground. Paint peeled off in long strips, a brick chimney leaned dangerously, a screened porch hung off one side of the structure.

But lights blazed from within, and they could make out low, muffled voices. A night wind had come up, and now it whispered through the sugar hackberry that had encroached upon the yard. In the distance an owl hooted, an alligator barked its hoarse cough.

Holding hands now, Carmela and Ava moved into the yard.

"Do you see a boat?" asked Ava.

Carmela shook her head. All she could see were cars. Six, maybe seven of them. All in various stages of disrepair, although a few must be drivable if their owners held jobs over in Lake Charles.

There was a low snort and then a rustle up ahead.

"Uh-oh," murmured Ava.

Carmela's hand dipped into her pocket.

"What are you—?" began Ava.

"Shhhh," said Carmela.

Slowly, gradually, a blue coonhound made his way toward them. He held his head low, but his tail was in a relaxed curl. The dog was cautious but wasn't presenting an out-and-out aggressive stance.

Casually, Carmela extended her hand, and the dog came toward her. He sniffed, gazed at her curiously, then dipped his muzzle into her hand and accepted her offering of dog treats. When he was finished chewing, she patted him gently on the side, feeling each rib through his soft fur. "Now," she whispered. "Now we'll take a look."

There was no shrimp boat in dry dock like in the photograph, no other wood fence or structure that matched up to what they'd seen. The garage had collapsed years ago, and there were no other outbuildings where Shamus could be held prisoner. So . . . it had to be the house or nothing at all.

Carmela and Ava crept closer toward a side window. Treading softly, holding their breath each time a tiny twig snapped or a bit of gravel crunched underfoot. Finally Carmela touched her fingertips to the outside windowsill and peered in.

The three Obelia brothers were home, all right. One lay fast asleep with his mouth open in an aging lime-green lounger. The other two were sprawled on an old sofa watching television. ESPN, some show about bow hunting.

Raising her head another six inches, Carmela tried to see what else was going on inside the house. Dishes were stacked in the sink, a table was piled with fishing gear, three metal lunch boxes sat open on a small counter.

"What do you see?" whispered Ava.

Carmela motioned for Ava to come forward and take a look. She did quickly, then ducked down, shook her head. Mouthed the word *nothing*.

Slowly, quietly, they backed away from the window. Curled up on a beaten-down patch of grass, the dog solemnly watched them go.

"You see anything?" asked Carmela in a low voice.

"They're weird looking," said Ava. "Like they've been raised by wolves or something."

"Aside from that?" asked Carmela.

Ava shrugged. "They all looked tired, as if they'd put in a hard day's work."

"That was my impression, too." Carmela thought about the lack of any kind of boat in the yard, the fact that these guys seemed dead tired after a day on the job, and decided these probably weren't the guys.

Ava made a quick cutting motion across her throat, and Carmela nodded. They'd struck out with the Obelia brothers.

Chapter 8

THEY were both quiet on the ride back to Delcambre, listening to the purr of the engine, trying to figure out their next move.

Ava bent down and scrounged in her handbag, pulled out the slip of paper that contained their notes. "Buford and Rusty Gallier," she said. "Worth a shot?"

Carmela blew her breath out slowly, tilted her head to the left, then to the right, trying to work the tension out of her neck. "Not sure," she said softly. It was after midnight now, and she was beginning to feel the first tiny pinpricks of dread. The feeling that this was a wild-goose chase and Shamus was still in very grave danger.

Grave danger, Carmela thought to herself. Or in a grave. Easy to dig a grave out here. Lots of tangled swamps and wild bayous where you could gouge out a shallow grave using a shovel or even a canoe paddle. Dump your body in, and nature would just take its course.

"There, over there," Ava was directing her. "Pull into that gas station, and I'll try to get some directions."

Like an automaton, Carmela cranked the wheel hard right and pulled into a desultory looking Spur station. Ava hopped out and dashed across cracked cement to the small cinder block building where a lone employee sat amid his retail selection of cigarettes, beer, pop, and beef jerky. She watched as Ava smiled, dimpled, and showed the young male employee her scrap of paper. Then the fellow reached for a map, unfolded it, and the two of them put their heads together, studying it.

"Mother of pearl!" exclaimed Ava as she jumped into Carmela's car. "If we ever find this place it'll be a miracle."

"You should have brought your saint candles," said Carmela.

"It's enough to know they're standing guard for us back home," said Ava. She studied some notes she'd scrawled alongside Carmela's initial notes. "Okay, go down this street back toward County Road 14. About a half mile." Ava sat silently as Carmela retraced their earlier route. "Now go about two miles until you see an old wooden sign for Evangeline's Cane Syrup and hang a right."

But when Carmela spotted the faded sign and saw the condition of the road, she couldn't believe it was even passable. "It's nothing but a trail," she moaned.

"Vacherie Trail, to be exact," said Ava. "And it does look bad."

"How far?" asked Carmela. She'd made the initial turn in, but now hesitated.

Ava grimaced. "Five miles."

"Five miles," repeated Carmela. *Should I try this?* she wondered. *What if I get stuck? It's gonna be miserable trying to get a tow truck way out here. Prob-*

ably wouldn't even get one until morning. Of course, if Shamus . . .

Carmela eased her foot onto the gas pedal and headed down the trail.

Buttonbush and swamp privet beat at the sides of the car as they swerved around puddles, sometimes driving up into long stands of rushes that threatened to encroach the trail. Still Carmela kept going, even though it felt like this trail would result in a big fat dead end.

THIS TIME CARMELA SPOTTED THE PLACE FIRST. She'd have missed it for sure if there hadn't been a tight left turn, and her eye hadn't caught a glint of silvered wood in the sweep of the headlights.

"There's something here," said Carmela. She flicked off her lights and came to a slow stop.

Ava peered through darkness that was made slightly murky by a ground fog that was rolling in. "I don't see anything."

"A little camp house," said Carmela, keeping her voice low. "Just off to the left."

Ava sat there, letting her eyes get accustomed to the dark. "Oh yeah," she said finally. "I see it."

Carmela opened the car door, stepped out quickly, and closed the door so the dome light shone only for a split second. "You coming?" she asked Ava.

But Ava sat absolutely still. "This is spooky, *cher.* I've got a bad feeling."

96

Carmela peered at the camp house a hundred yards away. "Join the club."

THEY CREPT THROUGH A STAND OF BLACK GUM TREES toward the camp house. At one point Ava stopped suddenly, batted frantically about her face with both hands, then shuddered. *Spider web,* she mouthed to Carmela, revulsion apparent in her eyes.

The ground here was soggy and boggy, the vegetation lush verging on tropical. As though the murky waters of the bayou had rolled in here, left its imprint, then receded just a bit. Held in check only by this spring's welcome dry spell.

They were at the camp house now, a building even smaller than the one the Obelia boys had inhabited. No lights shone, although the occupants could have been asleep. Or the place could be devoid of electricity.

Rusty metal traps, ugly things with tight springs and snaggleteeth, hung on the exterior walls. Hides belonging to alligator, nutria, and muskrat were tacked there, too.

Carmela and Ava edged their way around to an open area, talking in soft whispers.

Ava raised a hand and pointed. "There's a boat up on wooden saw horses!" she said in a loud whisper.

Carmela's heart thumped. "Does it have nets?"

Ava shook her head. "Can't tell."

They moved in closer.

"Nets," breathed Carmela. She could faintly make

out the telltale trappings on either side of the boat, the balls of shrimp nets. *Could Shamus be here?*

"Now what?" asked Ava, still whispering.

Carmela's top front teeth closed over her lower lip. *Now what indeed? Call out his name? Sneak in the house? Go back and get the cops?*

She stood there, feeling helpless and stupid. It had been her idea to take a gamble and come running out here. Now she seemed to be out of ideas; the generator had run dry.

Carmela scanned the yard. Her eyes took in the boat, a wrecked car, dilapidated washtub, old outboard motor, stack of firewood, and various odd tools.

Wait a minute, she thought suddenly. *There's no car. If somebody lives way out here, how the heck do they even get here?*

She frowned, looked around again. The shrimp boat was trashed. If there was another boat somewhere, she surely didn't see it. There was no light, no sign of life. No dog. No nothing.

"I don't think anyone's here," said Carmela. The thought made her feel bold.

Ava glanced at the camp house. "Only one way to find out, *cher.*"

Carmela stepped onto the first step. Winced as it emitted a loud *creak.* Still she climbed the rest of the way, then hesitated on the front porch.

Ava suddenly signaled to her. *Wait.*

Carmela stood motionless while Ava searched the ground around her feet, then picked up a sturdy-looking piece of wood. Ava climbed silently onto the front porch and hefted her chunk of wood over one shoulder like a baseball bat, indicating to Carmela that she'd stand guard. If anybody came flying out the front door after Carmela, Ava would be waiting there to deliver a solid whack to their head.

Murmuring a silent prayer, Carmela put her hand on the doorknob and pushed it open. A musty smell assaulted her. The scent of mice, old hides, decaying vegetation, and smoke. Standing there silently, she let her eyes get accustomed to the darkness, saw that the camp house was really just one big room. Table, a couple chairs, what looked like an empty cot, fishing gear stacked against the walls, a chain saw on the floor. And something curled up over in the far corner.

Slipping off her shoes, Carmela carefully, quietly, slowly, crept across the floor. Until she was ten feet, then five feet away from what appeared to be a huddled figure.

A trapper? Maybe a vagrant who'd found a place to crash for a few nights?

Whoever it was under a dark blanket, was snoring softly. Carmela flicked her little flashlight on, played the beam across the mound. Slowly, quietly, she bent down.

Perhaps it was the tiny shaft of light that stirred the sleeping figure. Or that her quiet motion had been detected. But a hand emerged slowly from beneath the ragged blanket and then a finger twitched. And there, on that right hand, was the dull glint of a Tulane class ring.

"Shamus," said Carmela. She didn't cry his name out loud, she just announced it in a normal speaking voice, as all her fear and anxiety dropped away. Like finally unloading a twenty-pound sandbag from your shoulders that you'd been toting around forever.

The blanket slipped slightly as the huddled figure stirred, then turned his head. Shamus, his face smudged and gray-looking, squinted up at her, clearly confused. Then he said, "I dreamed you were here."

"I am here."

Shamus blinked rapidly, tears glistening in the corners of his eyes. "Carmela," he whispered. "I knew you'd come."

"Damn right," said Carmela, her relief suddenly surging into anger. *Who did this to Shamus? And murdered Uncle Henry! Somebody's going to pay dearly!*

"Ava!" she called. "He's in here! Shamus is *here*." She threw herself down, fumbling at his bonds, tears rolling down her cheeks. "Gotta get you untied."

AVA'S MANICURE SCISSORS MADE SHORT WORK OF the duct tape that held Shamus's arms and legs, then they were hobbling through the swamp, the two women supporting Shamus on either side, rushing toward Carmela's car. Ava jumped in back, while Shamus gingerly eased himself into the passenger seat.

"We gotta call the police," Carmela murmured as she fished in her bag for her cell phone.

"Let's get out of here first!" cried Ava. "Not take

100

any chances right now." Shamus had been clear on the fact that nobody'd been around for a good five or six hours, but they were all well aware that the kidnappers, and there were two of them according to Shamus, could return at any moment.

Carmela spun her wheels and took off. Then they were flying back down the narrow trail, dodging palm fronds, overdriving her headlights. And like a feverish mantra, over and over, she kept asking Shamus, "Are you okay? Are you okay? Are you okay?"

Ava patted her shoulder gently. "He's gonna be okay, Carmela. Slow down or you'll get us all killed. These are mighty bad roads, and I'm rattlin' around back here like a damn beanbag."

"Was it Buford and Rusty Gallier?" Carmela asked, whispering a silent thank-you prayer to Bobbie the waitress.

"I dunno," Shamus told her. He had his arms wrapped across his chest and was shaking slightly.

Carmela eased off on the gas and did a quick assessment of her husband. He was stiff and hungry and looked slightly beaten down. But nothing a little tender loving care wouldn't fix. And once they got serious backup from the New Orleans Police Department and the local sheriff out here . . .

"I don't believe this," Shamus suddenly hissed. "I see lights coming toward us."

"We're almost at the main road," said Ava, sounding shrill. "Aren't we?"

"No, we're not," said Carmela. She'd measured the

distance using her mileage counter. They were only a little more than halfway back. And Shamus was right. Up ahead, she could see a faint glare, a car unmistakably weaving its way toward them.

"Douse the lights," Shamus told her. "And look for a spot where we can pull over."

Carmela fought to keep the car on the trail and see through the darkness. "There. Up ahead," she said. "I think the road widens a little."

"Pull in as tight as you can," Shamus instructed. "Don't worry about the car."

"What if we get stuck?" asked Ava.

"Then I'll push us out," said Shamus.

Carmela ran the car directly into a thicket of black haw and rocked to a halt.

"Heads down now," said Shamus. "And nobody say a word."

They made it by half a minute, maybe. They could hear the other car coming toward them, jouncing along, hitting ruts and potholes as it approached. Reeds and grasses slapping the undercarriage.

"Is it an Eldorado?" asked Carmela.

"Shhh," warned Shamus as the other car slid past them in the night, its single taillight glowing.

"You *did* kick out the taillight," whispered Carmela.

"Damn right," Shamus shot back.

Carmela raised her head a couple inches. "I don't think they saw us."

"Awright," said Ava. "Let's get out of here."

Carmela was about to heave a deep sigh when she

saw a sudden flare of red. The other car had just hit its brakes. "Rats, they did see us," said Carmela. She watched in the rearview mirror as the Eldorado backed into a stand of willow oak. Tires churning, its engine muttering, the Eldorado began to negotiate a turnaround. "They're gonna come after us!" she yelled.

"Hit it!" ordered Shamus.

Carmela flipped on the ignition and the lights, gunned the motor, and took off.

"Faster!" urged Shamus.

The Eldorado tailing them was a big car, a powerful car. An older model that had that throaty, full-bore sound. But it was nowhere near as agile as Carmela's little Mercedes.

"I feel like I'm smack-dab in the middle of a *Dukes of Hazzard* movie!" cried Ava as they wove and twisted their way down the trail.

Boom!

"Oh shit, oh dear! Now they're shooting at us!" cried Ava.

"Get down," warned Shamus. He reached a hand over the back of the seat, pushed Ava's head down.

Another shot rang out and there was a sharp *plink* of shattering glass.

"We're hit!" screamed Ava.

"They shot out a taillight," yelled Shamus. "Keep driving! Floor it!"

Carmela stomped down on the accelerator, and the Mercedes, always eager to guzzle a hit of gas, leapt forward. It was a solid car, built as all Mercedes are with high-end torque. Once you were moving at seventy or eighty miles an hour, even a little bit of acceleration could push that needle up to one twenty if you wanted to.

They hit the highway like a fighter jet smacking the deck of a carrier, spun wildly, skidded for a good twenty feet, leaving rubber all the way. Then they straightened out, gradually caught their collective breaths, and headed in the direction of Delcambre.

"Are they still behind us?" Carmela asked anxiously. Her adrenaline had kicked in big time, and she was shaking and shivering, her eyes wide with fright.

"I don't see 'em, I don't see 'em," chattered Ava.

Shamus reached over and put a hand on Carmela's shoulder to steady her. "You oughta drive NASCAR, darlin'," he said, pride evident in his voice. "You really dusted 'em."

Chapter 9

THE yellow-and-orange interior of an all-night truck stop on Highway 90 was not the ideal place to tell Shamus that his Uncle Henry was dead. But Carmela told him anyway. Ava was in the ladies' room, fixing her hair and touching up her makeup, even though it was now the middle of the night.

Shamus was shocked. "My God," was all he could say. "Uncle Henry." He put his hands to his forehead

104

and rubbed the space between his eyes with his thumbs. Wearing an oil-stained shirt, a dirty pair of jeans, and old sneakers without laces, Shamus looked like a disreputable hitchhiker instead of a bank executive and wealthy Meechum scion.

"The way we figure it," said Carmela, "Uncle Henry was shot first, and then they snatched you."

"And Glory?" asked Shamus.

"Glory's fine," said Carmela. "Well, not *completely* fine. She got so upset she hyperventilated and passed out. And then when she came to, she had a hissy fit and threw me out of the house again. But other than those little episodic events, she's okay. Okay for Glory, anyway."

"Jeez," said Shamus. He was still shaking his head and rubbing his eyes. "So much to take in."

"There was a five million dollar ransom demand," Carmela told him. "The so-called exchange was supposed to take place tomorrow at noon." She glanced at her watch. "Noon today."

"You say Edgar Babcock is heading up the investigation?" asked Shamus.

Carmela nodded.

"You got your cell phone with you?"

Carmela handed it over to him.

"I'm gonna go outside and make some calls," said Shamus. "Could you order me some food? I haven't had anything to eat since Saturday night, and I'm starving to death."

"Of course," said Carmela, feeling slightly guilty.

She'd eaten two meals since six o'clock.

"You told him?" asked Ava as she slipped into the booth across from Carmela, looking dewy and amazingly wide-awake. "About his Uncle Henry?"

Carmela nodded. "I did, and he's pretty darned upset."

"I can imagine." Ava gazed over Carmela's shoulder. "Shamus is pacing back and forth out there looking like he's ready to tear somebody's head off."

"He has a right to be angry," said Carmela.

"You'll get no argument from me," said Ava. "If I'd been tied up in that rattrap cabin like he was, I'd be bawlin' my eyes out. And probably pickin' cooties outa my hair."

Two minutes after Shamus's sausage and grits arrived, he returned to their table and sat down heavily.

"How ya doin'?" asked Ava. "My sincere condolences concerning your Uncle Henry."

"Thank you," said Shamus. "And thank you for coming along on this wild ride."

"We were afraid they might shoot you," said Ava.

"They surely would have," said Shamus looking both stunned and very serious. "I don't believe there would have been a fair exchange tomorrow." He paused, glanced up at the clock on the wall. "Today."

"Let's not talk about that now," said Carmela, edging closer to him. "You talked to the police?"

Shamus nodded as he helped himself to a bite of food. "Woke Detective Babcock up," said Shamus.

"Called Glory, too. You were right, she's pretty upset."

"That she is," said Ava, rolling her eyes.

"Do the police have anything at all?" asked Carmela. "Did they put a trace on that Eldorado? Have they found Uncle Henry's housekeeper yet? Are they sending the local sheriff out to roust whoever was living in that shitty little cabin . . . Buford and Rusty Gallier, I guess? Are they doing anything?"

Carmela's flood of words actually brought a grin to Shamus's face. "The big thing is they're hopping mad at *you*," he told her. "Edgar Babcock wants to talk to you first thing tomorrow. He's furious that you didn't tell him about the Polaroid on the door."

"Too bad," said Ava with a toss of her head.

"So you told Detective Babcock everything?" Carmela asked. Maybe she was in deep doo-doo.

Shamus nodded. "I pretty much had to."

"Well, that's rich," said Carmela, running fingers through her hair. "They're mad at me 'cause I helped solve their case?"

Shamus shook his head sadly. "Only *part* of the case. There's still Uncle Henry's murder. That's the *real* issue we need to focus on now." He stopped talking and ate a few more bites of food, though with far less relish than before. "Uncle Henry was like a father to me," he said, his voice slightly hoarse. "Taught me all about books and stamp collecting and photography. And banking, too."

"I know he meant a lot to you," murmured Carmela.

"He meant a lot to me, too."

Shamus reached over and squeezed her shoulder. "I know he did, darlin'."

"So what's going to happen now?" asked Ava. "Are the police going to take over from here?"

Shamus shook his head slowly. "That's the general plan, of course. Although I can't say things are exactly clicking for them."

"Like what isn't clicking?" asked Ava.

Shamus looked puzzled. "They say they *still* haven't traced the phone calls because they went through a Bahamian resender."

Carmela frowned. "But the callers, and I'm assuming it was this Buford and Rusty Gallier, are just a couple of sleazeballs who live in a swamp hut." She stared at Shamus. "Does that make any sense? Did those guys seem even remotely smart to you?"

Shamus shrugged tiredly and yawned. "Not to me. Then again, nothing is making sense right now."

Carmela pondered this for a few more moments. "Think about it . . . those guys barely had electric lights, let alone the ability to finagle a high-tech phone maneuver."

"You're saying they're not from the digital age," said Ava.

Carmela nodded. "Exactly. Which means the thugs who grabbed Shamus had to be just hired help. There's got to be someone else behind all this. Someone a whole lot smarter."

Shamus was nodding now. "You're right. I see

where you're going with this."

"So where would you start looking for this head honcho?" asked Ava.

"Probably start with Uncle Henry," said Carmela.

"Uh . . . excuse me," said Ava, nibbling daintily at a piece of toast. "But Uncle Henry is *dead*."

"But he had business dealings," said Carmela.

"I thought he was retired," said Ava.

"Only semiretired," said Carmela.

Now Shamus jumped in to explain. "For certain important institutional banking clients, Uncle Henry functioned as a conduit for venture capital."

Ava was suitably impressed. "That all sounds very hoity-toity and important. But what exactly is this venture capital thing?"

"Financing," said Carmela.

"Ah," said Ava, the light beginning to dawn. "Money. Well, isn't that how these crimes are usually solved? You look for the motive, then follow the money?"

"Ava," said Carmela. "I think you just said a mouthful."

TWO HOURS LATER, CARMELA AND SHAMUS WERE curled up in bed at Carmela's apartment in the French Quarter. Boo and Poobah, who were deliriously happy to see Shamus again, had somehow realized that an important event had just taken place. So they were zoned out on the floor next to them.

"You were very smart," said Carmela, snuggling

under the covers, "to send that note with the Avery clue."

Shamus beamed. "And you were very clever to demand a handwritten note."

"It was the least I could do," said Carmela. She inhaled Shamus's scent. He smelled warm and clean and steamy from the shower.

"Five million dollars," mused Shamus, as he pulled the comforter up over them. "You think I'm worth it?"

Carmela cuddled closer to him. "I'll let you know."

Chapter 10

IT was a French Quarter morning. Water burbled merrily in the courtyard fountain, sunlight streamed in through vine-covered wrought-iron grates on the windows, a faint *clip-clop* of a horse-drawn carriage echoed off the cobblestones as it carried tourists up and down the narrow streets to gaze at colorful little Creole cottages, elegant hotels, famous restaurants, and some of the best antique shops in the country.

Carmela was up and out of bed, bustling about her tiny kitchen, pulling out sausage, cheese, and eggs, throwing together one of her famous breakfast casseroles. She cubed her bread, tossed it into the pan where sausage and onions sizzled, threw in the rest of her ingredients, then added an extra squirt of hot sauce. Shamus liked *beaucoup* hot sauce and, today,

Carmela was willing to cater to his every whim.

Once she had her breakfast casserole in the oven, Carmela phoned Gabby, told her the good news but not all the details, then set the table. Humming to herself, Carmela grabbed oranges from the refrigerator and squeezed a couple glasses of fresh orange juice. When she stopped to consider *What next?* she heard the shower pattering away and knew Shamus was up and about. *Good,* she thought. *He's jumping back into things. That's a very positive sign.*

It hadn't been so long ago that Shamus had been unhappy and morose. Had sashayed out of their marriage and moved into his family's camp house, albeit a somewhat luxurious one, in the Baritaria Bayou to figure things out and work on his photography. That whole process had taken a while. But they'd finally reached a slow, tacit reconciliation and moved back in together. Now Carmela had legitimate concerns that his kidnapping, obviously a highly traumatic event, and the murder of his Uncle Henry, could send him rebounding into a precarious mental state again. God knows, the Meechum clan wasn't the most stable of families.

"Cawwww?"

"Huh?" said Carmela, spinning around.

A pair of bright eyes stared at her from inside a large brass cage. Eduardo, Uncle Henry's parrot. Carmela had given him several pieces of fruit yesterday, but no seeds.

Poor guy is probably hungry, she decided.

111

Carmela quartered an orange and held out a piece for him. The parrot gave an inquisitive cock of his head, stuck his beak out, and accepted the fruit. Deftly transferring it to one foot, he pulled at it hungrily.

"I promise I'll get seeds for you today," said Carmela. "And we'll run back and get your toys and perch, too. Okay?"

Bobbing his head as if to agree with her, Eduardo let loose a loud *"Okay."* Then, seemingly pleased with his verbal skills, said again, *"Okay, okay, okay, love you, love you, love you!"*

Which was followed by a loud pounding on Carmela's front door and Glory Meechum's voice demanding, "Carmela Bertrand, do you have a man in there?"

"Are you nuts?" asked Carmela as she pulled open the door.

Glory, gray hair arranged in a shellacked helmet, sensible black purse dangling from one pudgy arm, stared at her with menacing brown eyes that looked like raisins sunk into plum pudding. "I distinctly heard a man's voice," she thundered again.

"Maybe it was Shamus," said Carmela, deciding to have a little fun at Glory's expense. God knows, after last night's wild chase, she knew she deserved a little fun.

"Shamus is at his *own* house," said Glory protectively. "Where he *belongs*."

"No, I'm not," said Shamus, stepping around the corner, still towel-drying his hair. Carmela's oversized terry cloth robe was wrapped around his trim form. "I'm right here."

Glory's jaw dropped, her hard features turned suddenly soft, and she stumbled forward to embrace her brother. "Shamus, I was so *worried* about you. Even after you called last night, I could barely get back to *sleep*. Had to take another *pill*."

"I'm fine," Shamus told her, flashing his trademark boyish grin. "Better than fine."

"Uncle Henry . . ." began Glory, tears suddenly welling up, her broad shoulders sagging.

Shamus put his hands on Glory's shoulders. "I know, I know . . ."

"We've got to *do* something," whined Glory. She'd shifted from hostile to helpless in the blink of an eye.

"We will," Shamus told her. "In fact, I'm starting first thing this morning. Carmela had the bright idea of going through some of Uncle Henry's current business records to determine if any of this might be connected."

"You're a good boy," crooned Glory. "A smart boy."

What about me? wondered Carmela as she watched the two of them embrace. *What am I? Chopped liver? Combing through Uncle Henry's records was my idea.*

"Thank you, Glory," said Shamus, focusing a megawatt smile on his sister. "Your words really mean a lot to me."

The timer on Carmela's oven suddenly *buzzed.* "Breakfast is served," she announced in a suddenly guarded tone.

• • •

"ALL HAIL THE CONQUERING HERO!" SHOUTED TANDY as Carmela walked through the front door of Memory Mine. Gabby started the applause, then Tandy and Baby joined in.

"Gabby told us that Shamus sent you some sort of clue?" asked Baby, her blue eyes sparkling.

"Here, sweetie," said Tandy as she shoved a paper cup of steaming coffee into Carmela's hands. "Nice strong chicory coffee. And we brought croissants and strawberry jam from Croissant d'Or. Now sit down and tell us all about last night, okay?"

"We're absolutely dying to know," echoed Baby.

So Carmela went through the entire story, start to hair-raising conclusion, as the three women sipped coffee, munched their French croissants, and listened eagerly.

"A high-speed car chase where they actually *shot* at you?" shuddered Tandy. "How terrifying!"

"Remember," spoke up Gabby, "these were the men who *murdered* Shamus's Uncle Henry. They're dangerous people. Killers!"

Baby grimaced. "Do we know when the funeral will be?"

"Probably Thursday," said Carmela. The Meechum family had a family tomb in Lafayette Cemetery No. 1 over near the Garden District. Several generations of Meechum bones lay in repose there, so it was a good assumption that Uncle Henry would soon be joining them.

"What exactly are the police doing now?" asked Tandy. "Since you, smart and clever girl that you are, single-handedly found Shamus and handed him over to them on a silver platter."

"Still looking for the perpetrators, I suppose," said Carmela. "Shamus is down at police headquarters talking with them right now. Hopefully he can recall a few details that will turn into substantial leads."

"Let's hope so," said Baby.

"Then Shamus is going to grab Uncle Henry's files and meet me for lunch," continued Carmela. "We're going to put our heads together, see what we can figure out."

"Good girl," said Tandy.

Although it might be better if we put our hearts together, was Carmela's afterthought.

Then the phone started ringing, three more customers rushed into the shop, and all thoughts of investigations went spinning right out of Carmela's mind.

"Carmela?" said Gabby, suddenly looking frantic.

"I'm on it," Carmela reassured her.

One woman needed to create unique invitations for a Mardi Gras–themed hurricane victims benefit concert featuring a string quartet, but had no idea what to do. Carmela came up with the idea of taking dime store half masks and gluing small pieces of sheet music all over them. A hole would be punched below the left eye and eight-inch strands of colorful fibers tied through so they hung down like streamers. The invitation details would be typed on a plain sheet of paper, torn into a small, jagged piece, then glued just above the right eye. Then the entire mask would get a finishing coat of high-gloss gesso.

Another customer had some black-and-white photographs of an old family homestead that she wanted to include in a scrapbook. But the photos were all rather gray and flat. Carmela showed her how to enlarge them onto photo paper, then hand-tint the photos using special inks to add contrast and make the images far more dramatic.

At eleven thirty, just as Carmela was beginning to think about meeting Shamus, Edgar Babcock came barreling into her shop. He wasted no time and minced nary a word.

"What did you think you were doing last night?" he barked at her, his face just this side of a thundercloud.

"Making sure Shamus didn't get shot dead," Carmela told him in no uncertain terms. She put a hand on his elbow, guided him back toward the front of the store. "And kindly lower your voice, Detective. I have customers present."

Edgar Babcock glanced toward the back of Carmela's shop where three eager faces looked back at him. "Like they don't know what's going on?" he said.

"Never mind about that," she told him. "I want to know what *you're* doing. Did you send your crime lab out to that swamp shack? Did you talk to law enforcement out there? Did you find anything?"

116

"Matched the tire treads," said Edgar Babcock. "It was the same car that tore up your backyard, all right. The Eldorado."

"I could've told you that," said Carmela. "And the kidnappers, was it Buford and Rusty Gallier?"

"We're working on that," Babcock told her.

"Were they the ones who murdered Uncle Henry?" she asked. "Did any of the prints match?"

"Like I said, we're working on that," replied Edgar Babcock.

"If you're working on all these things," said Carmela, "juggling all these wonderful leads, how is it you don't have any definite answers yet?"

"Probably because you keep interfering," said Babcock, obviously frustrated now.

Carmela stared at him and frowned. "That's funny, I thought I was helping."

"Please," said Babcock. "Your kind of amateur help we don't need."

Carmela's mouth flew open, but before she could say a single word, Edgar Babcock held up his hands, as if calling a truce.

"Look," he said, "you've stepped on a few toes, but you got your husband back. Can you leave it at that? Let us do our jobs now?"

Carmela put her hands on her hips. "What about Uncle Henry?"

"We're making that homicide our number-one priority in the department," said Edgar Babcock. "But please . . . please don't make it yours, too."

SCURRYING THROUGH THE FRENCH MARKET, WHICH was located between Decatur and North Peters Streets, Carmela wove her way past bustling open-air food stands, souvenir shops, and produce stalls. This 150-year-old market was the perfect place to chow down on grilled alligator, stock up on pralines, grab a few jars of pepper sauce or a bag of kettle corn, and shop for Mardi Gras beads and T-shirts. In the spice stalls, pepper, cinnamon, and cardamom hung redolent in the air, while Cajun, Creole, Louisianan, and African American voices also blended together in another gumbo of accents and dialects.

Café Du Monde, the little café where Carmela was supposed to meet Shamus, sat at the uptown end of the market. It was a landmark institution, famous for its beignets and hailed as the original coffee shop to inventively blend chicory coffee with steamed milk to create what is now commonly referred to as café au lait.

"Shamus," said Carmela, plunking herself down across from her husband at one of the outdoor tables under the Café Du Monde's trademark green-and-white canopy. "What exactly did you say to Edgar Babcock?"

"Just that you were a first-class detective," said Shamus. He rose from his chair, bent across the little table, and delivered a kiss on top of Carmela's head.

Carmela accepted his kiss and then continued. "Because he came crashing into my shop like some sort of wild animal." She thumped her handbag down onto the table. "And yelled at me!" The yelling part really stuck in her craw.

"Oh yeah?" For some reason Shamus seemed downright amused.

"It's not funny," Carmela told him. She was looking for something more from Shamus than just his typical good old boy humor. Something that said, *This is serious stuff we're involved in.* But Shamus seemed relaxed and even a touch laid back. Definitely in a better frame of mind than last night, when Carmela had found him curled up on a bed of rags.

"You're a pretty tough cookie," Shamus told her. "In a face-off, I think I'd put my money on you."

"That's not the point," said Carmela. "It was embarrassing. Plus, *I* was the one who figured things out. Like where to find you. So I think I deserve a little credit, not a dressing down."

"C'mon," reasoned Shamus. "Blow it off. Don't act so put out. Look, I went ahead and bought us beignets and coffee." He patted a battered leather briefcase that sat beside him. "And I brought along Uncle Henry's current files just like you suggested. I thought we'd go through them together."

Somewhat mollified, Carmela stared at the paper basket that held her trio of beignets. "This is lunch?" she asked. "Shouldn't we go somewhere and get something a little more substantial? How about walking over to Brennan's or Tujague's?"

"Where else can you get all your basic food

groups?" laughed Shamus. "Sugar, fat, caffeine, and carbs."

"Please," said Carmela, holding up a hand. "As if I don't get enough of that already."

Shamus happily munched a beignet as Carmela shuffled her feet through what seemed like an inch of powdered sugar that had accumulated on the ground.

"When you talked with Babcock this morning," Carmela asked, "did he give you any indication that they might have some sort of line on these Buford and Rusty Gallier characters?" She paused. "Who are also, as I see it, Uncle Henry's murderers?"

Shamus's eyes suddenly turned flinty, and his voice was cold with anger. "There's no sign of 'em whatsoever. They've apparently slithered back into the swamp."

"Hmm," murmured Carmela. "Probably were just hired hands anyway. With someone else pulling the strings and giving orders. That's who the police really have to look for." Carmela took a bite of her beignet, watched helplessly as puffs of powdered sugar billowed onto the front of her black sweater.

"Who *we* have to look for," corrected Shamus. "Here . . ." He handed Carmela a stack of manila folders. "This is what you wanted to take a gander at. I had a hell of a time getting the okay from Glory."

"I'll bet you did," said Carmela, accepting the files. "So what are these? What exactly am I looking at?"

"These are people and companies that were turned down by Uncle Henry," explained Shamus.

"Turned down," said Carmela. "You mean on financing?"

Shamus nodded.

"Well, it's a start," said Carmela. "Someone might have an ax to grind."

Carmela hadn't been all that hopeful they'd find anything of value, but twenty minutes later her curiosity was piqued. There seemed to be a lot of companies desperate for cash infusions, and Carmela knew that fear and uncertainty often led to desperate acts. "This Landry Douglas, the oil guy, how well do you know him?" asked Carmela.

"Oh," said Shamus, giving a quick smile and reaching for that particular file. "He's a good guy. No sense looking at him. We do a lot of business with Landry's company, Terrapro Oil. They're drilling some very promising new wells."

"Awright, then what do you know about Huey Tippit?" asked Carmela, peering into another folder. "Tippit was turned down by Uncle Henry just last week. He requested five million dollars to finish a luxury condominium development over near Lake Pontchartrain." She looked up. "Five million dollars. Same amount as the ransom that was asked." *What was it Ava had said? You've got to follow the money.*

"I know Huey Tippit fairly well," said Shamus. "Frankly, I don't think he's got the stomach for murder."

"Okay," said Carmela. She munched her carbo-laden lunch and thumbed through more files. Probably, she decided, it was like looking for a needle in a haystack. These business files may or may not lead to the tiniest of clues. Or maybe Uncle Henry's murder had been a personal vendetta carried out against him. Carmela paused. Then again, why had Shamus been kidnapped as part of a package deal?

"We've got another half-dozen companies here that were turned down," Carmela told Shamus twenty minutes later. "Trammel Corporation, Pelican Software, Close-Connely Inc., Temperley Construction. Lots of companies that are still needing to rebuild. Ring any bells?"

"Not really," said Shamus. He had slid down in his seat and appeared to be lounging quite comfortably.

"How about Shipco International?"

"Nope."

"Sounds like a pretty big firm," said Carmela, taking a sip of coffee. "What do they do anyway?"

"Umm . . ." Shamus ran a hand along the side of his face. "Containerized freight, I think. Yeah, that's it, they handle stuff from all over the world. Guy who runs it is quite the hotshot entrepreneur. Lives in an enormous mansion over on Arabella Street near Tulane. And he started a chain of restaurants called Napoleon's Parlour."

"If the owner is so wealthy," asked Carmela, "why was he trying to get financing?"

Shamus gazed at her tolerantly, as if she were a small child who had just asked a very amusing question. "Are you kidding?" said Shamus. "Rich folks never want to use their *own* money. They'd much rather use somebody else's."

"Like a bank's money," murmured Carmela. "Okay, okay, enough said." Although she had lots of experience running a small business, she didn't have that much practical experience with *big* business. Although from what she'd gleaned from Shamus, the only real difference seemed to be that larger companies seemed to be managed a little sloppier.

The waitress came over with a fresh pot of coffee and dimpled prettily for Shamus.

"Refills here?" she asked.

"Aren't you just readin' my mind," he told her with a dazzling smile.

The waitress walked away with a slight twitch to her hips, and Carmela noted that Shamus craned his neck slightly to give her a quick appraisal.

"Hey, babe," said Shamus, leaning forward and putting a hand over his mouth to stifle a yawn. "I gotta take off pretty soon, haul my ass back to the bank. Got a meeting with the casino people. But if you could give the rest of these files a serious look, I'd really appreciate it."

Carmela had the urge to fling her remaining pastry at Shamus. Bonk it right off his head in a classic billiard side shot. "Maybe you should take this thing seriously, too," she told him. *Including our marriage,* she wanted to spit out. Instead she said, "Detective Babcock was pretty clear this morning that he doesn't want me doing any more investigating. If we were smart, we'd turn these files directly over to him. Let his people sort through them."

Shamus looked at Carmela with feigned surprise. "Glory would never allow that!"

"Tough," said Carmela.

"Come on, darling, *you're* the one with the real knack for figuring stuff out! I trust *you*."

Carmela gazed at Shamus, feeling slightly flattered and more than a little manipulated. "I run a scrapbook store," Carmela reminded him, "not the psy-ops division of the CIA."

"But you're so *clever*," whined Shamus. "Besides, when did you ever listen to the voice of authority? You're the original rebel gal."

They were silent for a while, as Carmela flipped through a few more files, reading them but not completely comprehending them. She was keenly aware that Shamus was pushing her buttons, and she hated it. Hated herself for allowing it to happen.

"You know," said Carmela, "a lot of these people are members of Mardi Gras krewes." It was true. Many of the venture capital requests that Uncle Henry had turned down had come from some rather prominent New Orleans businessmen. Of course, these were also the kind of guys who enjoyed three-martini lunches, popped big bucks for Jaguars and Hummers, and thought nothing of spending ten grand on a hunting trip.

"Then some of 'em will probably be there tonight," said Shamus.

Carmela blinked and stared at Shamus. "Tonight?" she asked. She was drawing a complete blank. "Is something going on tonight?"

"The Pluvius party," said Shamus. "Remember?"

"Mmm," said Carmela. "It's starting to come back to me." Shamus was a member of the Pluvius krewe, a rough-and-tumble group of rowdy business execs from fine old families. Pluvius staged a major parade through the French Quarter during Mardi Gras and put on a few token events the rest of the year. She'd forgotten they were getting together tonight for a sort of pre–French Quarter Festival meeting. A prelude to this weekend's annual French Quarter Festival. Although she suspected tonight's gathering was less about business and more of an excuse for krewe members to drink bourbon and brag about how much liquor they could hold.

"So we'll go to the party," said Shamus. "Schmooze, talk to folks, see if anybody's surprised to see me."

"Do you really think we should?" asked Carmela. "I mean, with Uncle Henry and all . . ." She didn't want to say they were in actual *mourning,* because the term seemed awfully dour and old-fashioned. But it felt like they should keep somewhat of a low profile in light of what had occurred. What was still going on.

"Do us good," said Shamus. "Besides, Uncle Henry would want it that way. Carry on, let you sleuth around a bit."

"I suppose," said Carmela, although attending a party still felt awkward.

"And then we'll go home," said Shamus.

Carmela was instantly on alert. "Home?" she said. "You mean back to Glory's house in the Garden District?"

"Of course," said Shamus. "Only it's really my home. Our home."

"Is it in our name?" asked Carmela. "Or even your name?"

There was a long pause, and then Shamus said, "Carmela, does it really matter?"

"Oh yeah," said Carmela. "It matters very much, since Glory is forever poking her big nose into our business. And when anything goes even slightly awry, I'm the one who gets the order to pack her bags and exit stage left. In fact," Carmela said, getting even more worked up, "I don't think we should move back into that house until Glory puts the property in *our* name."

There was an awkward silence as Shamus gazed at her sadly. "That could be a while, darlin'," he finally said.

Carmela crossed her arms and hugged her chest. "I can wait."

Chapter 11

W E didn't expect to see you back," said Gabby when Carmela came tripping into the scrapbook shop. "We thought you'd spend the rest of the day with Shamus."

So did I, thought Carmela. Instead she said, "No, I wanted to get back here. There's so much to do."

"Gee," said Gabby, looking surprised. "I though we were pretty much caught up."

Gabby had her there.

"Well, I started thinking," said Carmela, "instead of putting a display of handmade cards and tag art in the front window, why don't we do something with altered books?" *I have to do something,* she decided, *to get my mind off Shamus. Shake the feeling that he's showing classic symptoms of drifting off again.*

"That would be wonderful," said Gabby. "You know I've been dying to make one!"

"I heard that," called Baby from the back of the store. "And I want to learn how to do them, too. But first I'd like to know, what exactly *are* altered books?"

Carmela and Gabby retreated to the back of the store.

"They're really an amalgam of scrapbooking, painting, stamping, collage, and assembly," explained Carmela. "You start with an old, used book, one from a library sale or garage sale. Then you give it a new life. You might remove pages, carve out inside pages to create a diorama, or leave the pages intact and just add your own special visual touches."

"Tell Baby about the altered books you saw when you attended the scrapbook convention in Las Vegas," urged Gabby. She was already pulling out drawers and assembling paint, tags, and paper scraps.

"They were absolutely fantastic," said Carmela.

"Some altered books had been carved out to create religious reliquaries, others featured tiny dolls, Italian playing cards, vintage postcards, old letters, bits of antique jewelry, beads, and even pieces of quilting and embroidery."

"So anything goes," said Baby.

"Anything and everything," enthused Gabby. "In fact, Carmela and I have been stashing away old books for just this reason."

"And now's the time to work on them," said Carmela. "We're caught up with inventory, classes don't start for another couple weeks, and best of all, we've got the time." Although her excitement felt a little forced, she thought her words sounded plausible.

"Carmela, which one of your books are you going to work on first?" asked Gabby.

"The old Nancy Drew book," said Carmela without hesitation. It was a book she'd found sitting on top of a Dumpster behind Biblios Booksellers. Wren West, the bookstore's owner and Gabby's cousin, had been picking through boxes of hurricane-damaged books and was going to toss the old mystery book out. But Carmela had grabbed the thick blue book that had probably been published in the late thirties, dried it out, salvaged it, and now, appropriately enough, was going to put it to good use as her first experimental altered book.

"How about you, Gabby?" asked Baby as she adjusted her pearl-and-charm-encrusted Chanel neck-lace.

"I'm going to try doing a reliquary," said Gabby. "I've got an old oversized French poetry book that I found for fifty cents at a tag sale. I'm going to incorporate a sepia photo of my grandmother along with some lace, beads, and pretty paper."

"So you're both going to scoop out the insides of your books," said Baby. "How exactly do you do that?"

Carmela slid open a drawer and produced two large, gleaming X-Acto knives. "Very carefully," she answered.

JUST WHEN EVERYTHING WAS QUIET, WITH CARMELA, Gabby, and Baby working away diligently, Ava came flying in the back door. Carmela always kept it locked, of course, but Ava had demanded her own key.

"There's nothin' goin' on today," she complained, plunking herself down at the back table. "Hardly anybody is buying voodoo dolls or magic charms. And my love charms are just sittin' there like a puddle of puppy poop. Mercury must be in retrograde or maybe Mars is tangling with Venus again." Ava lifted a perfectly waxed eyebrow and gazed pointedly at Carmela. "Are Mars and Venus duking it out yet down here on earth?"

"Not yet," said Carmela, thinking back on today's luncheon with Shamus. "But they're getting close."

"We heard all about your adventure last night," Baby said to Ava. "You're to be commended for your courage under fire."

"T'warn't nothin' at all," said Ava.

"Have a cup of tea," offered Baby. She reached for a little orange teapot that was sitting on a nearby shelf, poured out a stream of pale green aromatic liquid into a tiny Japanese cup for Ava.

"Mm," said Ava, taking a sip. "Good. What is this?"

"Earl Green," said Carmela. "A special blend that I ordered from a tea shop in Charleston. The same place that orders colored bags and stickers from us."

"The Indigo Tea Shop," filled in Gabby.

Ava peered at Gabby, watching as she carefully sliced away at her book pages. "And what are you doing, Mrs. Mercer-Morris?" she asked, "besides coming close to nicking your pretty French manicure. Better be careful with that blade, it looks awfully sharp!"

"It is," said Gabby. "And this is a bear to do, but I'm determined to make it work."

"So what exactly *are* you doing?" asked Ava, stretching languidly, exposing a good two inches of toned, bare midriff.

"An altered book," Gabby told her.

Ava grinned. "I've heard of alter egos and altercations, but never an altered book."

"It was Carmela's idea," said Gabby, grinning back. They were all used to having Ava pop in from time to time. It was part of the fun of being in the French Quarter: lots of colorful shop owners who took a keen interest in each other. And since coming through the hurricane, they all seemed to be closer than ever.

"What are you wearing?" asked Baby, studying Ava's low-cut blouse. "It looks suspiciously like couture." Baby, who was married to a wealthy lawyer, who threw the occasional wildly extravagant party, and who also lived in a huge house in the Garden District, had more than a nodding acquaintance with haute couture.

"It's Michael Kors," smiled Ava, casually adjusting the blouse so it revealed even more of her youthful décolletage. "By way of that resale shop, The Latest Wrinkle, over on Magazine Street. You wouldn't believe what some women put on consignment! Last month I picked up an Ungaro jacket and Carmela got . . . What did you get again, honey?"

"Zac Posen slacks," said Carmela.

"I love those slacks," chimed in Gabby. "So tailored and elegant."

"Don't tell me you're abandoning all your leathers, feathers, and glitter T-shirts," said Baby, trying to keep a straight face. Ava was forever dashing in wearing a skull T-shirt or wrapped in a black velvet cape. Her crazy costumes were part of her exuberant persona.

"I'll never give up my crazy clothes," declared Ava. "It's every woman's God-given right to wear whatever makes her happiest. And I'm happy wearing lots of different things. Of course, I'm just as happy when I'm *not* wear—"

"Right," said Gabby, popping up quickly as two customers suddenly came into the shop. "Okay then."

Ava directed a slow wink at Carmela, then stood up, snatched one of the leftover croissants, and was out the back door as fast as her long, lanky legs could carry her.

"A true character," said Baby, shaking her head.

"And a true friend," said Carmela.

"Carmela," called Gabby from the front of the store. "Do we have any of those decorative brass keys left?"

"Should have," said Carmela, hoisting herself out of her chair and heading toward the front of the shop. She ducked behind the counter, raked her fingers through a cardboard box filled with plastic bags containing charms and tags, and found what she was looking for. Straightening up, Carmela spread a few bags out on the counter. "Two kinds," she said. "Large brass keys and small silver ones."

A woman with dark eyes, an angular face, short dark hair styled almost architecturally, and bright red fingernails tapped at a package that held a half dozen of the brass keys. "Perfect," she said. Then she pulled her thin mouth into a smile and introduced herself. "I'm Tina Tippit," she said.

Carmela tried not to do a double take. "Your husband is the real estate developer," she said. *Of course he is,* she thought to herself, *I just held his bank file in my hands not more than an hour ago.*

"Honey, truth be known, *I'm* the developer in the family," said Tina. "I handle land acquisition, construction, and marketing. Huey mainly deals with the sales aspect."

"You're doing those new condos over by Lake Pontchartrain," said Gabby. "I understand they're very elegant and upscale."

"Everything Tippit Builders does is upscale," said Tina. She smiled, revealing small, pointed teeth.

"What are the keys for?" asked Gabby.

"Promotion we're doing," replied Tina. "We've invited all our presale prospects to a party this weekend. Lots of champagne and schmoozing, or boozing and schmoozing as Huey calls it, then everyone gets to draw a key from the fishbowl. All the keys will be attached to cards, but one card will be a coupon for a free kitchen upgrade." She paused. "*If* they purchase a condo."

"Sounds like a good idea," said Carmela.

Tina focused on her. "You think so?"

"How many keys do you need?" asked Gabby, rummaging through the packages.

"Thirty should do it," said Tina.

While Gabby was ringing her up, Tina Tippit shifted her gaze to Carmela again. "I was very sorry to hear about the death of your husband's uncle. I knew Henry Meechum." She paused. "Do you know . . . are the police any closer to making an arrest?"

"I'm afraid not," said Carmela.

"Pity," said Tina, accepting her package from Gabby. "Terrible world we live in, isn't it?" She fluttered her fingers. "Well, ta-ta."

Once Tina Tippit had departed the shop, Gabby said, "Isn't she something? I read an article in the business section of the *Times-Picayune* about Tina Tippit being the top female real estate developer in all of Louisiana."

"Tina works with her husband, Huey," called Baby from the back. "But she's the one with the real money in that family. I understand she's quite smart. And tough, too. Very tough."

"I got that feeling," said Gabby.

"Me, too," said Carmela.

BY THE END OF THE DAY CARMELA HAD PRETTY MUCH completed her altered book. She'd hollowed out a four-by-six-inch square, added a background of dark blue velour paper, and painted in a sparkly yellow full moon. A tiny figure of a 1930s Nancy Drew, bent over and carrying a flashlight, had been colorized, mounted on foam core, then cut out and placed in the hollowed-out space of the book. Surrounding it were visuals of human faces, clocks, and question marks, as well as snippets of an old black-and-white photo that Carmela had taken of a mausoleum in St. Louis Cemetery No. 3.

"I love it," declared Baby as she perused the finished product. "Very spooky and mysterious. As soon as I finish this crazy memory quilt, I'm going to start making an altered book, too."

"Actually," said Carmela, "I'm thinking about doing another book."

"Good heavens," exclaimed Baby, "it seems like you're a veritable fountain of creativity. You never run out of ideas!"

"Ideas are my business," murmured Carmela, half to herself, half to Baby. She had, after all, started her career as a graphic designer for the *Times-Picayune*, New Orleans's plucky daily newspaper that, since its inception in 1837, had never skipped or missed publishing a single issue, including during Hurricane Katrina.

Then Carmela had moved on to working for Bayou Bob Beaufrain, designing labels for such products as Big Easy Étouffée and Turtle Chili. When Bayou Bob sold out to Capital Foods International and retired to Padre Island, Carmela had finally struck out on her own and founded Memory Mine. She discovered a little storefront on Governor Nicholls Street that had once been occupied by an antique shop. The former owners had left behind the enormous old library table, which now served as craft central in the back, and an old cupboard that, with a wash of paint and the addition of a few shelves, now housed her papers, foils, and stencils.

And Carmela had added flat files, wire racks that held a stupendous array of colorful paper, and floor-to-ceiling shelves that displayed albums, punches, photo mats, calligraphy pens, paper cutters, acid-free pens, brass stencils, scissors, and all the new scrapbook products that seemed to come out on a daily basis.

Yes, thought Carmela, as her eyes took in the shop she'd lovingly and literally built from the ground up, *ideas are very much my business, and I thrive on thinking outside the box. Which is probably why I'm noodling around ideas on how to catch Uncle Henry's killers. Much more so than even Shamus is.*

Chapter 12

G LITTERING green-and-gold scales adorned a gigantic humpbacked sea serpent. Next to him, a pink angelfish with red lips and googley blue eyes reclined against a giant half moon, silently watching the revelers of the Pluvius krewe.

The Pluvius den, located in the CBD, or Central Business District of New Orleans, was a huge warehouse of a building. The twenty or so floats that would be reconfigured for next year's Mardi Gras parade were parked around the outside walls. In the center of the building, a permanent bar and dance floor had been installed. Never let it be said that the party-hearty Pluvius krewe didn't live up to the reputation of the Big Easy.

"It's really jammed," said Carmela as she moved through the crowd with Shamus and Ava. Carmela had talked Ava into coming along tonight. First, because for as long as they'd been coming to these parties, Shamus usually ditched her so he could drink with his buddies. And second, because Ava was a pretty smart cookie when it came to asking questions and ferreting out answers. Men often went so ga-ga over Ava, they didn't realize how much information she was really weaseling out of them.

"Some of the Nepthys and Titania krewes are here, too," said Shamus. He raised a hand, cried, "Say howdy, Jimmy Joe," and was greeted by waves and exuberant whoops. "Can you ladies find your way to the bar?" Shamus asked, obviously in a frenzy to join his friends.

"Why not," said Ava, smoothing her clingy red dress down over her hips. "Looks like you wanna do the same thing I plan to do—say hi to the boys." But as Shamus galloped off into the crowd, Ava turned concerned eyes on Carmela. "Why do you put up with that crap?"

"His bad behavior?" asked Carmela. "Probably because he's pretty much always been that way."

"That's what attracted you to him? You like bad boys?"

"Nooo," said Carmela. "Not really. There were other . . . uh . . . fine points."

"And now you're back together with him," said Ava. Her tone indicated concern as well as disapproval. "I know we went out and rescued him last night," said Ava. "And that was a good thing. But I'm beginning to wonder . . . Who's gonna rescue you?"

"Something tells me our reconciliation may only be temporary," said Carmela. *Something? Hey, the warning signs are pretty much popping up everywhere.*

"Oh, honey," said Ava, suddenly concerned. "I surely didn't mean to pick at you. Are things with

Shamus really that bad? I mean, have they been bad?"

Carmela gave a tight nod. "They haven't been all that peachy."

"Then let's forget old Shamus for tonight and go get something to drink, okay?"

"Come to think of it, a glass of wine might just take the edge off," said Carmela. She wasn't a moper or a fretter. If she'd learned anything from her time with Shamus it was *que sera, sera*. What will be, will be.

"And I must admit there *are* some interesting men here," said Ava, looking around as they pushed their way toward the bar.

The Storyville Jazz Wompers were banging out their own version of *"See Ya Later Alligator"* as the two women shouted their drink order to the overworked bartender. Carmela wanted white wine. Ava ordered her new favorite, a concoction of bourbon, mint, and powdered sugar called a Dixie Julep.

Then they were pushing their way back through the crowd, looking for friends, absorbing the vibes, feeling the heat. It wasn't more than two minutes later that a good-looking man grabbed Ava and spun her out onto the dance floor. She rolled her eyes helplessly at Carmela, but her protest was mostly pro forma.

Carmela didn't mind. It was a party after all.

Sipping her wine, Carmela wandered through the crowd, saying hi to a few people, accepting the occasional condolence regarding Uncle Henry. Apparently no one else found it strange that she and Shamus were here partying tonight. And no one seemed the wiser about Shamus's recent disappearance, either.

At least the New Orleans Police kept that little incident under their collective hats, decided Carmela. *Thank goodness. Or thank goodness for the bank's sake, I guess.*

"Carmela!" cried a woman's voice at her elbow.

She whirled about to find Tina Tippit smiling broadly at her. "Tina," she said, "hello."

"Fancy seeing you again," said Tina. An unhappy-looking man stood next to her. Thin with thinning hair, an olive complexion, wary eyes, and features not quite as sharp as Tina's. "This is my husband, Huey. Say hi to Carmela, Huey."

Huey barely cracked a smile. "Hi, Carmela," he said.

"Nice to meet you," said Carmela, noting that Tina seemed to wear Huey as though he were a charm bracelet. *What had Baby said? Oh yeah, she's the one with all the money.*

"You must be very excited about your new condo development," said Carmela, for lack of any other common ground to talk about.

This time Huey Tippit exhibited a little more animation. "There's no other development can touch us on sheer luxury features," he said. "You move in to Pontchartrain Manor, it's basically turnkey. Everything's been carefully thought through and is already in place. Appliances, plasma screen TV, security system, gardens, you name it."

"Sounds lovely," said Carmela, wondering how

anyone from New Orleans proper could give up this highly atmospheric city with its shotgun houses, Creole cottages, plantation-style homes, columned mansions, and quaint French Quarter apartments. She knew the condos at Pontchartrain Manor were probably quite lovely, but she also knew they'd have white walls and beige carpeting. How different from the cracked brick walls, wrought-iron trim, Greek Revival motifs, and Caribbean palette of pale blue, green, and yellow that lent character to so many homes in the Bywater, French Quarter, and Garden District. And the gardens—there was absolutely no way Tina and Huey Tibbit's Pontchartrain Manor could ever come close to re-creating the tumbledown hidden charms of a New Orleans courtyard garden.

"You should come out and walk through our model," suggested Huey Tibbit. "I think you'd really like it."

"Maybe I'll do that," said Carmela. She could see Huey suddenly putting on his salesman's cap.

Tina waved a hand at her husband. "Carmela and her hubby already own a home in the Garden District. She's not interested in a condo."

Huey Tibbit focused a mirthless smile on Carmela. "You never know," he said. "Things change."

BY THE TIME CARMELA FOUND SHAMUS, SHE WAS ready to leave.

"Not yet, babe," he pleaded. "I'm just starting to have fun. Hey . . ." Shamus gestured to a tall, silver-

140

haired man on his left, "you remember Landry Douglas, don't you?"

"Uh, sure," said Carmela. She really didn't.

"He was at our wedding," prompted Shamus.

Landry Douglas shook Carmela's hand and gave a friendly grin. "The toaster griddle."

"Of course," said Carmela graciously.

"The invitation was by way of Glory," laughed Landry Douglas, "probably because I'm a bank customer."

"A *good* customer," echoed Shamus. He suddenly put an arm around Carmela and pulled her close. "Hey," he said, "did you remember we're supposed to attend the grand opening of that new casino Friday night?"

"I guess so," said Carmela, although her enthusiasm was seriously lacking. "Hey, when are you guys gonna have your meeting to talk about your gumbo booth at the French Quarter Festival this weekend? Assign times to the volunteers, of which I think I'm one." She thought the booth, meant as a fund-raising tool for Hurricane Katrina victims, was the main reason for this get-together tonight. Then again, maybe not.

"Soon," promised Shamus. "Real soon." He drained his glass and handed it to her. "Grab me another bourbon and branch, will ya, darlin'? I gotta confab with Landry about something."

At the bar, she ran into Ava and her dance partner.

"This is Ryder," giggled Ava.

141

"Hi, Ryder," said Carmela. "I'm Carmela." She was beginning to feel like it was either the first day of school or an AA meeting. *Hi, my name is Carmela, and I feel like an idiot.*

Ryder was tall, tanned, and very good-looking. Curly salt-and-pepper hair gave him an air of distinction, even though he was dressed in boots, jeans, and a dark blue Western-style shirt that had obviously been custom-tailored to his body.

"Of course," said Ryder, shaking Carmela's hand. "You're Shamus Meechum's wife."

"Right," said Carmela, wondering why everybody here knew everybody else. Except, of course, for her.

"Take a look at his boots," exclaimed Ava.

They all three looked down at Ryder's mahogany brown, spit-polished boots.

"Very nice," said Carmela.

"I sure wish I had a handbag to match," sighed Ava.

"Alligator," drawled Ryder. "In fact, the hides were harvested right on my farm."

"Gorgeous," said Ava, gazing into Ryder's eyes. "Simply gorgeous."

SHAMUS WAS TIRED AND OUT OF SORTS BY THE END of the night. He'd also drunk enough liquor that Carmela had decided she was the designated driver. When they pulled out of the dark parking lot and headed down St. Charles Avenue, Shamus breathed a deep sigh of relief.

"Good," Shamus muttered. "We're goin' home.

Glad you're finally seeing things my way." He rolled down the window, seemed to revel in the cool breeze as they swept along.

"Not exactly," Carmela finally said. "We're actually headed for Uncle Henry's house."

"What?" exclaimed Shamus. His handsome face was suddenly sullen.

"We have to pick up Eduardo's perch and a sack of birdseed," Carmela told him.

"Gimme a break," muttered Shamus. Then his hand snuck across the gear shift to rest on Carmela's knee. "C'mon babe," he said in a low growl, "let's just go to our place, okay? I'm tired as hell, and I sure don't feel like prowling through Uncle Henry's house at this hour of the night. The damn bird can wait."

But when they pulled up in front of Uncle Henry's house, lights glowed from within.

"What on earth?" said Carmela. She'd expected Uncle Henry's house to be completely dark. It was late, after all. Almost midnight.

"Huh?" said Shamus, his head lolling against the leather seat. Slumped down in his seat, he'd been dozing fitfully.

"Lights are on inside," Carmela told him.

"Maybe the police came back," said Shamus. He blinked rapidly, swiped the back of his hand across his chin.

Carmela considered this as the engine slowly ticked down. "I don't think so." She inhaled the night air, caught the heady scent of magnolia blossoms, wished everything with Shamus didn't have to morph into World War Three.

"Then who's in there?" asked Shamus. He was getting a little more curious. And nervous, too.

"Maybe Glory looking for something?" asked Carmela. She could envision Glory creeping around inside, muttering to herself, looking for bank papers or something.

"Nah," said Shamus. "Glory takes an Ambien at ten o'clock then sleeps like the dead."

"The housekeeper," murmured Carmela. "Maybe she finally came back."

"Mrs. Jardell?" said Shamus. "What the hell would *she* be doing in there?" Anger tinged his voice now as Shamus pulled himself into a sitting position, cracked open the car door, and gave it a hard shove with his shoulder.

"So you're going to check it out?"

"Hell yes," replied Shamus. He shifted his long legs, then scrambled out of Carmela's Mercedes. At the last moment his jacket caught on the door handle, and Carmela glimpsed a flash of silver. Shamus had a pistol tucked into his waistband.

"Shamus, no!" Carmela cried out. "Don't you dare—" But Shamus had already slammed the door. Now it was Carmela's turn to scramble from the car.

Shamus was halfway up the walk when Carmela caught up to him. "Be careful," she hissed.

"You bet I will," he told her as he bounded up the front steps two at a time.

Bam! Bam! Bam!

Shamus pounded on the front door. "Who's in there?" he demanded. Reaching into his waistband, Shamus pulled out his gun.

"What are you *doing?*" demanded Carmela. "Are you *crazy?* You can't wave a gun around like that. With all you've had to drink tonight you're gonna kill someone!"

"Sssh," said Shamus. He fumbled for his wallet, pulled out an old brass key, stuck it into the latch. He jiggled it for a few seconds, then the door swung slowly open to reveal a dimly lit foyer. "Just stay behind me," Shamus cautioned.

So, of course, Carmela leaned to one side and peered around him. "Who's there?" she called out.

"Sssh," said Shamus. He was so drunk he'd forgotten that he'd already pounded loudly on the front door.

"Mrs. Jardell?" called Carmela.

There was a shuffle of footsteps, and then a woman's voice called back, "Is that you, Carmela?"

It was Mrs. Jardell.

Shamus charged down the hallway into the kitchen, Carmela following on his heels. When they got there, a young man with oatmeal-colored hair, pale skin, and a suspicious face was sitting at the table. The sleeves of his white T-shirt were rolled up to reveal faint blue tattoos.

"Who the hell are you?" Shamus asked in a belligerent albeit righteous tone.

145

"Who are *you?*" asked the young man back.

Martha Jardell moved in to intercede. "This is my sister's boy, Johnny Kenner," she told them. Mrs. Jardell was in her seventies, although she could pass for ten years younger, and always wore a sensible housedress and sturdy shoes. Tonight was no exception.

"If he's your sister's boy, what's he doing here?" demanded Shamus.

Martha Jardell hesitated. "I had to go pick him up. That's where I've been for the past couple days. We were up in Cottonport and just got back this evening."

"Then you know about Uncle Henry?" asked Carmela.

Martha Jardell nodded sadly. "I read about it in the newspaper. Terrible thing. I tried to call you on your private line, but you were never home." She gazed at Carmela, curiosity on her face. "Did they arrest the person who did it?"

Shamus pointedly ignored Mrs. Jardell's question. "And why exactly did you come back here?" he demanded.

"Actually, we stopped at your house first," said Mrs. Jardell. She glanced at Carmela, seeming to note the look of consternation on her face. "But like I said, you weren't home."

"So you came over here," said Shamus. "Just went ahead and let yourself in."

Martha shrugged her shoulders, looked around sadly. "I work here. Worked here, I guess I should say.

With Mr. Henry gone . . . Anyway, I wanted to pick up a couple things and . . . have one last look, I suppose. I spent a lot of time in this old house with Mr. Henry." Mrs. Jardell had always called Henry Meechum, Mr. Henry.

Shamus's head swiveled toward Johnny Kenner, who had been watching him closely, his mouth pulled into a sneer.

"What have you got there?" demanded Shamus.

Johnny set a silver sugar bowl down on the table. "Nothin', man," he said.

"Keep your hands off that," warned Shamus.

"Maybe you oughta take it easy," sneered Johnny. "Stop freakin' out and pop a chill pill."

"Shut up!" snapped Shamus. "I know why you people came here; you're probably looking for something to steal." He reached a hand out toward Carmela, snapped his fingers. "Cell phone please?"

Reluctantly, Carmela pulled the phone from her bag and handed it to Shamus. She figured he was going to call Glory. Wake her up from her drug-induced stupor.

Instead, Carmela watched in shock as Shamus fumbled with the buttons, then finally punched in 911.

"Shamus, what are you . . . ?" began Carmela. "You're calling the *police?* You can't be serious!"

"Never been more serious," said Shamus. He spoke on the phone for several minutes, telling the dispatcher there'd been a break-in, demanding they send a police cruiser immediately.

"You're going to have Uncle Henry's housekeeper

arrested?" said Carmela. She was incredulous, just couldn't believe what was happening here.

"Hell yes," said Shamus. "And her thieving nephew, too."

Carmela's eyes blazed as she addressed Shamus in a clipped tone of voice. "This isn't right," she told him. "Mrs. Jardell didn't have anything to do with Uncle Henry's death. She was out of town, and you know it."

"I *don't* know that," snarled Shamus.

WHILE SHAMUS WAS TALKING TO THE POLICE OFFI-cers, and Mrs. Jardell and her nephew Johnny were being questioned and unceremoniously led outside, Carmela sought refuge in Uncle Henry's library. With its mingled smells of old leather and brandy and well-oiled furniture, the library had always seemed a cozy, homey place. Gazing at the floor-to-ceiling book-shelves lined with fine leather-bound books, Carmela thought about what a peaceful retreat it must have been for Uncle Henry.

Of course, this was where poor Uncle Henry had been murdered. So maybe not so peaceful for him after all.

Carmela exhaled slowly as her eyes moved across Uncle Henry's office to his leather chair to the corner table stacked with books, to his desk with a single book resting upon it. Her eyes lingered on the book she'd dug out of the leather chair and placed there that fateful Sunday. Remembered vividly the frenzied moment when she'd found Uncle Henry slumped in his chair, shot through the head.

How could someone kill a kindly old man in cold blood? she wondered. Then again, she knew that the world was a very different place today. Now even children snuck guns into school and occasionally murdered their young classmates.

Carmela shook her head as if to clear it. Tonight had been like some bizarre trip through a nightmarish funhouse. The too-raucous party at the Pluvius den . . . Shamus going ballistic over Mrs. Jardell's return . . . trading barbs with her nephew.

Carmela's eyes again sought out the single book with the cracked binding. She'd pulled it from beneath the cushions of Uncle Henry's chair and set it there. Certainly hadn't bothered to look at the title.

Now her curiosity was aroused. She switched on a floor lamp, felt a distinct shift in the room's atmosphere as light spilled into the dark corners of the library. All the room needed now was a crackling fire, a couple nice dogs stretched out nearby, and, of course, an occupant.

Carmela reached for the book, held it up to study the title.

Geology of Louisiana.

Not exactly a best seller, she decided. *And not even in very good shape.* The binding was barely there, the pages worn and tattered.

An idea suddenly popped into Carmela's mind. One that embodied a sort of karmic symmetry. She opened her handbag, dropped the book inside.

A board creaked behind her, and Carmela whirled around. Shamus was standing there. Looking unsteady and more than a little unhappy.

"I loaded the perch and birdseed into your car," he told Carmela. "Just like you wanted." He sighed heavily. The alcohol and all his ranting had caught up with him. "Now I'm going home. Across the alley to our *real* home. If you know what's good for you, you'll come along with me."

Carmela stared at him. "If I know what's *good* for me?" she repeated, her heart sinking like a rock. "Shamus, right now I'm not sure *you're* good for me."

"Suit yourself," he muttered, then turned on his heel.

Carmela heard Shamus's angry footsteps down the center hallway, flinched as the door slammed behind him. Squeezing her eyes shut, she put a hand to her heart, and thought, *I can't believe this is happening again.*

Chapter 13

A RRESTED?" gasped Gabby, pushing back a hank of baby-fine hair until it rested behind her ears. "Shamus actually had Uncle Henry's housekeeper arrested?"

"Tried to anyway," said Carmela. "Along with her nephew." She'd just arrived at Memory Mine this Wednesday morning and was retelling last night's sad story.

Gabby stared at her, brown doe eyes looking sad and questioning. "But why would he do that?"

"Shamus was in a mood," said Carmela. "I think what he really wanted was for the police to question them."

"Shamus was drunk again?" asked Baby in a matter-of-fact tone. She'd arrived bright and early this morning, vowing to finish up her paper memory quilt. "Sounds like Shamus hit the Pluvius party pretty hard last night."

"We both did," said Carmela. "But some of us had less to drink than others."

"So tell me more," said Gabby, cupping one hand and gesturing for more information. "The house-keeper had just stopped by to . . . what?"

Carmela shrugged. "Search me. Maybe Mrs. Jardell was picking up some of her stuff, or she intended to leave a note, or maybe she was just taking a last look around. But I'm pretty sure she wasn't there to steal. She'd worked for Uncle Henry for three, maybe four years. They got on well, and I know he trusted her."

"So why was her nephew with her?" asked Gabby.

"Again," said Carmela, "I have no earthly idea. Perhaps he drove her over. She could have been nervous about going into a house where her employer had just been murdered."

"That's a happy thought," said Baby.

"Or she was looking for something," said Gabby, her eyes going even wider. "You never know."

"Looking for what?" Carmela asked with a crooked

grin. "The clue in the cookie jar? The mystery in the Mixmaster? Hardly. I really think the poor woman just stopped by to express her sadness in a personal way."

"At midnight," said Gabby.

"She could be a night owl for all I know," replied Carmela. "What she *isn't* is a murderer."

"I agree," said Baby. She stood up from the back table, teetered toward Carmela and Gabby on four-inch-high Gucci stilettos. "I remember when Mrs. Jardell cleaned for the Housemans, who lived just across the street from me. They loved her very much and said she was extremely reliable."

"Then why isn't she still cleaning for the House-mans?" asked Gabby.

"Because, darling," said Baby, as she fiddled with her green-and-white silk scarf strewn with a bits and bridle motif, "they pulled up stakes and moved to Palm Beach."

TWENTY MINUTES LATER, CARMELA FOUND HERSELF dealing with a beleaguered customer whose precious family photos had been damaged during Hurricane Katrina.

"Is there anything you can do?" asked a tearful Celia Baker. "Some of the only photos I have of my momma and grandparents are sandwiched in there."

Carmela stared at the clump of photos that had been melded together by toxic floodwaters. The photos had long since dried and were now inexorably stuck together in an eight-inch-high slab.

"I tried to pry a few photos off the top, and they just ripped apart," lamented Celia.

Carmela nodded. "I can see that. If we want to try to save at least some of these photos, we need to rewet them all over again."

"Are you serious?" asked Celia.

"The thing to do," explained Carmela, "is to soak the entire clump for at least twenty-four hours. In a bath of clean water containing a high concentration of a photo wetting agent."

"Then they'll just come apart?" asked Celia. "They'll be as good as new?"

"I wish it were that easy," said Carmela. "No, then I'd have to gently peel the layers apart, keeping my fingers crossed there isn't any serious emulsion damage. Then I'd wash each photo again separately and either dry them between layers of photo blotter paper or use a commercial photo dryer."

"You can really do this?" asked Celia, looking apprehensive and hopeful at the same time.

"I've been helping salvage family photos ever since the flood, and I've had about an eighty percent success rate," Carmela told her. "So, if you're willing to let me try . . ."

"Please," said Celia. "Please try."

"What do you think?" asked Gabby, once Celia had departed the shop. "Think you can save 'em?" She pointed at the gunky stack, a testament to the terrible tragedy that had touched all of their lives.

Carmela sighed. She'd had so many people asking

for help with their photos, and her heart went out to all of them. She knew how devastated she'd feel if all the photos of her daddy, momma, and grandparents were lost forever.

"I'm going to do my best," she told Gabby.

"Want me to fill a bucket?" asked Gabby.

Carmela thought for a moment. "No, I'll take the photos home and do them. All the equipment I need is still there. Right now I'm going to work on something else."

SEARCHING THROUGH CABINETS, HUNTING AROUND IN their one-of-a-kind drawer, the one Gabby jokingly referred to as the "kookaloo drawer," Carmela searched for items, charms, papers, and tidbits that would work well in her new altered book.

Ephemera was, of course, the buzzword of today. Ephemera referring to old letters, papers, books, diaries, postcards, cruise ship tickets, trolley tickets, and the like. In fact, entire shops dedicated to the business of ephemera were starting to spring up like mushrooms.

Carmela had decided that Uncle Henry's book, the old geology book she'd picked up last night, was a sort of ephemera. It was chockablock full of old maps, handwritten notes, and such. Which also made it a perfect candidate for an altered book.

She was going to hollow it out and create a kind of reliquary, then add a tribute poem as well as a few items that were both decorative and meaningful. It would be her personal memorial to Uncle Henry.

"We do have a crucifix," said Gabby, handing Carmela a small wooden cross.

"Where'd you find it?" asked Carmela. She'd poked around and hadn't found one.

"Back room, bottom drawer of your desk."

"I thought I looked there," said Carmela. "Guess I'm awfully distracted, huh?"

"You have a right to be," said Gabby. She gazed at the paraphernalia scattered around Carmela. "And I love what you're doing." She picked up the old geology book and flipped through it. "This book isn't in very good shape, but it's got loads of character."

"Which is why I figure it'll make a good altered book," said Carmela. "It was probably due to be retired anyway."

While Gabby waited on customers, pulling out drawers of Lokta tie-dye and Indian silk paper, and demonstrating some of the new templates, Carmela was feeling her way slowly with the design of this altered book. Creating the first one, the Nancy Drew book, had been fairly simple. But coming up with a solid concept for this altered book was proving to be a difficult task.

Carmela finally settled on hollowing out the old map book in the form of an arch, removing more than half of the pages, then gluing the rest together. Once that task was done, she cut a piece of bottle-green corrugated paper to fit into the arch, then snugged it in as background. The next step was to select a rubber stamp of a Grecian urn, stamp it using bronze ink on terra-cotta paper, then cut that image out and highlight the urn with metallic rub-ons.

Carmela paused for a moment to consider her work so far. The urn looked very dimensional and elegant against the green background. So far, so good.

The next pieces she added into her hollowed-out book were an articulated metal sun charm, a wine-colored glass heart, and a miniature parchment scroll rolled up and bound with a tiny bit of gauzy gold ribbon.

She'd found a map page in the book that had been flagged with a leather bookmark. It was a map of Louisiana with a small blue circle drawn just to the northwest of Baton Rouge.

Uncle Henry had grown up near Baton Rouge, so Carmela supposed that was the area where his family homestead had been located. Now that snippet of map went prominently into the altered book, too.

A sheet containing a poem Carmela had written many years earlier was pasted on the left inside cover of the book then painted over with clear crackle glaze.

Carmela added a few dots of glue to the crucifix, attached it inside the book, then affixed a black silk cord to the book's outside spine. A dark bronze tassel with three jet-black beads were added to the cord for extra effect.

She was finished.

Gabby, sensing this, excused herself from the customer she'd been showing die cuts to and tiptoed across the room to peer over Carmela's shoulder. "I love it," she breathed.

"Really?" asked Carmela. "You think it's okay?" Whenever she experimented on her own and went a little bit far afield, there was always that niggling bit of self-doubt.

"It's spectacular," said Gabby. "In fact, I think you should bring it with you tomorrow."

"To the service?" said Carmela. "Oh no, I couldn't." Then, warming up to Gabby's idea, said, "I mean, I shouldn't." Uncle Henry's memorial service was going to be held in Lafayette Cemetery No. 1. Right outside the Meechum family crypt.

Baby crept over to join them. "You *have* to bring it," Baby insisted once she'd inspected Uncle Henry's tribute book. "In fact, it should be displayed prominently."

"Probably put it right on top of the casket," suggested Gabby.

"Perfect," purred Baby. "Nestled in a wreath of tiny white flowers." She took a step back, studied it again. "It really does convey a lovely sentiment."

"I'm sure Glory will have something to say about that," said Carmela. She figured Glory would undoubtedly hate it. Would probably view the altered book as some sort of voodoo symbol.

"I'm sure Glory will love it," promised Gabby, who always tried to see the good in people.

"We'll see about that," said a skeptical Carmela.

157

• • •

JUST AS GABBY WAS ABOUT TO FOLLOW BABY OUT the door to pick up po'boy sandwiches for lunch, Martha Jardell showed up. She came rushing into the shop, breathless and upset.

"Mrs. Jardell," said Carmela, noting the look of fear and worry on the older woman's face. "What's wrong?"

Martha Jardell didn't mince words. "My nephew's been arrested. Can you help me?"

"Arrested for real?" asked Carmela. "You're sure? He's not just being held for questioning?"

"For real," said Martha. Normally a spunky and optimistic woman, she now looked haggard and defeated.

Carmela thought about how Shamus had bullied and badgered the cops last night. Obviously this mess was Shamus-induced, completely his fault. And, once again, she was being called upon to bat cleanup.

"Okay," Carmela said to Mrs. Jardell, "you come on back and sit down. Take it easy." She shot a glance at Gabby. "Gabby?"

"Mm-hm?" said Gabby, immediately at Carmela's elbow.

"When you pick up po'boys can you also grab a cup of coffee for Mrs. Jardell?"

"Of course," said Gabby. "I'm on my way." And she was out the door in a heartbeat.

"Now," said Carmela, pulling out a chair for Mrs. Jardell, "sit down and tell me everything."

Mrs. Jardell eased herself down and turned worried, red-rimmed eyes on Carmela. "Johnny, my nephew, was arrested because he was in Mr. Henry's house last night. Your husband says he was stealing things and may even be connected to Mr. Henry's death."

Now it was time for Carmela to look worried. She liked Mrs. Jardell, knew her fairly well. In fact, Mrs. Jardell had helped out once during a dinner party, a sorry affair she'd given for various and sundry Meechum relatives. Mrs. Jardell had also come across the alley fairly often to lend a hand at cleaning, too. Whenever Carmela had offered to pay her, Mrs. Jardell had always shook her head and told her, "No need, I'm still on the clock with Mr. Henry."

"What exactly did Shamus say was stolen?" asked Carmela.

Mrs. Jardell looked apprehensive. "A valuable coin collection, a bronze statue, and a few other things."

Carmela had no real knowledge of these items but figured if Mrs. Jardell was involved, it had to be a bogus charge. Probably, Glory had come in and taken those things. Trust Shamus and his sister to be grand masters at miscommunication.

"Here's what I'll do," said Carmela, patting Mrs. Jardell's hand. "I'll talk to Shamus, and I'll also call Lieutenant Edgar Babcock. He's the one handling the homicide investigation."

Mrs. Jardell gave a visible flinch as she continued to gaze into Carmela's eyes.

"I know," said Carmela. "It's hard to believe anyone

would want to murder Uncle Henry."

"He was a wonderful man," said Mrs. Jardell. "A true Southern gentleman."

And by far the nicest of all the Meechum relatives, thought Carmela.

"And you say you were out of town Sunday morning?" asked Carmela. She figured it wouldn't hurt to reconfirm facts, even though she was still positive Mrs. Jardell had no involvement in Uncle Henry's death.

"I was up in Cottonport," said Mrs. Jardell, "picking up Johnny."

"That's right," said Carmela. "You mentioned that before. Okay then, I'll call you as soon as I talk to the police."

"Bless you, Carmela," said Mrs. Jardell, struggling to her feet. "Thank you for your help."

Chapter 14

WHERE'S Mrs. Jardell?" asked Gabby as she came steamrolling through the front door, laden with white take-away bags.

"Gone," said Carmela.

"Well, I've got her coffee," said Gabby. "And po'boys for us."

"What kind?" asked Carmela, feeling the first flutter of hunger pangs.

"Fried oysters for you, roast beef for me," said

Gabby, rattling the white bags enticingly.

"Fried oysters?" exclaimed Carmela.

Gabby stared at her. "Don't you like them?"

"I adore fried oysters," said Carmela. "But they're not the healthiest item on the menu."

"Today we're chucking aside diets, fear of cholesterol, and aversion to trans-fatty acids in favor of eating some *real* food," Gabby told her. "Some New Orleans *comfort* food."

"Comfort food it is then," said Carmela, knowing full well that New Orleanians enjoyed the unhealthiest diet in all the United States. "Because I'm starving."

Approximately one minute later, Carmela had set a land speed record for digging into her fried oyster po'boy and dialing up Detective Babcock at the same time.

"Are you people crazy?" was her opening salvo when he came on the line. "Do you know that two of your officers harassed Martha Jardell last night? She's Uncle Henry's *housekeeper,* for crying out loud."

"Carmela?" came Detective Babcock's questioning voice.

"You bet it is."

"Don't forget about Mrs. Jardell's nephew, Johnny Kenner," said Detective Babcock in a slightly amused tone now. "We also arrested her nephew."

"Please tell me," said Carmela, her voice dripping with acid, "how that makes any sense at all."

"Pure harassment," said Detective Babcock. "Hallmark of the New Orleans PD."

"What the . . . ?" stammered Carmela.

"The nephew you met last night? Who, by the way, goes by the name of Johnny Kool? He's actually a fairly bad dude. Was just released, in fact, from Avoyelles Correctional Center. Did eighteen months for felony armed robbery."

Carmela suddenly remembered the faded blue tattoos on Johnny's arms. *Prison tattoos?* she wondered. *And that's where Mrs. Jardell had been? Picking him up?*

"Are you serious?" Carmela asked in a strangled voice, knowing this single new piece of information could change everything.

"We just deal with the facts, ma'am," said Edgar Babcock pleasantly. "So it would appear that Shamus did the exact proper thing last night."

Carmela lowered the phone and held it against her chest. Shamus had acted like a stupid, bumbling ass. He'd threatened people with a gun, pigheadedly ordered in the police, and, in so doing, had managed to do the right thing. Truly, she decided, the world had gone mad.

Babcock spoke into Carmela's sudden, shocked silence. "The other thing that throws a monkey wrench into things is your Mrs. Jardell. She happens to be a prime beneficiary in Henry Meechum's will."

"She is?" said Carmela. "Really?" Frowning, she took a slurp of Diet Coke and a quick bite off her po'boy. Decided she had made a wrong turn somewhere along the line and apparently become a rotten judge of character. Case in point: First she'd taken Shamus back, now she'd been pulled in by Mrs. Jardell's sad tale. Was she naive or just plain gullible? Whatever the answer, it wasn't good.

"Carmela, are you eating something?" came Lieutenant Babcock's questioning voice. "Because I seem to detect a certain amount of surreptitious activity."

"A po'boy," Carmela admitted, savoring the pungent taste of the oysters, the greasy crunchiness of their batter coating. "Lunch."

"Ah," said Edgar Babcock. "That explains the slurping."

"I was definitely not slurping," protested Carmela, as she wiped a big, squirty splotch of mayo from her upper lip. Po'boy sandwiches were notorious for being humongous in size and for being "dressed." In other words, loaded to the gills with mayo, tomatoes, lettuce, pickles, red peppers, and sometimes even coleslaw.

"So here's the thing," said Edgar Babcock, sounding very business-as-usual now. "We'll check out the timelines on those two and get back to you."

"Okay, sure," Carmela said distractedly, wondering if Johnny Kool's first act out of prison had been to murder Uncle Henry. She hung up the phone, turned as she heard the bell jingle over the front door, and suddenly saw a wall of red roses advancing toward her.

"What on earth . . . ?" Carmela dashed out of her office to the front of the store.

Two deliverymen were struggling with giant sprays of roses. Gabby was frantically trying to direct them. The few customers that were in the shop were suddenly smiling broadly. Women always loved roses.

Gabby scurried toward Carmela, legs churning in her tight pencil skirt, and held out a gift card. "For you," she said.

Carmela peeled the card open and read the few lines that were penned there. "These roses are from Shamus," she snorted.

"How romantic," sighed Gabby.

"Take 'em back," Carmela ordered the first delivery guy.

But the deliveryman just gazed at her placidly. "Ma'am, this is only the beginning. We've got six more bunches sitting outside in the truck. We were also told you might try to refuse them, so we have strict instructions to leave them here anyway." Then, as an added explanation, he said, "we got tipped extra."

"Oh dear," said Carmela.

"Oh *yes*," enthused Gabby. "They're *gorgeous*. We've just got to keep them."

"Where on earth are we going to put them all?" murmured Carmela.

"Everywhere!" exclaimed Gabby as the phone suddenly shrilled and she made a quick dive through a bank of roses to grab it.

"Lord love a duck!" exclaimed Tandy as she suddenly stepped through the front door. "It looks like

Valentine's Day came early!" She pulled her bright red half-glasses out of her handbag, put them on, and peered around. "Or someone's having a Mafia funeral."

"Shamus sent them to Carmela," said Gabby, as she held up the phone. "And, speak out the devil," she said in a stage whisper, "he's on the line now."

"I'll take that call in my office," Carmela said softly.

"Hey babe!" came Shamus's exuberant voice once Gabby had transferred the call. "Did you get the roses?"

"They're just being wheeled in now," said Carmela. "A spectacular effect. It looks like we're all set to decorate floats for the Rose Bowl Parade. Or maybe welcome a horse and jockey into the winner's circle."

"You know I'm sorry about last night," said Shamus. "Really sorry."

"So flowers are supposed to make up for your acting like a complete and utter ass?" asked Carmela. She was still angry with Shamus, even though Mrs. Jardell and her nephew warranted being checked out. She wondered if Shamus knew about Johnny's background and Mrs. Jardell's place in the will. She figured he had to. Glory would have blabbed immediately.

"I figured a gazillion flowers couldn't hurt," said Shamus. "And, please, can we dispense with any verbal jousting? My head's not quite right today."

"I wonder why that is," said Carmela in a snarky tone of voice. "Want me to have Ava whip up a medicinal potion for you? A touch of henbane, a nip of mugwort?"

"And don't get on my case for having a few extra drinks, either," said Shamus. "Look, I called to apologize."

"For . . . ?" said Carmela. *Where to start?*

"Everything." When Carmela didn't answer, Shamus added, "That means I want to make up."

"You're such a charm school dropout, Shamus." *And utterly transparent,* she thought.

"What are you talking about?" Shamus pretended to be hurt.

"I can read between the lines," said Carmela.

"What?" said Shamus. "That I wouldn't mind a little 'make-up sex'? Sounds like a fine idea to me."

The notion had occurred to Carmela more than once that Shamus acted nasty and obstinate just for the pure pleasure of having "make-up sex."

And wouldn't you know it, Shamus's voice was suddenly coy. "I could be free by two, darlin' . . . then we could get together and have a little afternoon delight."

"Hmm," said Carmela. *Over my dead body.*

"You know I can't live without you," said Shamus.

"I need time to think things over," Carmela told him.

"C'mon, babe," wheedled Shamus. "What's to think about? We love each other, don't we?"

"There's never been any doubt in my mind about that," responded Carmela. "But our problem has nothing to do with loving each other; it has to do with *living* together."

"So we're oil and water," said Shamus. "Big frickin' deal, lots of people are opposites. Opposites attract; you know that."

Carmela did know that. She'd always been the polar opposite of Shamus. Working-class to his upper-class. A trifle too sensible to his devil-may-care attitude. But that wasn't the heart of the problem. It was his . . . Carmela drew a deep breath . . . his carelessness. His carelessness about their relationship. A relationship needed to be nurtured and cared for. Mutual respect was critical; so was communication. And Shamus just seemed to exist in his own little world.

"Listen, darlin'," said Shamus. "You've got to come home sometime."

"I'm gonna stay in the French Quarter for a while," replied Carmela.

"Honey, I don't want you living there. Mrs. Jardell may be under surveillance and her nephew sitting in jail, but those kidnappers still know where you live. I have a feeling this whole thing is far from over."

"Then I'll keep both dogs with me," said Carmela, knowing Shamus was trying to scare her and detesting him for it.

"Better you should keep my gun."

"No thanks," said Carmela. "I don't need *that* kind of trouble."

"GABBY SHOWED ME THE BOOK YOU MADE FOR Henry Meechum," said Tandy, once Carmela was off the phone and back puttering around her shop. "I think it's quite lovely. Of course, everything looks lovely in here what with all the rose bouquets strewn about. Or am I just seeing things through rose-colored roses?"

Carmela gazed about Memory Mine. There were roses in the center of the craft table, roses on top of the flat files, roses on the front counter. In fact, probably too many roses.

"I'm going to stick some of these bouquets in the front window," Carmela told Tandy and Gabby, "so we can at least maintain a partial view of our inventory." She picked up two glass vases, slipped behind the counter, and snugged the vases into her display of paper and albums. Decided they did look rather nice there, after all.

But when Carmela lifted her eyes to look out the front window, the familiar form of Glory Meechum suddenly came into view, strutting down the sidewalk, a determined look on her face.

What's in the ozone today? wondered Carmela. *Why is everyone suddenly drawn here like a moth to the flame?*

Glory launched herself through the doorway and into Carmela's scrapbook shop. "Carmela," Glory thundered without preamble. "You have something that belongs to me!"

Carmela, who still hadn't gotten used to these rude and grandiose intrusions by Glory, fought to keep her temper and her blood pressure under control. "What are you talking about?" she asked, holding her voice steady, too.

"Shamus gave you *confidential* files from the bank," said Glory as her lower lip began to curl. "And I've come to get them back." Glory slammed her black leather purse down on Carmela's front counter like a judge wielding a gavel. "Crescent City Bank is a major corporation, and I sit squarely on the board of directors."

"Shamus asked me to look at those files with him," said Carmela. "He asked me to *help*."

"Your help is neither needed nor wanted," said Glory. "So kindly hand them over."

"The files aren't here," said Carmela in her most casual tone, even though she knew darned well they were stacked on her desk in the back office.

"Where are they?" demanded Glory. Now she'd pulled her lower lip into a distinct pout. When Glory Meechum didn't get her way, she morphed into a two-headed Godzilla monster with the personality of a rambunctious four-year-old.

"Umm . . . I think they're at home," said Carmela.

Glory narrowed her eyes, wary of some sort of trick. "Your home?" she asked.

"Yup," answered Carmela.

"Where Shamus is?" asked Glory. "In the Garden District?"

"No," said Carmela, "that would actually be *your* home. Unless, of course, you care to sign the deed over to us."

"Dream on," sneered Glory. "You think I don't know what you have up your sleeve? If I deeded that

169

house over, you'd probably divorce Shamus in a heartbeat. Then you'd hire some smarmy high-powered attorney and have that house handed to you on a silver platter."

"You certainly have a delightful strategy mapped out for me," said Carmela. *Damn Glory. If it wasn't for her, my marriage to Shamus wouldn't be half as difficult as it is.*

Glory lifted her chin and pulled her mouth into an evil grin. "Tell me you two aren't close to *divorce*," she said, relishing the word as it rolled off her tongue. "Just tell me to my face."

She had Carmela there. Things weren't looking good at all.

But Carmela, who'd been harangued by Glory time and again, refused to crumble under her verbal assault.

"We're just fine," replied Carmela. "Better than fine."

"Of course you are," snarled Glory as she leaned in close to Carmela. "Maybe if you didn't spend all your free time focused on your so-called *investigation* or misdirected your efforts on criminals like that Mrs. Jardell and her no-good nephew, you might be able to get your own life straightened around."

Carmela felt Glory's hot breath in her face, felt a fleck of Glory's spittle hit her cheek. Then Glory snatched up her purse and lurched for the front door. But not before Carmela caught the look of smug satisfaction on Glory's broad face.

"Whoa," called Tandy from her perch at the craft

170

table in back. "Who let the T. rex out of its compound? Or is the electricity down again on the entire island?"

Chapter 15

CLATTER *clatter. Knock . . . knock knock knock.*
"Come in," called Carmela. Standing at the kitchen counter, she was busily grilling chicken breasts and chopping walnuts while Boo and Poobah sprawled on the tile floor, keeping a watchful eye out for tidbits. Eduardo the parrot napped on his perch, happy he'd finally eaten his fill of seeds.

"I've got a date with Mr. Wonderful," drawled Ava as she teetered in on strappy bronze stiletto heels.

Turning around, Carmela caught a flash of shapely leg, a glitter of sequins that looked like the movie chase lights down at the Prytania Theatre, and a wide expanse of tanned, toned midriff.

"A date?" Carmela laughed. "Or an audition for a Vegas show?" Ava was glammed to the max tonight. A gorgeous mauve top sprinkled with matching sequins and a floaty ankle-length cream chiffon skirt that was slit up the side.

"Oh, come on, honey," said Ava, making a dainty pirouette. "The top is Roberto Cavalli, and the skirt is pure discount store."

"Whatever it is, it sure works," said Carmela with an admiring glance. Her friend, the former beauty queen, had quite a knack for pulling together spectacular outfits. Although when Mardi Gras rolled around, with all its parties and balls, that's when Ava really pulled out the big guns: marabou-trimmed mules, turkey feather boas, leather bustiers, and masks. Ava had a real knack for creating the most gorgeous leather masks.

Ava plopped down on a kitchen chair and pulled a tiny mirror from her black silk bag. Smiling broadly, she applied a coat of mauve lip gloss. "I read this fashion article that said you should never be too matchy-matchy with your outfits. That it's a good idea to mix things up. You know, fancy with basics."

"I hear you," said Carmela, who herself favored pairing the occasional designer jacket with a pair of jeans and had once worn a leather jacket to a Mardi Gras ball. "The thing is," she said, assessing Ava's outfit with a wicked grin, "you're going to have to watch out for magpies."

"Huh?" said Ava, caught off-guard.

"With all those sparkles, they'll likely pick you over for sure."

Ava smiled languidly and slid her hands down to her exposed tummy. "Do you think I should get my belly button pierced?"

"Uh . . . no," said Carmela. "I think it hurts a bit. They use this pliers-type instrument that is far worse-looking than the tool I use for inserting grommets."

Ava wrinkled her nose. "On second thought, I guess I'm not that into pain."

"So where arc you off to tonight?" Carmela asked.

"Dinner and a movie?" *Dressed like that, I don't think so.*

"Dinner, yes," said Ava. "After that, your guess is as good as mine." She gave Carmela a broad wink.

"So I take it you're going out with . . ."

"The stud muffin," finished Ava. "Ryder. My *nouveau amour* from last evening." Ava arched one carefully made-up brow and leveled a gaze at Carmela. "And you, *cher,* are once again ensconced back here in your little *pied-à-terre.* All by your lonesomeness."

Ava's blunt assessment brought Carmela back down to a thudding reality. "Shamus and I had words again," she said. She'd already called Ava earlier and told her about the Jardells, hinted at the Shamus thing, too.

"You and Shamus have more than word issues," said Ava. "You have a major *problema.*"

"We love each other," said Carmela defensively.

Ava threw her hands up in the air. "I never said you didn't love each other! But love is generally the simplest part of a relationship. It's all the other piddley-ass shit that gets in the way, makes you want to pluck your eyeballs out."

"Why do you suppose that is?" asked Carmela.

"Search me," said Ava. She reached down and scratched Boo's tiny triangle ears. Boo, attracted by the flash of sequins, was giving Ava an adoring look. "I think it all goes back to biblical times," said Ava. "With Adam and Eve and serpents and apples getting stuck in their throats."

"Serpents got apples stuck in their throats?" asked Carmela mildly.

"No," said Ava. "But that's pretty much the timeline for when all the problems and crappy miscommunication between men and women got started."

"A comforting thought," said Carmela, wondering if there was the least little shred of hope for her and Shamus.

LEFT TO HER OWN DEVICES, CARMELA PUTTERED about in her kitchen again, halfheartedly making a chicken salad her aunt Eulalie had passed down to her. This Chicken Salad Eulalie consisted of chicken breasts, grapes, mayonaise, curry, and chopped walnuts. But once Carmela got all the ingredients mixed together, she decided she wasn't that hungry. So she stuck the bowl of Chicken Salad Eulalie into the refrigerator, telling herself that maybe tomorrow night she'd have more of an appetite.

Instead, she busied herself making Spicy Sausage Balls. They were a particular favorite of Shamus's, and he had specifically requested that she bring a plate of them to the reception at Glory's house that would follow the funeral service tomorrow.

As her sausage balls sizzled, Carmela fed the dogs, then snacked on a piece of cheese. Wandering around her apartment, she glanced at the stack of bank files she'd trucked home with her. These were the files Shamus had been so hot for her to go through. The same files Glory had demanded be returned.

Get it together, she thought to herself. Never had she seen a brother and sister so consistently at odds with each other, yet so ruthlessly devoted to each other. Glory viewed Shamus only in glowing terms; Shamus constantly defended Glory and all her bizarre foibles.

And who was left in the middle of all this? She was, of course.

And who would probably be forgotten after tomorrow? Poor Uncle Henry, that's who.

Carmela frowned. That wasn't right. Uncle Henry had pretty much been the only Meechum, except for Shamus, who'd been at all civil to her. He'd treated her like she really was his niece. Had offered to lend her money once when Memory Mine was struggling.

So didn't Uncle Henry deserve a little more consideration? Of course, he did.

If the police hadn't been able to shake anything loose, could she? The idea burned in Carmela's brain like a hot penny.

She glanced at the manila folders again, felt their presence tug at her. Shamus had been so sure they'd discover a clue within these files. Then, he'd seemed to abandon that theory when Mrs. Jardell and her nephew had conveniently shown up.

Carmela picked up the stack of files, moved toward the leather chair. She sat down, toed the ottoman toward her, stretched her legs out slowly, feeling tired but a little keyed up at the same time.

Letting her mind wander, Carmela's fingers tapped the files in her lap. Poobah lifted his head, cocked a crooked ear, then went back to his snorey dog dreams.

Slowly, Carmela opened the first file.

It was the file on Landry Douglas, owner of Terrapro Oil. Shamus had told her he was a good guy, above reproach, so she put that file aside.

The next file was the venture capital request from Huey and Tina Tippit. She wondered if they'd gone elsewhere for their five million to finish their luxury condo development.

Carmela paged through the rest of the stack. It was the same as before. Companies who had been turned down in their financing requests, though none had specifically asked for the amount of five million dollars.

She pawed through files for Pelican Software, Close-Connely Inc., Trammel Corporation, and Temperley Construction. All were privately held companies, so it was difficult to glean a lot of data on them. The last file in the stack was the one for Shipco International. They were—Carmela scanned the documents—containerized freight. With a subsidiary corporation called Bonaparte's Parlour. A chain of restaurants that served French and Cajun-influenced food.

Wait a minute . . .

Carmela backpedaled through the sheaf of papers.

The CEO was listed as Ryder Bowman.

Ryder? thought Carmela. *Ava's Ryder? The guy she's out with right now? The stud muffin?*

Carmela closed her eyes and thought for a moment. What had Shamus told her? Oh yes, that the CEO of

176

Shipco International was a hotshot who lived in an enormous mansion. And that he'd started a chain of— Carmela snapped the file shut—restaurants.

Like a puzzle piece suddenly tipping into place, an image popped into Carmela's brain. A clear picture of a pair of spiffy brown alligator boots that Ryder Bowman had been wearing last night.

He'd bragged that the skins were from his own farm. In fact, his exact words had been *"harvested"* from his own farm.

Alligator farm, thought Carmela, getting a sudden chill. For all practical purposes, a farm of that nature had to be located somewhere out in one of the bayous.

She wondered if Ryder's encounter with Ava had not been so accidental after all. That he might be trying to get close to Shamus and Shamus's family.

Pulling a hand-knit afghan across her, Carmela wondered if Ryder Bowman, proud owner of his own alligator farm, might also have direct contact with swamp creeps like the two men, supposedly Buford and Rusty Gallier, who had killed Uncle Henry and kidnapped Shamus. The notion both stunned and chilled her.

CARMELA DROWSED, HALFHEARTEDLY WATCHING A late-night TV talk show until she saw a faint light go on in Ava's upstairs window. Then she tiptoed to the phone and dialed her friend's number.

Ava, seemingly possessed with that second sense, knew it was Carmela.

"I'm in love!" Ava screeched into the phone.

Carmela could almost hear her shriek across the empty courtyard.

"So soon?" asked a dismayed Carmela. "You've only had one real date." Ava was inflicted with what Carmela called the Zsa Zsa syndrome. In other words, Ava fell in love an awful lot.

"Well . . ." Ava's yawn turned into a purr. "I sure am in like."

"How much do you really *know* about this guy?" asked Carmela, struggling to find an opener.

"Are you kidding?" said Ava. "We went to Antoine's and talked the whole time. Of course, first we feasted on Dom Perignon and Oysters Rockefeller and grilled pompano. Then we yacked our little heads off. Do you know," continued Ava, "that Ryder is a real *player?* He owns a major shipping company!"

"A shipping company," repeated Carmela.

"I just *knew* you'd be impressed," Ava bubbled happily. "I sure was. And guess what else? Ryder invited me to the opening of that new casino Friday night. Isn't that just too fantastic?"

"Sure is," said Carmela. "Do you know what else he's involved in? What his other business interests are?"

There was another yawn and then Ava said, "Why are you asking all these questions, *cher?*"

Should I say something to her? wondered Carmela. *No, I can't spoil her evening with my unfounded suppositions. I just can't.* Instead she just said, "no reason, Ava. Sleep tight."

Chapter 16

T HURSDAY dawned dreary and cool. A storm front had pushed its way in from the Gulf of Mexico and now low-hanging gray clouds blanketed the city like a shroud.

A perfect day for a funeral, Carmela decided as she stood among the pack of mourners that was beginning to congregate in Lafayette Cemetery No. 1. This city of the dead, established in 1833, was one of the oldest cemeteries in New Orleans and the location of the Meechum family tomb. Glory had decided against a formal church service, citing the precedent that all Meechum family members received their send-off to the great beyond amid these cracked and aged crypts, tombs, and monuments.

Carmela figured the real reason was that Lafayette Cemetery No. 1 was centrally located in the Garden District and just a few blocks from Glory's palatial home. Glory didn't much enjoy traveling outside her comfort zone.

Carmela watched as Uncle Henry's casket bumped down the narrow pathway between jagged stone tablets and towering mausoleums and approached the makeshift catafalque. Borne on the shoulders of a half-dozen Meechum relatives, the casket dipped and bobbed, a testament to the heavy oak and brass Eternalux model that Shamus had tearfully selected. And then Shamus was front and center, looking very sedate and serious in his charcoal-gray suit as he supervised exact placement of the casket and overflowing baskets of flowers.

Gravel crunched beneath Carmela's feet as she approached Shamus from behind. The altered book was clutched in her hands. "Shamus?"

Shamus whirled around at the sound of her voice. "Huh?" he said.

"I want to show you something." Carmela held the book out to him as though it were an offering.

Shamus focused on the reworked black leather book, slowly taking in the crucifix, the poem, the various little embellishments. And the veil of funereal seriousness that had blanketed his face suddenly crumpled. "Did you make this for me?" he asked, his voice suddenly tremulous, bordering on reverential as he continued to study Carmela's handiwork.

Carmela had, of course, intended the book as a tribute to Uncle Henry, a sort of memorial. But Shamus looked so touched that Carmela instead just answered, "Yes."

"You've gotta be the sweetest woman ever lived," said Shamus. He put his arms around Carmela and pulled her closer. Nuzzled her, gave her a tender kiss.

A little warning bell dinged in the back of Carmela's head. *Be careful, he's drawing you in again. You think he's a changed man, but he's really not.*

Shamus focused his attention on the book again, rapidly blinking back tears. "This is so special," he said, his voice hoarse. "I think we should put it on top of Uncle Henry's coffin." He placed the book on top of the polished wood, positioned a spray of white roses behind it. "And I . . ." tears clouded his eyes as he fingered the left-hand page . . . "I want to read this poem aloud." His voice quavered slightly, then he favored Carmela with a soft, sad smile. "Is that okay with you? You know I recognize the poem."

Now tears shone in Carmela's eyes, too. "Of course," she told him. "Whatever you want is fine by me."

The moment was, of course, broken by Glory Meechum. Leaning heavily on a chubby, beet-faced Meechum cousin, she approached Uncle Henry's casket. "What on earth?" she said, peering at the altered book. "What's that silly little picture book doing there?" Glory spat out the words *"picture book"* as though she was referring to a pile of fresh manure.

"What this actually is," said Carmela, trying to be as nonconfrontational as possible, "is an altered book. I tried to pull together various tokens and symbols that reminded me of Uncle Henry."

Glory peered at the book again, then put a hanky to her bloated face. "How morbid."

"It's staying," Shamus told her.

"Suit yourself," sniffed Glory.

THE SERVICE WAS SEDATE, POLITE, AND SURPRISINGLY sad. Thadeus Busby, a longtime friend of Uncle Henry's, talked about how they had served together

181

during the Korean War. How Henry Meechum had been awarded a silver star for his valor during Operation Cleaver, the tank and infantry raid into the Iron Triangle. A young Meechum cousin sang *"Amazing Grace,"* and the crowd of mourners joined in as best they could, stronger on the choruses than the stanzas. And now the minister, a skinny beanpole of a man in a slightly worn black suit, was working his way through a fairly standard sermon on life, death, and resurrection.

Gazing around at the mourners, Carmela was surprised by the large turnout. There had to be more than one hundred people here today. Friends and relatives as well as business and banking acquaintances.

In the shadow of a towering spire stood Tina and Huey Tippit. Tina's large, oval-shaped dark glasses covered most of her face, and she seemed extremely subdued. Huey just looked bored.

Detective Edgar Babcock was here, of course. Studying the crowd, looking fairly natty in his dark suit, doing his best to look inconspicuous.

As Carmela's eyes continued to rove about, she found some very familiar faces, too. Tandy, Baby, Ava, and Gabby were all crowded together over near a tall, obelisk monument. Tandy was taking pictures like crazy, scrapbooking the funeral, no doubt. Then again, Tandy scrapbooked everything.

And, much to Carmela's sad surprise, Mrs. Jardell was standing off to one corner. All by herself, weeping silent tears. Carmela hoped that Glory wouldn't go careening over to the poor woman and harass her or try to shag her away.

Then it was Shamus's turn to take his place at the head of the casket. Stepping into position, he surveyed the crowd solemnly, then reached across the polished wood and picked up Carmela's altered book.

Carmela gazed at Shamus, and their eyes met, sharing a brief moment. Then he began his recitation of "On Heavenly Wings," a poem Carmela had written in honor of her father after he was killed in a barge accident on the river. The sheer simplicity of the words and Shamus's fine reading were both heartfelt and heartrending.

> *High in the Heavens*
> *The angels conferred*
> *With a whisper of wings*
> *And one soft spoken word.*
>
> *The messenger beckoned*
> *Caused many to grieve*
> *As on a wing and a prayer*
> *Their brother took leave.*
>
> *But with earthly bonds broken*
> *A joyful soul sings*
> *Borne to the Kingdom*
> *On heavenly wings.*

By the time Shamus finished there wasn't a dry eye in the house.

"You came!" cried Carmela, embracing her friends in the crowd of people that milled about the casket, offering condolences to Glory, Shamus, and the rest of the Meechum relatives. "You darlings."

"Of course, we came," said Baby. She looked sleek and sophisticated in her cream-colored Chanel suit. "Henry Meechum was a neighbor and a dear, sweet man. When Del and I first moved to the Garden District from Gentilly he generously gave us cuttings from all his plants."

"Are you coming to the reception?" Carmela inquired of her friends. Gabby had volunteered to go down to the French Quarter and run Memory Mine for the afternoon, but Carmela was hoping Baby, Tandy, and Ava might come along to lend their moral support.

But Baby gave a resolute shake of her head. "Pass," she told Carmela. "I simply can't abide Glory Meechum. The woman's an absolute witch."

"Well, Ava and I are coming," said Tandy. "I've never been inside Glory's house, and I'm dying to see if she's really as fussy about her housekeeping as everyone says she is."

"Believe me," said Carmela, "she is." Glory definitely had a touch of OCD, obsessive-compulsive disorder. Last year she'd gone through five housekeepers, worn two large area rugs threadbare, and burned out three Dirt Devils with her constant vacuuming. Carmela never missed an opportunity to run the dogs, complete with muddy paws, through Glory's house. It put the woman into a catatonic state that lasted for at least a week.

Ava dangled a little red velvet bag in front of everyone. "I brought magic charms to ward off Glory's evil eye, just in case. Dried goat's blood and bat's teeth."

Tandy gave Ava a seriously disapproving look. "It isn't really," she said, tucking her chin in.

Ava giggled. "No, not really. This is actually a new good luck charm I'm going to be selling at my shop. Arrowroot, bergamot, and cinnamon. What do you think?"

"Sounds like a topping for French toast," said Gabby.

"*Smells* like a topping for French toast," added Baby, leaning forward to take a sniff.

"I thought maybe Carmela could use a hit off it," said Ava. "For extra luck and fortitude."

"If we're going to Glory's," said Tandy, "I think we could *all* use a hit off it."

CARMELA STOOD IN GLORY'S PRISTINE, LYSOL-smelling kitchen clutching her covered Pyrex dish and feeling like a complete idiot. "I'm the only one who brought something?" she asked. All around her, young men and women in spiffy black-and-white uniforms scuttled about, arranging slices of ripe melon around wheels of Camembert cheese, preparing crab rolls, and heating miniature quiches. The catering crew.

Shamus's wide shoulders suddenly appeared in the

doorway. "Sausage balls," he exclaimed, snatching the dish from Carmela's hands. "I knew I could count on you, babe. Fantastic. These little treats are my all-time favorite!"

Carmela's eyes blazed. "You knew this reception was catered?"

Shamus popped a sausage ball into his mouth and munched heartily. "Sure." With his exuberant chewing the word came out *"Shuuuhh."*

"But you had me make sausage balls," said Carmela. She felt a hot pluck of anger right behind her eyeballs, feared she was going to lose it. Fought the urge to slip off one of her high heels and whack Shamus upside of the head.

A crooked grin creased Shamus's face as he continued to chew. "You know I'm crazy for your sausage balls, darlin'. You get that sweet-sour thing cookin', and there's nothing like it." He popped two more into his mouth. "Dang, these are good."

Wordlessly, Carmela walked out of the kitchen. The moments they'd shared earlier, when Shamus had first seen the altered book, when their eyes met just before he read the poem, were all but forgotten now. He was a clod, she told herself. A cretinous, idiotic clod. And that went for his relatives as well. If she could whisper a prayer or click her heels together and be magically transported somewhere else, she'd do it. Anywhere else. Even an IRS audit would be preferable to this ghastly reception.

"Sweetie," said Ava, grabbing Carmela's arm. "Are

you okay? You're looking a little flushed."

"I . . . I am a little hot," admitted Carmela. She was hot under the collar. But this was not the time nor place to let her Chernobyl temper explode. Oh no, that would come later.

"Here," said Ava, reaching to help with Carmela's jacket. "Slip your jacket off."

This morning, when Carmela had been scurrying around, trying to get ready, she couldn't decide if her black dress would be too cool or if her black suit would be too warm. Had settled, instead, for the dress with the suit jacket over it.

A compromise. Lots of that going around these days.

"Do you think Mrs. Jardell will have the nerve to show up here?" asked Ava as Carmela struggled to regain her composure. "I saw her on the sidelines at the cemetery. Do you know . . . is she still under suspicion because she was named a beneficiary in Uncle Henry's will?"

Carmela nodded. "She is. And her nephew's still in custody."

"Damn," said Ava, arching her eyebrows. "Think he did it? This Johnny Kool?"

Carmela gave an ambivalent shake of her head. "Not sure."

Ava frowned. "Who else could have?"

"No idea," sighed Carmela.

"And you were doing so well," said Ava. "Figuring out how to find Shamus, pawing through those bank files . . . You've got good investigative skills, girl."

"Now everything's coming up cold," Carmela told Ava. "Or, rather, somewhat ambiguous."

"But Johnny Kool could have offed Uncle Henry so that his aunt inherited the money," said Ava. "And Mrs. Jardell could still be completely innocent."

"I suppose so," said Carmela. That scenario had occurred to her, but it seemed awfully far-fetched.

"And you were suspicious about Tina and Huey Tippit. Because of the five million dollars."

"I still am," said Carmela. "And I'm wondering why they turned up at the funeral service."

"I think they're here, too," said Ava, her predatory eyes scanning the crowd. "Who else?" she prodded.

Carmela decided she *still* didn't want to say anything to Ava about Ryder Bowman. The stud muffin. After all, the only connection she had was his bank file and the alligator/swamp thing. And that was tenuous at best.

"Ladies," said a voice behind them.

Carmela and Ava turned to find Edgar Babcock surveying them with a bemused look on his face. He was balancing a plate of appetizers in one hand, looking all the world like one of the guests. "Still engaging in a little freelance detective work?" he asked.

"Who . . . us?" said Ava.

"Just chatting," murmured Carmela.

"Sure you are," said Edgar Babcock mildly.

"You know," said Ava, flashing an enticing smile. "I

have some St. Sebastian candles on close-out right now. He's the patron saint of police officers."

"Is that right?" asked Babcock. His right eyebrow twitched, indicating he was slightly amused.

"Or," continued Ava, "I could give you a really sweet deal on St. Andrew. Of course, he's the patron saint of fishmongers."

"I think I'll have to pass on both of those for now," said Edgar Babcock. Then he turned his full focus on Carmela. "You have something for me."

"I do?" asked Carmela. *What's he talking about?* she wondered.

Edgar Babcock dropped his voice. "The files."

"Oh, the files," said Carmela, giving him a look of wide-eyed innocence.

"Shamus told me he gave Henry Meechum's business files to you," said Babcock, sounding stern now. "Better he should have turned them over to us right away."

"Isn't that Shamus something," said Ava, thrusting a hip out subtly. "Probably should get hauled in for obstruction of justice."

But this time Edgar Babcock remained focused on Carmela. "I want those files today," he told her.

"You're welcome to them," said Carmela. She wasn't about to arm wrestle Lieutenant Babcock for the files. Besides, she'd been through them twice and still hadn't come up with any stunning revelations.

"You're still, uh, at your place in the French Quarter?" he asked.

Carmela gave an imperceptible nod. Her place. Yeah, right.

"Maybe I could stop by and get them tonight," proposed Edgar Babcock. He picked up a toothpick, stabbed murderously at something on his plate.

Carmela peered suspiciously at his mound of appetizers. "What have you got there?" she asked.

"Sausage balls," said Lieutenant Babcock. "And are they ever good."

"SO SHAMUS SOLD YOU OUT FOR A COUPLE SAUSAGE balls," said Ava, once Lieutenant Babcock had moved on.

"These days I get the feeling he'd sell me out for a lot less," said Carmela. She twisted her mouth into a mirthless grin. "And Shamus was the one who was so all-fired hot for me to help solve Uncle Henry's murder. He thought we could handle things quietly, not bring any unnecessary embarrassment to the bank."

"He didn't want the bank embarrassed, or Glory didn't want the bank embarrassed?" asked Ava. "Seems to me Shamus is no stranger to embarrassment. There was that hurling incident at Mardi Gras and the oyster-eating thing at Arnaud's."

"And don't forget the goat incident at Tulane," said Carmela, rolling her eyes as the two of them strolled across the room toward the bar.

Once again, Glory had enlisted the aid of her gardener, Gus, to pinch-hit as bartender. This time Gus was wearing a white shirt, black vest, red tie, and pants that seemed a little too short for his lanky build. Carmela figured Glory probably didn't trust the caterers to handle the liquor. Probably afraid they'd pilfer a lousy fifth of bourbon. Or steal her cache of mini drink umbrellas.

"Glass of red wine, please," said Ava.

Gus gave Ava a sad, hangdog look. "Sorry, miss," he said in a papery voice. "We're only serving white wine. Miss Glory doesn't want any stains on the carpet."

"Then how about a nice dry martini," said Ava. "Unless she's worried about a couple olives getting mashed down into the nap. Which I'd be more than happy to oblige with."

"And for you, Miss Carmela?" Gus looked nervous, as though he was afraid Carmela was going to order some extravagant drink involving grenadine, madori, or some other brightly colored liqueur that his boss had strictly forbidden.

"Just a glass of—" began Carmela, then she stopped short as Glory suddenly bulled her way up to the makeshift bar.

"Gus, give me two more glasses of Scotch," Glory demanded.

Gus bobbed his head, completely forgetting about Ava and Carmela's drinks. "Coming right up, Miss Glory."

Carmela stared at Glory, and Glory stared back. Then, reluctantly, Glory said, "Carmela, this is one of the bank's outstanding customers, Mr. Landry Douglas."

There were subdued hellos as Carmela said, "We met the other night."

Landry Douglas nodded, pleased she'd remembered. "Nice to see you again."

Ice cubes *clinked* into glasses as Gus struggled mightily to fill the bar order.

"Shamus's wife owns a little paper shop in the French Quarter," said Glory, tossing out her statement as a sort of non sequitur. Then her chubby fingers grasped Landry Douglas's arm, and she attempted to pull him away.

"It's a scrapbook shop," said Carmela, in a tone that indicated she wasn't amused by Glory's deliberate misnomer.

"Scrapbooking is very big right now, isn't it?" said Landry Douglas. He smiled at Carmela, seemingly interested, favored her with a look that said, *I know Glory's being terribly rude.*

"The number-one craft in America," Carmela replied. "Something like one in four families are engaged in some sort of scrapbooking, journaling, or genealogy book project. By the end of next year, scrapbooking is supposed to be a fifteen billion dollar industry."

Now Landry Douglas simply beamed at her. "A woman who understands business," he said.

Glory waved her hand dismissively. "Scrapbooking's just a fad."

"I don't think so," interjected Ava. "Carmela's really smart at gauging the market."

"Did you know," said Landry Douglas, "that back in the eighteen seventies Mark Twain, who absolutely delighted in collecting quotes and articles, developed *Mark Twain's Patent Scrapbook*?"

"Interesting," said Glory. Her flat tone indicated she could care less.

"And by the turn of the century," continued Douglas, "something like fifty versions of his albums were available?"

Carmela grinned. "How do you know this?" What he'd said was all true.

Landry Douglas grinned back at her. "I'm a student of history." He took a sip of his drink. "And, I have to admit, my wife's a fanatical scrapbooker."

WHEN CARMELA FINALLY LOCATED TANDY, SHE WAS deep in conversation with Tina Tippit.

"Have your *heard* about these condominiums, Carmela?" asked Tandy. "They sound absolutely stupendous."

"Just enough to whet my interest," lied Carmela. "Although I haven't seen the sales brochure yet."

"I'll get you one," promised Tina, "now that things are really moving forward."

"Pardon?" said Carmela.

Tina put a fluttering hand to her chest. "Huey was chatting with your sister-in-law earlier. And Glory has agreed to extend us five million dollars in additional financing! I'm thrilled to say that puts us directly into phase three."

"Ooh . . . what's phase three?" inquired Tandy.

"Construction of twenty more units and the launch of our marketing campaign," Tina told her excitedly.

"Gosh," said Tandy. "I guess I'm in the presence of some pretty high-test women today." She grinned at Tina. "You're a real estate developer." Tandy shifted her gaze to Carmela. "And Carmela is a small business owner. Of course," said Tandy, dropping her voice, "Carmela's also a crackerjack detective. Ava was telling me earlier how Carmela was . . ." Carmela put a hand on Tandy's arm to stop her, but it was too late . . . "putting together a few clues and doing some serious sleuthing concerning the murder of Henry Meechum."

Tina licked her lips and shifted an unflinching gaze toward Carmela. "Is that a fact?"

"Not really," demurred Carmela. *Ssh, Tandy,* she thought, *don't say any more.*

But Tandy pushed on. "Our Carmela's a very clever lady. This wouldn't be the first murder mystery she's solved."

"GLORY," SAID CARMELA, ONCE SHE SAW THE RECEPTION was winding down. "We need to talk."

Glory focused bleary eyes on Carmela, instantly conveying the fact that she'd once again mixed alcohol with meds. "Whadya want?" she slurred. Glory had positioned herself between the bar and the front door, so she could bid good-bye to folks and still get as many refills as needed.

"You promised five million in financing to Tina and Huey Tippit?"

Glory glared at Carmela. "And why is it you're poking your nose into bank business?"

"Do you realize that Uncle Henry turned them down two weeks ago? And that five million was the exact amount of Shamus's ransom demand?"

Glory put a hand on one hip and took a long pull on her drink. "We have the murderer," she said, enunciating each word in an exaggerated manner. "He is in custody."

"Shamus, Lieutenant Babcock . . . I think they might have made a mistake," said Carmela. She knew it was going to be difficult to convince Glory of this, but she had to try.

Glory continued to stare at her belligerently. "A mistake," mimicked Glory. "So you're telling me that everyone is wrong . . . except you. Aha. Are you by any chance personally acquainted with this Johnny Kool character?"

"Not really," said Carmela. "But I know Mrs. Jardell. She's a fine, honest woman, and if she says her nephew didn't do it, that's good enough for me."

"Even though she stands to profit from Uncle Henry's death?" Glory seemed to be taking great pleasure in their exchange.

Carmela had finally made up her mind about that issue. "Yes. Even though Mrs. Jardell will inherit money, I still don't believe she or her nephew is involved."

"Carmela," sneered Glory, "you're such an easy mark. Way too trusting, and always a little too friendly with the hired help. This Johnny Kool person was in *prison,* for heaven's sakes. For armed robbery."

"His story is that he was with a bunch of guys and didn't know they were even planning a robbery." Mrs. Jardell had been very clear in explaining this to Carmela. Apparently, Johnny's parole board had believed this story, too, and given him an early release.

Glory rolled her eyes, and Carmela had the urge to grab a bowl of clam dip from the table and pour it over Glory's head. But then she'd ruin a perfectly good bowl of clam dip.

"You two having a nice chat?" asked Shamus. He had a look of apprehension on his face. Like he'd just encountered two pit bulls who'd squared off against each other and were about to go at it tooth and nail.

"Peachy," said Carmela between clenched teeth.

"We need to talk about the Skyline deal," said Shamus, turning his attention to Glory. "When you have time."

"Of course," said Glory, a dreamy look suddenly spreading across her face at the sight of Shamus. "By the way, I'd like the two of you to put in an appearance at the opening of the new Le Rive Casino tomorrow night. We have an awful lot to be proud of. Crescent City Bank arranged the financing. Twenty million dollars in short-term bonds."

"Last I looked," said Carmela, "I wasn't part of Crescent City Bank."

Glory gave a disdainful snort. "You are Shamus's wife," she said. *"For now.* Thus your presence is required."

Chapter 17

WHAT are you doing back here?" asked Gabby. Her pistachio-colored cashmere sweater was slung casually over her shoulders. She looked like she was almost ready to lock up.

"Ava dropped me off," Carmela told her. "We couldn't handle the reception anymore."

Gabby looked immediately sympathetic. "Glory?"

Carmela nodded. "Oh yeah."

"Thank goodness she seemed fairly subdued during the service this morning," said Gabby. "Of course, most folks are subdued at a funeral."

"That was then; this is now," Carmela told her. "Glory started drinking like a stevedore once the reception got under way. So, suffice it to say, she's no longer subdued."

"Sorry," said Gabby.

Carmela dropped her oversized handbag on the front counter. "Busy afternoon?"

"Not so much," said Gabby. "Oh, but we sold the last eight packs of vintage travel stickers. To Jody over at Trinity Travel. Do you want me to order more?"

"Sure," said Carmela. She looked around, dug in her handbag, pulled out the Uncle Henry altered book. "I think we might be low on alphabet tiles and grosgrain ribbon, too. And it might not be a bad idea to order some more of those plastic scrapbook organizers. A lot of our customers seem to be heading off on weekend scrapbook retreats."

Gabby lifted a hand and indicated the book. "That sure looked nice sitting on the casket this morning. And Shamus's reading of the poem was very touching. Everyone around me was practically in tears."

Carmela turned and gently placed the altered book in the front display window next to the Nancy Drew book. "I'm glad I brought it along today," she said as her cell phone shrilled. She threaded her way back around the counter, almost knocking over a display of modeling clay, and scrambled for the phone in her handbag. "Hello?" she said.

"I've got a fantastic idea," came Ava's enthusiastic voice. "Let's go shopping!"

"Oh Ava," groaned Carmela, "it's been such a grindingly long day."

"All the more reason to blow off steam."

"And money," responded Carmela. Now that she and Shamus were on the fringes of being estranged again, she definitely had to keep a watchful eye on her cash flow.

"C'mon, *cher*," wheedled Ava, "I really need something new to wear tomorrow night."

"You've got a date tomorrow night?"

"Sure do. The grand opening of that Le Rive Casino!"

"Oh yeah," yawned Carmela. "I'm supposed to go to that, too. Something about Crescent City Bank putting up big bucks for it. I get the feeling it's kind of a command performance for the bank."

"Yowza!" shrieked Ava. "That means we *both* need brand-new killer outfits."

"I don't know," said Carmela, hedging. "Where were you thinking of starting your hunt?"

"Where else but The Latest Wrinkle?" proposed Ava.

"Our friendly local resale shop," said Carmela.

"Resale, yes," said Ava. "But great, great stuff. Thanks to all the tasteful and moneyed ladies of New Orleans who wear an outfit once or twice, then get colossally bored with it. Their loss is our gain." Ava paused. "Or, if they gain weight and can't wear the outfit, is their gain our loss? No, that's not quite right," she muttered.

"Oh, man," said Carmela, still on the cusp of hesitation. "I really should get home and walk Boo and Poobah."

"Tyrell already did that," said Ava. "Just twenty minutes ago. He fed your little fur monsters, too, as well as that wretched, squawking bird. So you've got nary an excuse." Tyrell Burton was Ava's assistant, an

African American who attended Tulane. With his grandmother's Haitian background, Tyrell spun the most perfect legends and lore to Ava's customers and sold a ton of merchandise. Only problem was, Tyrell had just received his MA in history and was supposed to head off to Stanford in another month to begin work on his doctorate.

"How are you ever going to find anyone as smart and reliable as Tyrell?" asked Carmela. He was a whiz at business, too, and had helped put Ava's entire inventory on computer. As much as one could inventory magical charms.

"I have no idea," said Ava, suddenly reminded of Tyrell's impending departure. "I get hysterical just thinking about trying to replace him. And whoever I find, he definitely has to be quirky," added Ava. "After all, we are in the business of selling voodoo charms."

"He?" asked Carmela. "It's got to be a he?"

"More fun to look at," purred Ava.

MAGAZINE STREET, FROM WASHINGTON AVENUE TO Audubon Park, was an elegant, old-world tapestry of picturesque wooden cottages as well as stately and historic brick buildings with sleekly redesigned storefronts. Here, antique shops, art galleries, coffee shops, and elegant little boutiques had found the perfect home.

The Latest Wrinkle, located between Harmony and Pleasant, was situated in a cottage, formerly a single-family home, that had been added on to in back.

Furnished with antique Oriental carpets, brass floor lamps with fringed shades, and velvet fainting couches, The Latest Wrinkle featured antique wooden breakfronts and chiffoniers filled to capacity with silk blouses, T-shirts, cotton drawstring slacks, and sweaters. Rack after rolling rack held precious loads of designer clothes that had been brought in for resale. Antique shelves had offerings of brand-new shawls, scarves, and costume jewelry.

Mardi Gras masks hung on eggplant-colored walls alongside oil paintings and framed Mardi Gras invitations. A sprawling library table covered with a velvet piano shawl displayed gently worn pairs of Manolo Blahnik, Christian Laboutin, and Jimmy Choo shoes.

Ava wasted no time. She spun through the shop like a determined professional shopper, grabbing a black silk wrap dress, a long red dress with a mermaid-looking flare at the bottom, and a short gold dress that was slightly deconstructed.

Carmela, checking the racks carefully, came up with a short plum-colored chiffon cocktail dress.

"Look at this," said Ava, holding up the red dress, obviously her favorite find du jour. "I think this is a Valentino, even though somebody cut out the label." She spoke in the kind of reverential tone most people reserve for church.

"Oh it is, for sure," said Melanie, the manager of the shop. She was fashion model skinny with pale skin, long blond hair, and prominent cheekbones. Tonight she was poured into a tight black knit dress. "We have

201

one very prominent lady, I don't *dare* reveal her name, who always brings her ball gowns to us once the Mardi Gras season is over. And almost all of them are couture."

"You hear that?" said Ava to Carmela. "Couture." She reached over, grabbed a tiny, feathered hat from a display. "Isn't this adorable," she said, popping the brown-and-gold feathered creation on her head, then sweeping her long hair up with her hands to study her image.

"But not with the red dress," cautioned Carmela.

Ava removed the tiny hat from her head and plopped it atop Carmela's head. "But maybe with *your* dress," she suggested.

Carmela straightened the hat as she gazed at herself in the slightly wavy and ornately gilt three-way mirror. Sauvignon blond-streaked hair topped with an almost-matching pouf of feathers. The look, much to her surprise, was amazingly *chic.*

"Wonderful!" declared Melanie. "It's very *you.*"

"And youthful," said Ava. "Try on the dress."

So of course Carmela's plum-colored dress fit like it had been custom designed for her. And Ava's red mermaid dress also clung to her in perfect, form-fitting style.

"But is this appropriate for a casino opening?" wondered Carmela. The plum dress was by Nina Ricci. Sleeveless, low cut, the skirt hitting just at the knee. Very Audrey Hepburn–looking but in a modern way.

Ava slipped on a pair of black satin pumps. "The

operative word is *casino,* darling. Which means anything goes. Blue jeans, cocktail dresses, even glittering gowns!"

Carmela appraised herself in the mirror again. She
did look cute, she decided. Damn cute.

"Well, I'm gonna get this red dress," said Ava. "This
will make the stud muffin think he died and ascended
to heaven."

"Or at least third base," grinned Carmela. "Okay, as
long as we're going all out, I'm going to ante up for
this dress, too."

"Just the dress?" asked Ava.

"Just the dress," said Carmela. She'd already
checked the price tag on the hat.

"Hey, Spenderella," cajoled Ava, "the feather hat
makes the outfit. Gives it a sort of British flair. Very
Camilla."

"Are you serious?" gasped Carmela. "This bit of
feathery fluff costs two hundred and fifty dollars!"

"Yeah, but it's couture," said Ava, as if that justified
the extravagance. "And probably cost over a thousand
dollars new. Besides, you can put the whole shebang
on Shamus's credit card. You still have Shamus's
credit card, don't you?"

Carmela nodded at her image in the wavy mirror,
admiring the way the feathers twined with her blond
hair. Oh yeah, she sure did have Shamus's credit card.

Ava came up behind her, put her hands on either side
of Carmela's waist. "Then go for it," she urged in a
cajoling voice.

Carmela giggled even as she considered Ava's words. Felt like Ava was the little devil sitting on her left shoulder telling her to go for it. But who was the little angel plopped on her right shoulder telling her to restrain herself? Shamus? Glory?

Oh no, I don't think so.

After the beating she'd taken from Glory Meechum today, maybe she did deserve a treat. Glory had all but ordered her to attend the casino opening tomorrow night. And Shamus had stood there, nodding his agreement like some silly bobble-head doll.

"Okay," said Carmela. "The dress and the hat."

Melanie rushed in for the kill. "Ladies," she announced, "have you checked out our jewelry counter yet?"

THIRTY MINUTES LATER, CARMELA AND AVA WERE parked in a booth at Tipitinas, the original good-time music bar on Napoleon Street. A group called the St. Claude Street Band was cranking out their chanka-chanka Cajun rhythms. Carmela and Ava were acting as a mutual admiration society for their newly purchased earrings.

"The pearls look good?" asked Ava. She put them on, cocked her head, enjoying the feel and motion of the drop earrings.

"Gorgeous," replied Carmela. She herself had picked up a pair of gold coin earrings, a pair that Ava had declared *molto* Italian and very "designery."

Ava chattered on. "Remember that scene in the

movie *Casino* when Robert De Niro marries Sharon Stone, then takes her home and gives her all those fur coats and a treasure chest filled with Bulgari jewelry? That's gotta be my all-time favorite movie scene."

"Better than Rhett carrying Scarlett up the stairs in *Gone With the Wind*?" asked Carmela. "Or the final scene in *Pretty Woman*? Or, hey, what about the ending of *Sleepless in Seattle*?"

"All great romantic scenes, I give you that," said Ava. "But the Bulgari jewelry scene is still the best. I positively get *chills*."

They ordered drinks, listened to the band thunking away onstage, relaxed.

After a generous glass of Chardonnay, Carmela finally got up the courage to reveal to Ava her vague suspicions about the stud muffin.

Ava listened to her friend, then nodded knowingly. "I can see where you're coming from, what with Ryder owning an alligator farm and all that. And the fact that Shamus was kidnapped by a couple swamp rats. But I just know you're wrong. Dead wrong."

"I hope so," said Carmela. "Truly."

"Oh, you are," said Ava. She winked at Carmela, raised her arm to signal the waiter for another round. "But just to make sure, I promise to keep a keen eye on Ryder."

Great, thought Carmela. *Now if we can just figure out who's gonna watch over you.*

Chapter 18

BOO and Poobah set up a rousing chorus of howls when Carmela returned home that night.

"Ssh, hush," she told them as she let herself and her multiple purchases in. The dogs had been fed, they'd been walked, but Carmela decided to take both dogs out for a quick spin around the block again, pooper scooper and plastic bags at the ready. Then, still feeling monumentally guilty that she'd left them alone all day, Carmela gave each pup one of her home-baked dog treats, the ones she called Baby Boo's Baby Food Cookies, once they got back to her place.

Now, the thing of it was, *she* hadn't eaten. Compound that with a measly piece of toast for breakfast, a minuscule piece of cheese at Glory's, and the two glasses of Chardonnay at Tipitina's, and you had yourself a potent recipe for an alcohol-induced hunger headache.

Bustling into her small kitchen, Carmela decided to set things right. She downed a couple aspirin, figured she could throw together a nice, quick casserole. Maybe even whip up a tin of buttermilk biscuits.

Flipping through her recipe cards, Carmela pulled out her recipe for Chicken and Broccoli Divan. It was a homey recipe she'd picked up from her momma. Then she set about shredding cheese, melting butter, and chopping bread crumbs.

But wait. She didn't have fresh broccoli.

Hold everything; maybe there was a package of frozen broccoli stuck in the icy recess of her freezer.

Carmela dug past a clump of frozen shrimp, a forgotten loaf of sandwich bread, a package of mystery meat wrapped in white butcher's paper, and a pint of chocolate mint ice cream that was so old it had an inch of freezer burn on the outside of the carton. She finally found that box of frozen broccoli wedged way in the back.

Okay, good.

But as she pushed all the frozen food she'd dislodged toward the back of the freezer, a little white box slithered past her, tumbled down, then smacked hard on the floor.

Bending down to grab the wayward box, Carmela was shocked when she recognized the fancy gold lettering on the box's top flap: Willoughby's Cakes & Tortes.

Flipping open the box, Carmela gazed solemnly down at the little marzipan bride and groom anchored solidly to the top tier of her wedding cake. The tiny couple, feet mired in icing, hands joined but eyes staring straight ahead as if lost in their own private worlds, were covered with a thin layer of white frost. As though they'd been traversing the nether regions of the Arctic for a very long time.

Frosty, thought Carmela. *If that isn't an telling prediction I don't know what is.*

Without hesitating, she reached down and snapped off the head of the miniature groom in a gesture of pique. She let the little marble-sized appendage roll around in the palm of her hand for a few seconds, then flipped it toward the garbage pail, where it landed inside with a loud *thunk*. Carmela decided a psychiatrist would probably have a field day analyzing that single action.

Oh well, at least I didn't feed the little groom's head to the dogs. That would have really been creepy.

Deciding the rest of the duo wasn't any use to her now, unless she wanted to dump the bride completely and pursue a headless horseman theme, Carmela tossed the rest of the wedding cake couple into the garbage, too.

Then she tossed the broccoli into a pot that was bubbling away on her stove, dug around for a can of cream of broccoli soup.

Once she had her casserole in the oven, the buttermilk biscuits were a cinch. Flour, sugar, baking powder, shortening, and, of course, buttermilk. Carmela was humming away, cutting out biscuit rounds using a juice glass, when there was a loud knock at the door followed by howls from the dogs.

Probably Detective Babcock come to collect those files, she decided. She had them all stacked on the table, ready to go.

Wiping her flour-dusted hands on a kitchen towel, Carmela went to the door and edged it open, throwing a body block on both hounds. Edgar Babcock stood there, a look of supreme befuddlement on his face.

"I've got some bad news," he told her.

"Shamus!" Carmela cried, clapping a hand to her breast and steeling herself for bad news. *I shouldn't have snapped off the groom's head like that. Makes for bad karma. Or very bad juju, as Ava would say.* "What happened now?" she asked, apprehension evident in her voice. *Please don't tell me he's been decapitated or something like that.*

Edgar Babcock held his hands out as if to steady her. "Take it easy. This has nothing at all to do with Shamus. Or any other family member. The thing is . . . your shop was broken into."

"What?" shrilled Carmela. "Memory Mine?" In her mind's eye she suddenly pictured expensive scrapbook paper strewn everywhere, glue sticks, paint, and embossing powder coloring the white tile floor like a Jackson Pollock painting.

"The good news is," said Edgar Babcock, "the burglars didn't really get in."

Now Carmela squinted at him. "Memory Mine was broken into but not really broken into?"

"Someone tried to jimmy the lock," Babcock explained.

"Front or back?" asked Carmela, even though she was pretty sure of the answer.

"Back door. A couple guys coming out of Cat Daddy's Bar down the alley saw some asshole pounding away on it. They shouted at him, but he took off running."

"As opposed to just offering himself up for arrest," said Carmela. She'd tried to make her words sound droll, but decided they'd come across a little shrill.

"Hey," said Babcock, holding up his hands in a defensive posture. "Don't shoot the messenger. I'm only here because I caught the report over my radio. And I figured there might be a remote possibility that this break-in tied in to the murder of Henry Meechum." He hesitated. "Or Shamus's kidnapping."

"Really," said Carmela, lifting an inquisitive eyebrow.

Lieutenant Babcock spread both hands in a gesture that said, *Why not?*

"So now you're asking me what I think?" Carmela said, surveying him and taking a step back.

"I suppose so," said Babcock, suddenly seeing where this was going and looking unhappy.

"I thought you told me to stay out of this," said Carmela. "To leave investigating to the *professionals*." The words came rolling off her tongue like an accusation.

Edgar Babcock pursed his lips. "Okay, so now I'm asking for your help. Or I at least want to know if you have a hunch about something. If you see some sort of connection."

"Huh," said Carmela. "A connection."

"Look," said Babcock, beginning to get frustrated. "I don't know what the hell is going on here either."

"That makes two of us," said Carmela, reaching down to grab the dogs' collars and pull them away from Edgar Babcock. For some reason they were extremely attracted to his pants. Maybe he had a dog or a cat. Or maybe he just had interesting pants.

"You haven't kept me up to date on anything," continued Carmela. "Did the crime scene people turn up anything at the swamp house where Shamus was kept? Do you know when Johnny Kool was released from prison? And exactly how much money does Mrs. Jardell stand to inherit?"

"Okay, okay," said Babcock. "Touché. My team is working on all those things. And I promise I'll let you know—soon."

"Do I have to go down there now?" Carmela asked suddenly. "Is the back door lock completely trashed? Could someone get inside my shop?"

"No, no, the lock's screwed up all right, but it'll hold until morning. Besides, I told the beat cops to keep an eye on things."

"Thank you," said Carmela, calming down slightly. "And thanks for coming by."

"No problem," said Babcock. "Just be sure to call a locksmith first thing, okay?"

"Will do," said Carmela, wondering how Gabby was going to take this. Gabby was a little paranoid to begin with. And her husband, Stuart, was the original Chicken Little. The sky was *always* falling as far as Stuart was concerned. In fact, in the aftermath of Hurricane Katrina, Stuart, who was as far from a holistic being as the CEO of a Swiss pharmaceutical conglomerate, had resorted to herbs, New Age music, and some sort of ginseng tonic to help relieve his stress and anxiety.

"Here," said Carmela, scooping the bank files off the table and handing them over to Edgar Babcock. "I guess these are what you really came for."

Detective Babcock tucked the stack of manila folders under his arm. "If you think of anything, let me know, okay?" He glanced down at his knees, where Boo was performing a muzzle lock.

Carmela hesitated. "There is one thing," she said. "Actually, a couple things."

Babcock waited for her to continue.

"Could you check on Tina and Huey Tippit?" Carmela asked. "The thing is, Uncle Henry turned them down on five million in financing, then Glory went and approved it."

"Interesting," said Edgar Babcock. Juggling the files, he managed to pull a small notebook from his pocket and jot down a couple notes. "What else?" he asked.

"Uh . . . could you also check on a guy named Ryder Bowman?" asked Carmela. "He's the CEO of a company called Shipco International."

"Ryder Bowman," said Babcock in a tone that indicated he might be familiar with the name. "What makes you think this guy might be involved?"

"Alligator farm," said Carmela.

"Alligator farm," repeated Babcock. "Okeydokey."

"Look," said Carmela, hating Edgar Babcock's condescending tone and feeling more than a little stupid. "Just run his name through the system or whatever it is you law enforcement people do, awright?"

"Sure," agreed Babcock, but his eyes danced with mirth.

"And what do you know about casino financing?" asked Carmela.

"You mean for Le Rive?" asked Babcock. "Just that Henry Meechum was peripherally involved."

"Aren't casinos usually run by gangsters?" asked Carmela. "Organized crime?"

Babcock lifted an eyebrow. "Maybe back in the days of Vito Genovese and Sam Giancana. But now reputable financial institutions are involved."

"Awright," said Carmela as Edgar Babcock headed out the door, "but if you stumble across anything in those files, be sure to let me know." She closed the door, latched it, let loose an enormous sigh.

Picking up the packages she'd dropped on the sofa earlier, Carmela toted them into the bedroom. She pulled out the dress, smoothed it gently, hung it on a padded hanger in her closet. Took the feathered hat, set it on top of her head. Wandering back out to the kitchen, Carmela put a scoop of the chicken and broccoli divan in a ceramic bowl, grabbed two buttermilk biscuits, arranged it all on a wicker tray. Carrying it over to her leather chair, she passed by Eduardo's cage. Suddenly excited, the bird jumped from his lower perch to his top perch, eyeing her carefully.

"Pretty," the bird called out. *"Pretty lady."*

Carmela had to laugh out loud. Eduardo had noticed her hat with the feathers and interpreted her as a kind of kindred spirit.

But even as she chuckled, Carmela wondered if the break-in at her shop *was* connected to something larger. Wondered what someone thought was so tempting inside her shop.

The files, she thought suddenly. *Did someone know I had those bank files sitting at my store? And if so, who?*

Chapter 19

M ONEY," said Gabby the next morning. "It had to be someone looking for money. After all, today is Friday. So there's almost a week's receipts inside the safe."

"But it's not *that* much money," responded Carmela. Memory Mine was profitable, but it was far from being a cash cow. Besides, Carmela decided, an awful lot of people paid with credit cards these days, so they didn't have to hassle with carrying cash. And who on earth knew how to crack a safe these days? Didn't that pretty much go out with John Dillinger and his gang?

"Doesn't have to be a lot of money," argued Gabby. "Look at all the convenience stores that get robbed these days. What do those stickup artists come away with anyway? Maybe twenty bucks, a couple packages of stale Twinkies, and a few cartons of Marlboro Lights."

"Marlboro Lights?" said Carmela, as she shuffled through the morning mail. "Burglars are concerned about reducing their intake of tar and nicotine?"

"Maybe," shrugged Gabby.

"Whoever tried to break in was after *inventory*," insisted Baby. She had shown up early and was finishing the last three pieces of her memory quilt. "I've heard countless stories of retail shops being robbed by people who had aspirations of setting up their own stores."

"Are you serious?" exclaimed Gabby. "That sounds more like a hijacking."

"It happened over in Slidell," said Baby. "Two good old boys cleaned out part of Baugher's Hardware Store so they could set up their own store in one of those public storage lockers."

"So maybe Carmela's going to have some serious competition," laughed Gabby.

"I already do," said Carmela. "That darling little shop over in Chalmette."

Gabby thought for a long moment. "You mean . . . um . . . Jill? Oh, you two attended that big industry show in Las Vegas together, didn't you."

"Here's the thing," said Carmela. "There's a good chance this was just a garden variety break-in. Remember when Barty Hayward had his antique shop next to us?"

Gabby and Baby both nodded. Gabby said, "I remember."

"Barty was broken into a couple times," said Carmela. She still figured last night's break-in had to be about the bank files, but she didn't want Gabby and

Baby to get any more upset than they already were.

"Carmela's probably right," said Gabby, accepting the explanation. "Come to think of it, Roumilott's Jewelry down the street was broken into last month. They lost all their diamonds and South Sea pearls."

"Well, there you go," shrugged Baby. "Back to square one."

AN HOUR LATER, ORDERS HAD BEEN WRITTEN UP AND e-mailed to their suppliers, inventory was straightened on shelves and sitting in harmony with Shamus's rose bouquets. With walk-in traffic tapering off somewhat, Carmela decided she was ready for something new. A new project perhaps.

Ducking into her tiny office in back, Carmela scrounged around, found what she was looking for, then stepped back out and set three empty silver soup cans in the middle of the back craft table.

Baby smiled up at her. "Oh my, is it lunchtime already?"

"Not quite," said Carmela. "But I've been threatening to find a use for all our extra scraps and snips of paper. And now I think I've got it figured out."

Getting interested now, Gabby studied the three empty soup cans. "I bet you're thinking of desk accessories," she said. "Like pencil or brush holders?"

Carmela nodded.

"Ooh, show us," urged Baby, who always had boundless energy when it came to a new craft project.

Pulling open one of the flat files, Carmela scooped

up a handful of paper scraps and laid her colorful treasures on the table. She sorted through them for a few moments, pulling out various textures and prints, then said, "I think I'm channeling *Out of Africa.*"

"That sounds fairly compelling," said Baby.

Carmela took a piece of French silk paper with a beige marbled finish and wrapped it around one of the silver soup cans. Working gently with the paper and using her glue stick, Carmela soon had the can covered completely, even folding the paper over the top lip of the can to carefully camouflage it.

"Great," said Baby as she watched. "Now what?"

Taking two one-inch strips of shiny tortoiseshell-looking paper, Carmela wound one around the top of the can and one about an inch up from the bottom. Once those paper strips were fixed into place, Carmela glued on a few crinkly gold and brown fibers, then took a brass zebra embellishment and glued it on near the top.

Baby squinted at Carmela's handiwork. "You certainly completed that little project in a flash," she said.

Carmela pushed a tin can toward her. "It's easy. You try it."

"Not sure what kind of design to do," said Baby. "My home office is a little more old-world."

"What about using this eggplant-colored suede paper?" offered Carmela, pushing a strip toward her. "You could sponge some gold and bronze acrylic paint onto it for added color and texture, then add some of this gray velvet ribbon strung with small pearlized beads."

"Love it," declared Baby. "But the finished project sounds so much better when you describe it. I don't suppose you'd want to—"

"Yoo-hoo!" called a strident voice as the front door of the shop flew open. "Yoo-hoo, Carmela!"

Carmela turned in her chair and blinked. She wasn't sure she'd ever actually heard anyone utter the phrase *yoo-hoo* before.

Mrs. Purdy, the leasing agent for Carmela's apartment building and a vision in purple, was pushing her way toward them. Mrs. Purdy wore a purple silk pantsuit that had to be a holdover from the eighties and large purple-framed glasses with Coke-bottle lenses. She was mid-sixties and also carried a faint purple streak in her white, slightly teased hair. Ava, who didn't care much for Mrs. Purdy, always called her Mrs. Goody Goody Gumbo.

Carmela bounded out of her chair and met Mrs. Purdy halfway. "Mrs. Purdy," she exclaimed, her voice conveying surprise at this impromptu visit. "What can I do for you?"

"I tippy-tapped on your apartment door earlier this morning," said Mrs. Purdy in a high, singsong voice, "but the only answer I got came from a pack of yapping dogs." She eyed Carmela sharply. "Just how many dogs do you have in there, anyway? Eight dogs? Ten?"

"No, no, just the two," Carmela assured her. "I hope that's not a problem."

"Not specifically," replied Mrs. Purdy blithely. "But

218

I did want to show the apartment to a prospective tenant."

Caught off guard, Carmela stared at her. "Show the apartment?" she stammered.

"As you know," said Mrs. Purdy, "space is at a premium in the French Quarter. So many folks are utterly *taken* with the idea of living in these historic buildings, and your lease is up at the end of the month." Mrs. Purdy delivered this information in rapid-fire succession.

"But I . . . I'm not leaving," Carmela blurted out.

Mrs. Purdy dropped her chin and peered over purple-rimmed glasses. "I was under the impression you'd moved back in with your husband, dear." Her statement carried a vague note of disapproval.

"Well, I did," began Carmela.

"So why do you need the apartment?" pressed Mrs. Purdy, suddenly looking more than a little curious.

Not wanting to spill out her entire litany of marital problems in front of Mrs. Purdy, Carmela just said, "because I need it."

Mrs. Purdy's jaw hardened; she suddenly looked unhappy. "For how long?"

"Not sure," replied Carmela. At this point she had no earthly idea if she'd be moving back in with Shamus or if she'd have to hole up in the French Quarter for the rest of her natural born days.

"That's a rather unsatisfactory answer," pronounced Mrs. Purdy. "As a leasing agent, I need to *know* unequivocally if you're going to renew or not. Otherwise I have three other parties who have shown great interest."

"What about a short-term lease?" asked Carmela, scrambling.

Mrs. Purdy shook her head, and her white hair, purple streak included, moved slowly, like clouds passing. "That's not really acceptable. These other parties have already expressed a willingness to commit to a long-term lease."

Carmela considered this critical information for a split second. She didn't want to find herself on the street with no place to go, and she wasn't certain about moving back in with Shamus. "How about a six-month lease?" she hedged. "Is that long-term enough?"

Mrs. Purdy's face lost none of its disapproval as she slowly opened her notebook and made a couple random jottings. "A one-year lease would be prefer-able," she replied.

Carmela took a big gulp. "I suppose I can commit to that," she said.

"Good," said Mrs. Purdy, snapping her notebook shut, happy to have bullied Carmela into compliance. "Excellent."

Of course, the solution was a long way from excel-lent, but it was the best Carmela could manage for now.

CARMELA WAS HUDDLING WITH MR. PETERS, THE locksmith, at the back door when Shamus called.

"I'll pick you up promptly at seven," he told her.

"I'm only doing this for you," she replied. "Not because Glory has demanded I be present tonight as some sort of familial prop."

"God, you're an angel," said Shamus. "You've never let me down, Carmela. I can always count on you."

Carmela didn't say a word. She wondered if she could count on him for rent money.

"Be sure to dress real fancy," Shamus added. "This shindig tonight is a *very* big deal. Crescent City Bank has pretty much bankrolled this new casino, so we're all kind of like guests of honor. There'll be lots of champagne and caviar and stuff." He let loose a forced laugh, obviously cognizant that Carmela was barely tolerating this conversation. "Fish eggs," he added gamely, hoping for a reaction. Any reaction.

"I'll be ready," said Carmela, not the least bit impressed by the idea of imported caviar or Shamus's feeble attempt at humor.

"I'm wearing my Armani tux," said Shamus. "Still fits like a dream, of course." He paused. "Do you by any chance know where my red cummerbund is?"

"You could try looking in your closet," advised Carmela.

"Right," said Shamus. "I'll do that. Okay, watch for me tonight, babe, I'll be the good-looking guy in the James Bond tuxedo."

"Are you bringing your gun along, Mr. Double-O-Seven?"

"You bet I am," said Shamus emphatically. "Who knows, those assholes could try to kidnap me again!"

Chapter 20

LIGHTS blinked and flashed in a dizzying array of colors. Slot machines clanked and thunked loudly with silver dollar payoffs. And men and women in black-tie dress, their faces flushed with excitement, hoisted flutes of champagne to toast the opening of New Orleans's brand-new Le Rive Casino.

Carmela had been on board the super-sized riverboat for all of five minutes and already had the beginnings of a tension headache. And why not? The minute the motorized skiff had deposited them on deck, Shamus had dashed off somewhere, probably to be feted as the heir apparent for Crescent City Bank. And now she was left standing in the middle of a casino that was utter bedlam. Guests rushed from clattering slot machines to pinging poker machines to green-felt blackjack tables. All were eager to enjoy casino gaming and anxiously hoping for a serendipitous visit from Lady Luck.

And everyone, except her, seemed bowled over by this super luxe casino with its plush red carpeting, cascading chandeliers, and riverboat atmosphere. Carmela wondered how long she had to politely endure this spectacle before she could be ferried back to shore again.

"Carmela!" shrilled Ava. She came galloping up in her red mermaid dress, fish tail churning, and wildly threw her arms around her friend. "You made it!"

"Just barely," said Carmela, tugging at her dress. The designer creation that had seemed so perfect the night before now felt a trifle short on her. And the chiffon fabric seemed to ride up a bit as she walked. Carmela certainly hadn't noticed *that* in the shop.

"You look *très chic,*" exclaimed Ava, her eyes quickly taking in Carmela's outfit. "I don't remember that dress being quite so short, but the mini length looks very sexy on you anyway. Extremely va-va-voom! And the hat . . ." Ava clapped her hands together gleefully . . . "the hat is to *die* for!"

Self-consciously, Carmela put a hand up, fingertips grazing the puff of plumage that nested in her short, choppy hair. "I think a bird *did* die for this."

"God, don't you just adore this scene?" asked Ava, gazing around and letting loose with an excited little shiver. "So many movers and shakers to rub shoulders with. Can't you just smell the money!" She batted her eyelashes, and Carmela could see that they were tinged with iridescent copper.

"Speaking of money," said Carmela, "where exactly is your Mr. Ryder Bowman tonight? You did accompany him, right? Or, rather, he accompanied you."

"The stud muffin's over there playing baccarat," said Ava, waving a hand in a grand gesture. "Le Rive's not going to offer baccarat when they open to the general public, but they have it special tonight

223

because of all the fat cats."

"It's like blackjack?" asked Carmela. She wasn't a gambler, wasn't particularly enchanted with the notion of gaming. But she knew she'd probably have to try her hand at something tonight. Kill a little time, be polite.

"Baccarat's like mini blackjack," explained Ava. "You only play to nine."

"To nine," said Carmela, tucking this fact away.

Ava hesitated, suddenly not so certain about her pronouncement. "Or maybe you play to eleven." She grabbed two flutes of champagne from the tray of a passing white-coated waiter and shoved one into Carmela's hands. "Come to think of it, I'm not really sure. But I do know that rich people *adore* it."

EVERYONE WAS IN ATTENDANCE HERE TONIGHT, Carmela decided. In the span of about ten minutes she ran into any number of friends and acquaintances. Baby and her husband, Del, were there, looking very amused with the goings-on and very much in love with each other.

And as she edged up to a wide expanse of bar to trade in her champagne for a glass of red wine, she met Jekyl Hardy, a dear friend who was an antique dealer and one of the premier Mardi Gras float builders. Lean and tan, with dark hair pulled back into a sleek ponytail, Jekyl was always hyperalert.

"Isn't this fantastic?" Jekyl asked, gesturing toward the thousands of glass bottles that sparkled behind the bar. "More than sixty-five premium vodkas and forty malt scotches. A real testament to New Orleans's appetite for excess, wouldn't you say?"

"It surely is," said Carmela. There was a reason New Orleans had earned the nickname, the Big Easy.

Jekyl's dark eyebrows shot up as he peered at Carmela in mock horror. "Oh, heavens. Do I get the feeling *you* don't like this scene either?"

Carmela did a pantomime gesture of a half faint, worthy of a silent screen star, then threw an arm companionably around Jekyl's shoulders. "I despise it, too," she murmured in his ear.

Jekyl took a heroic sip of bourbon and gave a harsh grin. "Guess I'm just an old-fashioned boy, but I much prefer an *intime* dinner party in an elegant French Quarter apartment."

Carmela grinned in return. Jekyl Hardy was a French Quarter habitué himself, and she'd attended more than a few of his marvelous dinner parties. In fact, Carmela would have much preferred to be mingling with soft-spoken guests in Jekyl's fairy-tale apartment than to be here now.

Jekyl's third-floor walk-up in a 150-year-old brick building boasted dark blue shellacked walls, a pitted marble fireplace, and antique smoked mirrors in gilded frames. Both the living room and parlor contained overstuffed furniture covered in old-fashioned brocades and dark damask fabrics. Lamps cast dim shadows, Chinese carpets were slightly scuffed but quite authentic, hardwood floors creaked and sagged.

The overall impression, like the city of New Orleans itself, was an aura of genteel decay and decadence. One kept expecting Tennessee Williams to emerge from the shadows.

"A little bird told me you moved back to your apartment," commented Jekyl.

"A little bird named Ava?"

Jekyl nodded happily, gestured for another drink.

"She's right," said Carmela, wondering if everyone knew about her sort-of-single-again status, if that's what it really was.

"Are you planning a short-term stay or long-term stay?" Jekyl asked casually.

"Don't know," said Carmela, for she really didn't. And why did Jekyl suddenly sound like Mrs. Purdy?

"Just remember, dear girl," responded Jekyl, "even the great Napoleon Bonaparte went into exile twice." Napoleon was Jekyl Hardy's personal hero. Jekyl had several white marble busts of the French emperor displayed prominently throughout his apartment.

"Yes," replied Carmela. "But Napoleon *died* in exile."

ON HER WAY TO THE LADIES' ROOM, WHERE SHE FIG-ured she could kill another few minutes, Carmela ran into Byrle Coopersmith and her husband Charles. Byrle was one of her regulars at Memory Mine. A fanatical scrapbooker, rubber stamper, and card maker who loved the sheer joy of expressing herself creatively.

"Hey," said Byrle, once they'd all said their hi-how-are-yous, "thanks for your suggestion about doing a memory scrapbook. We think Charles's Aunt Mina is doing a whole lot better because of it."

Charles nodded eagerly. "She really is."

"Sometimes all it takes," said Carmela, "is a visual prompt." She was a major advocate of creating memory scrapbooks for seniors who were having difficulty remembering family and past events. By putting together family albums with photos that were clearly captioned and dated, as well as life and family timelines, seniors with memory problems could refer to these memory prompts and not feel so embarrassed, lost, or alienated. It was Carmela's wish that scrapbookers everywhere helped create these albums for seniors.

"Have you tried your hand at any of the blackjack tables yet?" asked Byrle.

"On my way now," said Carmela. But as she swept around a corner, she ran smack-dab into Tina Tippit.

"Carmela," said Tina, pulling her mouth into a Cheshire cat grin. "We meet again."

"Nice to see you," stammered Carmela. *Goodness, why do I keep running into this woman?* she wondered. Then, because she wasn't sure what to say, added, "How are the condos progressing?"

That was the exact opening Tina needed. She immediately launched into a builder's diatribe that included details on zoning regulations, ceiling joists, and setbacks and clearances. When Tina finally exhausted herself on those subjects, she veered into details about tough new EPA standards and property taxes.

"Sounds like you've got a full plate," commented Carmela, wondering how best to extricate herself from this rather one-sided conversation. Drywall and piping just weren't that scintillating.

"Seems like you're awfully busy, too," said Tina. "I was most interested to hear that you were personally looking into the death of Shamus's uncle." Tina Tippit stopped, peered carefully at Carmela. "More people should play the concerned citizen," she added. "The world would be a far, far better place."

ON THE WAY BACK FROM THE LADIES' ROOM, Carmela finally encountered Shamus again. He was standing with a big, burly man dressed in a slightly too-tight tux, and Shamus seemed to be laughing at all the man's jokes.

"Carmela!" Shamus waved wildly at her to come join them. "Come on over here."

She cautiously approached the two men.

"Carmela," said Shamus, "this is Zig Crawford. He's the general manager of Le Rive Casino."

Zig Crawford's red face beamed at her. "Call me Crawfish, honey, everybody does."

"Yo, Crawfish!" whooped Shamus as the two of them clinked their glasses together hard, slopping drinks everywhere.

"So you're Shamus's better half," said Crawford, peering at her with a genial smile. "The lady with the fancy scrapbook store. I bet you're just doing a hell of a job with that."

"Trying to," said Carmela.

Zig turned his megawatt smile back on Shamus. "Well, we're just pleased as punch with your husband and his entire clan. They put up a shitload of money to help launch our new casino."

"It's lovely," Carmela told him. She didn't feel it was appropriate to tell Zig Crawford that she thought his casino resembled a movie set for a tacky bordello. "Too bad Uncle Henry isn't here to see this. I understand he was involved in helping set up the financing."

"Henry Meechum," said Zig, dropping his voice to a reverential tone.

"Uncle Henry knew a good thing when he saw it," agreed Shamus.

"But your husband is a financial genius in his own right," crowed Zig Crawford.

Carmela lifted an eyebrow. "Really." This was the first she'd heard of any financial genius genes in this generation of the Meechum family. For the most part, the current crop of Meechums had simply inherited the Crescent City banking empire and just served as stewards, trying best not to rock the boat or make too many bad loans.

"Now don't go tellin' everybody about those oil futures," warned Shamus, grinning widely. "That's just between you and me."

"Shit," said Crawford, favoring Carmela with a broad wink and playfully smacking Shamus on the arm, "I bet you must've told twenty people about them already."

CARMELA WAS TRYING TO FIGURE OUT BLACKJACK. Did she hit on fourteen and sit tight on sixteen? Or did it depend entirely on what cards the dealer was holding? And what about fifteen? That seemed like one of those iffy numbers right there in the middle. Why did everyone else at her table look like they knew exactly what they were doing, and she didn't? Did she have enough chips to hang in the game? And if she got tired of playing, could she just gather up her chips and walk away? Clearly, she needed some sort of lesson in gambling etiquette.

Rescue came in the form of Ryder Bowman.

"You just hit on fifteen," said a low, melodious voice over her shoulder.

Carmela turned and found herself looking into appealing blue eyes that shone out from a suntanned face. "I should have just sat tight?" she asked him.

Ryder gave a laconic shrug. "Probably not. The dealer was only holding a twelve. You were probably screwed anyway. Unless you were counting cards."

"Should I have been?" asked Carmela in all seriousness.

"Not really," said Ryder, laughing. "Even if you could master that dark art, most casinos generally frown on it. Here . . ." He picked her chips up, handed them to her, and helped her up from her seat. "You seem like more of a craps player."

"I don't know a thing about that game either," admitted Carmela as they crossed the main floor of the casino together. "Except that people standing around a craps table always look like they're having loads of fun. All that whooping and hollering."

"See?" said Ryder. "You *do* know something about gambling."

They wandered over to the craps table, and Ryder showed Carmela where to lay her money on the big, green-felt table so she could place a field bet.

"What's that?" asked Carmela as she draped her arms over the table rails.

"The casino pays even money for three, four, nine, ten, and eleven. And two-to-one for two or twelve," Ryder told her. Then, signaling the waiter, Ryder ordered a fresh glass of red wine for Carmela.

Carmela wondered why men always seemed to have that innate ability to signal waiters and get exactly what they wanted. Were they more authoritarian than women? Were they better tippers? Or was it just a guy thing?

"You won!" exclaimed Ryder. "Want to keep going?"

"Absolutely," said Carmela. She was beginning to enjoy herself for the first time tonight.

"We're gonna go big eight this time," said Ryder. "That means you're betting that an eight will be rolled before a seven comes up."

"Are you wearing your alligator boots tonight?" Carmela asked Ryder, as they watched the dice bounce off the sides of the table.

He plucked at his trouser leg, revealing elegant black calfskin shoes. "Sorry to disappoint," he told her. "Hey, you just won again."

Carmela, feeling more and more confident, placed her own field bet this time. "Where is your alligator farm located, anyway?" she asked. Louisiana boasted more than a hundred alligator farms, and they seemed to be scattered all across the state. She was, of course, curious to find out exactly where Ryder Bowman's alligator farm was located.

"It's over by Houma," Ryder told her. "In Bayou Terrebonne. You know the area?"

"I've been there." Houma was southwest of New Orleans, but on the way toward Avery Island.

"Your friend Ava is quite a girl," Ryder said, suddenly changing the subject.

"Ava's my best friend," said Carmela. "Which of course means I only want the best for her."

Ryder's earnest eyes sought out Carmela's. "I hear you," he said. "But please realize we're just beginning to get to know each other."

"Okay," said Carmela. "I hear you."

Under Ryder's careful tutelage Carmela played craps for another ten minutes or so and, surprisingly, won almost two hundred dollars.

"This is smokin'," she told him, finally getting into the swing of things. "And fun, too."

"You got the hang of it fast," Ryder told her. "You're a quick study."

"Dang," marveled Carmela. "Maybe I should give that baccarat thing a whirl, too."

"You stay put right here," Ryder told her. "Nobody's doing all that well at baccarat tonight. There was this one guy at my table, Huey something, who was *way* down. And I mean like thousands down."

"Huey Tippit?" Carmela asked suddenly.

Ryder shrugged. "Yeah, that could've been the guy's name. I don't know, I don't remember exactly."

"Is Ryder bringing you good luck?" asked Ava as she sauntered over to join them.

"Look at this," said Carmela, indicating her sizable stack of chips.

"There's only one more thing you need to learn about gambling," Ryder told Carmela as he snaked an arm around Ava's nipped-in waist.

"What's that?" Carmela asked eagerly.

"Quit while you're ahead."

AS CARMELA STROLLED BACK TOWARD THE CASHIER'S cage, warming up to the evening, debating whether or not to cash in her chips, Glory suddenly loomed in her path. It was as if the Goodyear blimp had descended and crushed out the party.

"Carmela," said Glory in an imperious tone. "I sincerely hope you're on your very best behavior tonight."

Carmela stared tiredly at Glory. "What do you think I'm going to do, Glory? Start a food fight? Lead a wild conga line? Pull my dress down and swing topless from the chandeliers? For your information, I didn't even want to *be* here tonight. I showed up only because Shamus *asked* me to, not because you issued some silly edict about familial support."

Glory's hard eyes bore into Carmela, then her pudgy face took on a cagey look. "I must say, Carmela, you're being awfully tolerant, considering the situation."

"What are you talking about?" asked Carmela, knowing full well Glory was trying to goad her into something.

"I'm talking about Shamus," replied Glory, almost purring now. "As you well know, boys will be boys. Especially our Shamus. And last I laid eyes on him he was engaged in a rather intimate conversation with a certain young lady." Glory hesitated a moment, allowing her words to have their full impact on Carmela. "Zoe Carvelle."

Carmela was taken aback but tried not to let Glory see her sudden discomfiture. "Shamus and I trust each other, Glory," replied Carmela, trying her very best to take the high road. "And we're not going to be pulled apart by any foolish, vicious, and unfounded implications on your part."

But as Carmela walked away, Glory's words gnawed greedily at her heart. The fact of the matter was, Shamus *did* have a roving eye. He genuinely liked women and had done his share—*more* than his share—of dating when they were separated. Worst of all, if Shamus really was flirting with Zoe Carvelle tonight, it was because she was a beauty, albeit an empty-headed one, that he'd been involved with not all that long ago.

Feeling blindsided and suddenly wounded, Carmela strode through the casino, slipped through a pair of French doors, and found herself on the wide wood-planked deck that ran around the outside of the river-boat.

It was quiet out here and calm, with only a small cluster of people maybe forty feet away from her. Carmela could barely hear their words, just quiet mumblings.

Staring at the twinkling lights across the river, Carmela leaned on the railing and gazed toward the city of Chalmette. Smokestacks poked up, other commercial buildings rose in the distance. From just upriver came the mournful *toot* of a tugboat. Probably guiding some barge filled to capacity with grain toward the Gulf of Mexico.

Letting her chips drop from one hand into the other, Carmela stared into the velvety dark, letting the laughter, the clink of glasses, the shrieks from the craps table fade slowly into the background. The group standing on the deck down from her glided back inside, and she was left with her quiet view and her silent yearnings over her marriage.

Gazing across at the far bank of the Mississippi, Carmela decided even the warehouses and docks looked romantic and peaceful in this soft, dark light. If only she could find such—

There was a slight *creak* behind her, as though the deck had gradually shifted, and then an arm snaked hard around her neck.

"Sha—" she began, but with the pressure growing suddenly, painfully tight, she knew it wasn't Shamus. This was no practical joke.

"Couldn't leave well enough alone, could you?" an angry voice hissed in her ear.

Male? Female? Carmela wasn't sure who her attacker was. But whoever it was, they were heroically strong. And nasty. She tried frantically to suck in air, but nothing seemed to be getting to her lungs like it was supposed to.

Carmela's chips went flying as both her hands flew up and she fought to claw away the strong arms that imprisoned her. "Let . . . go!" she finally managed to choke out.

But the pressure remained firmly at her neck.

He's putting pressure smack-dab on my hyoid bone, she thought to herself, knowing she'd picked up that nasty bit of trivia from some police or forensic TV drama. *Cutting off my air supply.* That terrible thought and the lack of oxygen made her woozy. And nearly frantic.

"Had to go snooping around," said the rough voice.

Suddenly, Carmela's attacker bent her forward over the railing. She felt cold metal press rudely into her chest and a swoop of wind as her dress rode up in back. But she also gained something precious in that fleeting moment—a gulp of air.

Just that one inhaled breath gave her the strength and courage to fight back. Straining forward even more, leaning far out over the riverboat now, Carmela balanced against the rail and launched a series of hard kicks at her attacker's legs. And was rewarded when the sharp heels of her stilettos not only connected with her attacker but dug into his legs! There was an angry *yowl* in her ear and a marked loosening of her attacker's grip.

This was the break Carmela needed. With all her strength, Carmela jackknifed herself forward and propelled herself over the rail in a perfect somersault.

Chapter 21

T HE water was far colder than Carmela had anticipated. And black as crude oil. As Carmela plummeted downward through the water, she experienced an almost out-of-body sensation of falling, falling, falling. Of water molecules simply slipping aside to accommodate her tumbling body, as though her entire being was a steak knife cutting through warm butter.

At the same time, her muddled mind projected a strange mix of reality and *déjà vu*. It was like watching a scene from the movie *Titanic* and, at the same time, physically experiencing the horror of being inexorably sucked down into murky water. Then, after what seemed like endless liquid moments, her free fall into the depths of the Mississippi seemed to abate, and Carmela began kicking. Kicking for her life.

Up, up, she swam, lungs burning from lack of oxygen. Finally she was thankful for all those years at summer camp when she'd been goaded by well-meaning counselors to swim that hundred meter relay, to dive off the high board, to lose her fear of water.

But as Carmela's head finally popped above the water's slick surface and she was finally able to suck the first of many welcome gulps of air, her thankful-ness was replaced by fear. This part of the Mississippi was a working river, of course, populated by a huge number of barges, boats, and oceangoing ships. Fig-uring she might be in immediate danger of being mowed down by a giant ship or pulled under by their wake, Carmela didn't wait around. She immediately paddled around to the other side of the riverboat and struck out for shore. Her hands clawed and slapped at the water, her legs kicked like crazy as she willed her-self to focus. Focus on the nearest point of land and let that be her compass heading.

In the dark, Carmela could make out the familiar low roof of the French Market. It was hard to believe she'd sat there at the Café Du Monde with Shamus just four days ago, sipping chicory coffee, bantering back and forth. Now it seemed like a lifetime. Of course, a normal life with Shamus seemed like a life-time ago, as well.

Kicking and splashing, Carmela inched her way closer to shore, knowing she probably looked like some sort of tired animal struggling desperately to get to land. Then her fingertips grazed rock, and she was hauling herself out of the river behind the French Market. Staggering to find her footing, Carmela grasped the skirt of her dress and wrung it out like a dishrag. Then she sat down hard on the grassy bank of the Mississippi and allowed herself the luxury of a few tears.

Emotions in turmoil, Carmela pinballed between feeling scared, completely disoriented, and downright angry. Someone had just tried to do serious harm to her, someone who was apparently incensed by what they'd termed her "snooping around."

Carmela knew, of course, that her attacker had to have been referring to her recent activities. Her semi-investigation into Shamus's kidnapping, the ransom demand, and Uncle Henry's murder. Someone on that riverboat tonight had been nervous about how close she was getting to uncovering some very real answers.

As Carmela sat there, alternating between dripping and drying, one of the local street musicians wandered by. He was a grizzled African American man, a local denizen who went by the name of Tommy B. Tommy B played a wicked saxophone, usually garnering several hundred dollars per night from appreciative tourists over in Jackson Square. He was always accompanied by his aging Jack Russell terrier.

"You need help, ma'am?" Tommy B asked her. His face was unreadable, but his voice was kind. The Jack

Russell stretched his nose out to sniff tentatively at Carmela, then retreated a few steps.

Carmela wrenched off a shoe and dumped out a stream of muddy water. "Do you have a cell phone I could borrow?" she asked the musician. Her voice was a tired croak.

"Course I do," said Tommy B. He pulled a shiny silver phone from his vest pocket and handed it to her.

Carmela called the person she always called in emergencies, the only person she could ever really count on: Ava. She didn't tell Ava the exact nature of her predicament, but when Ava answered on her cell phone, Carmela made her situation sound dire enough that Ava agreed to jump on the first skiff available and come running.

"You're very kind," Carmela told Tommy B as she returned his phone.

"No problem," he told her. "Just tryin' to help."

She was grateful he didn't ask about her bizarre situation. Or comment on how awful she must look.

"OH MY LORD!" CRIED AVA ONCE SHE ARRIVED. SHE put a hand to her mouth, trying to stifle her plaintive cries as Carmela quickly related all the sordid details.

"You got *pushed?*" asked Ava. "Someone tried to choke you to death and then pushed you off the damn boat?" Anger filtered in amid Ava's shock.

"Actually," said Carmela, "I jumped. Or somersaulted, if you want to be technically correct. Not that

I had a lot of options at the time." She hiccupped loudly, gazed piteously at Ava. "Guess I must look pretty bad, huh?"

Ava knelt down beside her, touched a hand gently to Carmela's shoulder. "You look like the proverbial drowned rat, *cher*."

Bedraggled feathers felt like wet fingers dragging themselves across Carmela's forehead. A most irritating and uncomfortable feeling. "With this hat still pinned on I probably look like a drowned bird," Carmela sighed.

"I'll put it as kindly as I can," said Ava. "The hat did not survive."

Carmela pulled the mass of wet feathers from her head, stared at it glumly, then pitched it into the river where it floated sadly on the surface.

"And you don't have a clue in heaven who attacked you?" asked Ava.

Carmela shook her head, spraying beads of water. She felt like Boo or Poobah after one of their forced baths. "No, but whoever it was, he was awfully strong."

"So a man," said Ava.

"I think so," said Carmela. "Or a woman who hits the gym like clockwork."

"Good heavens, who'd want to do that?" shuddered Ava.

"Not me," said Carmela, struggling to her feet and trying to pull her dress down toward her knees. Her impromptu dip in the river seemed to be causing her dress to shrink up even shorter. *Oh well, to hell with modesty,* she decided.

"You don't think it was Glory, do you?" asked Ava.

Ava's words brought Carmela up short. "Damn. That never occurred to me."

"You think she'd try to kill you?" asked Ava. "Is she crazy enough?" Ava stared at Carmela with huge eyes. "Wait a minute, what am I saying? Of *course* she's crazy enough. Glory's a raving lunatic."

"You're spot-on there," said Carmela, "but I'm pretty sure it was a man's voice . . . whisper."

Noting that Carmela had begun to shiver, Ava put her arms around Carmela and started rubbing her friend's shoulders. Then Ava frowned and plucked a big piece of gunk from Carmela's hair. "I guess there's a reason they call it the Big Muddy," she said, flicking the black gob away. "Although, after your little adventure tonight, they should change it to the Big Guncky."

"I gotta take a shower," said Carmela, shuddering. "I'm probably gonna get cholera or mange or something."

"Horses get mange," said Ava. "And dogs."

"Whatever," said Carmela, gazing down at her bare legs, which were slicked with brownish-green mud. "Jeez, I look like I just had a really bad spa treatment."

Ava agreed. "The mud wrap without the wrap."

That little bit of humor made them both chuckle.

"Honey," said Ava, "you were just lucky you didn't get smacked in the head by a barge. Or bitten by an alligator."

"There are gators in the Mississippi?" asked Carmela as Ava helped her struggle to her feet. "I thought they were only in salt marshes."

"No, no," said Ava. "That's all changed. During Hurricane Katrina, even a couple sharks got blown upriver. They could have swum down Canal Street if they wanted to and fed on the looters."

"Take a bite out of crime," added Carmela.

They limped together across North Peters Street, and Ava signaled for a cab. A yellow cab parked in front of the Catfish Grill and Chill saw them, pulled ahead, then swung around in a wide U-turn to pick them up.

"Are you sure you don't want to go back to the party?" Carmela asked Ava. "Won't the stud muffin be worried about you?"

"No problem," said Ava. "I told him I had an emergency, that I'd see him tomorrow."

"Thanks," sighed Carmela. With Ava at her side she suddenly felt a hundred times better.

"I'll tell you something," said Ava, as they clambered into the cab. "You sorted one thing out for sure."

"What's that?" asked Carmela.

"It was somebody from that riverboat attacked you, so you just narrowed down the field."

"Maybe," yawned Carmela.

"Somebody on that boat is not only worried about your investigation," continued Ava, "they think you're getting way too close!"

Chapter 22

"WHERE did you disappear to last night?" asked Shamus. "It seemed like you dropped clean out of sight."

"I certainly did," said Carmela. She was on the phone, still flaked out in bed, just beginning to feel the few aches and bruises she'd garnered from last night's reckless plunge. The dogs lazed at her feet. The TV was tuned to MTV, where Sheryl Crow was belting out her latest hit.

"I wish you'd have told me you were going to leave," complained Shamus. "Glory wanted the whole family together for a group photo. I think Zig is planning to hang it in the VIP room."

"Isn't that grand," sighed Carmela.

"You've certainly developed a snarky attitude," Shamus told her. "What the hell is wrong with you, anyway?"

Tiny sparks of fury ignited inside Carmela's brain. "What's wrong?" she asked. "What's *wrong?* How about the fact that I rescued you from some shit hole swamp camp just five days ago, and now you couldn't care less! Or that you begged me to help solve Uncle Henry's murder but allow Glory to carp at me and tell me to stay the hell out of the way! How's that for openers, Shamus?"

Carmela was wound up now, about to tell Shamus exactly what happened to her last night, then suddenly changed her mind. Decided it was better to stay on track with what was *really* bugging her.

"And how is it possible," asked Carmela bitterly, "that you and I were getting along so well just a week ago, and now we're a complete and total disaster?"

She blinked back tears, struggled to keep her voice strong, to not betray the fear and despair that was bubbling up inside. Did she hate Shamus? Did she love him? Did he still love her?

"Carmela," came Shamus's pleading voice. "I love you."

She hung on the phone listening to him, but unwilling and, truth be known, unable to respond.

"You believe me, don't you?" asked Shamus.

Carmela thought about Glory's needling words last night. Wondered if Shamus really *had* been scampering about, flirting with his old girlfriend, Zoe Carvelle. "I'm not sure anymore," she said finally.

"Look," said Shamus. "We gotta talk. In person. Today. I want my family back together."

"We don't have a family," murmured Carmela. *And the way things are going, probably never will.*

"Sure we do. You and me, Boo and Poobah," reasoned Shamus. "It's all we need; it's a good family. My gosh, we've even made plans. We were going to enter Boo in that big dog show, Pup America. Can you imagine how she'd feel if we didn't put on a united front for her?" Shamus's voice had taken on a plaintive whine, not unlike Glory's.

"Boo will survive just fine," said Carmela. "And we

can still be there for her."

"But she needs to perceive us as a couple," said Shamus. "Now, can we *please* get together and talk?"

"You'll be busy with the parade," Carmela pointed out. "Remember, today's the French Quarter Festival."

"I know, I know," said Shamus, sounding slightly exasperated now. "And I've got some people I have to meet with. Listen, are you going to be at your shop?"

"I can be," said Carmela. "I mean, I will be for a while. Then I have to help man the Gumbo to Geaux booth for the Pluvius krewe. I don't really want to, but I got talked into it."

"When?"

"Last winter."

"No, I mean when are you working at the gumbo booth?" asked Shamus.

"Oh, later this afternoon," said Carmela.

"Then we'll get together late afternoon, darlin'," promised Shamus. "I've got an investment thing I want to talk over with you, too."

"You've always got an investment thing hanging out there," sighed Carmela. Shamus wasn't exactly the smartest tack in the box when it came to investing. Even though Zig Crawford had been talking him up big time last night.

"This is different," said Shamus. "It's surefire."

"Sure it is," said Carmela.

"Carmela," said Shamus, "I just know things are going to turn out for us. In a positive sense, I mean."

246

Carmela, who hadn't yet told Shamus about extending the lease on her apartment, sighed heavily. "We'll see," she replied.

CARMELA DITHERED ABOUT HER APARTMENT FOR THE rest of the morning, halfheartedly picking at the clutter that seemed to be spread everywhere, knowing that Gabby would have already opened Memory Mine in anticipation of the larger crowds that would flow into the French Quarter.

Once Carmela eventually got herself down there, too, she figured they'd keep the shop open until about three o'clock or so, then close when all the jazz concerts and other activities started to fire up for real.

The mauve Nina Ricci dress Carmela had hung in the shower last night was a dry, disheveled wreck today. Wrinkled, faded, still looking river water dingy even though she'd done her best to rinse it out. When she'd first put on the dress it had perked her spirits; now the little rag only served to remind her of a very bad experience. And who needed bad memories when there were plenty to go around?

Snatching the dress from its padded hanger, Carmela rolled it into a ball and arced it into her wicker hamper, deciding she wasn't ever going to slip into *that* little frock again. Or into the Mississippi River for that matter.

So why did I toss the stupid dress in the hamper? she asked herself. *Knock, knock, puddin'head. Throw the thing away for good.*

Carmela pawed through the wicker hamper, found the dress, and pulled it back out. Judging from the pile of clothes lumped inside the hamper, Carmela decided she'd better contemplate doing some serious laundry one of these days. Of course, Shamus had squirreled a bunch of his dirty stuff in there, too.

Carmela hauled out a blue chambray shirt, some men's socks, and a yellow T-shirt that said *Full of Bull* in red funky type. No kidding.

These were clearly Shamus's things, and Carmela decided that, rather than dealing with all his crap, she'd toss everything into a plastic garbage bag and then toss that bag directly at Shamus's head. Let him crouch in front of the Kenmore and try to figure out the spin cycle on his own.

Except the chambray shirt had a terrible smell emanating from it. Carmela lifted it up, sniffed gingerly, and wrinkled her nose as the pungent odor of gasoline wafted up at her. This shirt, she decided, deserved its own bag.

She sped into the kitchen, dodging the minefield of orange slices and carrot rounds that Eduardo had tossed on the floor to create a virtual parrot salad bar.

Then Carmela remembered. This shirt didn't belong to Shamus at all. It was the shirt he'd been wearing when she found him curled up on the floor of the camp house over near Delcambre. Shamus had been snatched from their house in the Garden District wearing only his birthday suit and a terry cloth robe. This shirt belonged to the kidnappers. This shirt was . . .

248

"Evidence," she murmured out loud, staring at Eduardo.

The notion intrigued her. But what exactly should she *do* with the shirt, now that she'd determined its worth? Tell Shamus about it? Call Detective Babcock and turn it over to him? Or, better yet . . .

Hang onto it for the time being?

See if she could decipher some sort of connection, given the facts she'd already gleaned.

Carmela scampered over to her dresser, pulled out a large drawing pad that was stashed behind it. Blowing off a few clinging dust bunnies, she carried the pad of paper over to her dining room table and grabbed a fat black marker pen.

"Okay," she muttered to herself. *"What exactly are the facts?"*

Twenty minutes later, she had a working outline of what she knew, or at least suspected, so far:

Uncle Henry shot, Shamus kidnapped
Why?—Ransom (5M)
Who?—Companies that dealt with Uncle Henry
    (almost 3 dozen)
Swap rats in Eldorado—hired hands?
Tina and Huey Tibbit need 5M
Johnny Kool—prison record
Mrs. Jardell—beneficiary in will
Ryder Bowman—alligator farm, might know
    local swamp rats?
Other Factors:

Burglars tried to break into shop—looking for
   bank files?
Glory—trying to hide something?
Uncle Henry involved in casino financing?
Someone attacked me last night!
Shirt smells like oil or gasoline

Carmela stared at the list, then added one more thing
under the Ryder Bowman line: "Ryder trying to get
close via Ava?"
   She surely hoped she was wrong.
   Staring up at Eduardo, who sat on his perch looking
very regal, feathers the color of a bright green gem,
Carmela said, "What do you think, little bird?"
   Pleased at the attention paid to him, Eduardo
flapped his wings and bobbed his head. "Evidence,"
he crowed back at her. "Evidence."

Chapter 23

FINGERS flying across the computer keys, Carmela
struggled to finish designing the handout menus
for the Pluvius krewe's Gumbo to Geaux booth.
   The Gumbo to Geaux name had, of course, been
Carmela's idea. Gumbo being that marvelous roux-
thickened soup that was generally chock-full of shrimp,
fish, sausage, and okra. And geaux being a reference to
the little plastic geaux cups that French Quarter bars
gave their customers so they could wander around the
Quarter, get in trouble, and still sip their drinks.

Gumbo to Geaux wasn't going to knock restaurants like K-Paul's Louisiana Kitchen, Galatoire's, or the Court of Two Sisters off the map. The little stand, which the Pluvius krewe had just finished building an hour ago, would serve only gumbo, hush puppies, and ice cold beer. An order of each selling for just five dollars.

"How are you doing with your flyer thingy?" asked Ava. She was wandering about the shop, scanning the shelves, trying to put together a basket of scrapbook items for the silent auction.

Carmela had completely forgotten she'd promised this little donation until she sat down at her computer and saw the reminder Post-it note. It was a good thing Ava had strolled in and Carmela could wrangle her friend and put her to work, since Gabby was busy waiting on customers who seemed to be pouring into the shop in droves.

"Almost done," said Carmela. She looked over at her friend. "You okay?"

Ava shook her head. "When I woke up this morning, which was slightly later than normal, there wasn't a single bottle of Diet Coke in the fridge. That, for me, is basically a doomsday scenario. So I'm wandering around still feeling like a deadhead."

"Gotta have that hit of caffeine," agreed Carmela. "But, luckily, there's a can of Coke stashed in that little refrigerator under the shelf there. Behind a left-over box of pralines."

"Bless you," sighed Ava, diving for it.

Carmela fussed with her menu for a few more minutes. She was pleased with the funky, bouncing script she'd selected and was really in love with the Italian carnival icons she'd used to add a touch of graphics to the little handouts. "I wish we had time to use the deckle edge scissors on these," lamented Carmela. "Or maybe a punch."

Ava grabbed one of the sheets as it came flying out of the laser printer. "Are you kidding? These little menu flyers are drop-dead gorgeous. I mean most folks would just scrawl something in Magic Marker and then dash over to Kinko's. You put real thought into your design, you really *care*."

"I love doing this stuff," admitted Carmela. "It's my passion."

Ava nodded. "I do believe it is. Which is why you're also an inspiration to your customers."

"You're feeling better already," said Carmela.

"Doesn't take long," said Ava, stifling a burp.

Carmela nodded toward the wicker basket that dangled from Ava's arm. She'd selected papers, a couple punches, some stencils, an X-Acto knife, colored tags, and a few rubber stamps. "Why don't you toss in a couple packets of beads. And maybe some charms, too," suggested Carmela.

"Alrighty," said Ava. "I wasn't sure what the value was supposed to be on this thing. Didn't want to give away the proverbial store."

"The guidelines said the retail value should be around fifty or sixty dollars. But it's okay if you go higher. Lord knows, this is all for a good cause."

Ava bent down and unfurled a roll of stickers from the lower shelf. In her tight jeans and sunflower-yellow scoop-necked sweater she was the image of Marilyn Monroe in *The Misfits*. Although Carmela was also wearing blue jeans and a Persian red V-neck knit shirt, she somehow didn't feel quite as diva-looking as Ava. Then again, Ava's jeans were a whole lot tighter, and she'd pulled her sweater down over her suntanned shoulders so the straps of her matching yellow bra peeped out. Cute, but also a little racy.

"Okay," yelled Carmela as the last sheet spat out from the printer. "We're done here. Let's hustle our butts over to Jackson Square!"

IN 1850, THE PLACE D'ARMES WAS RENAMED Jackson Square in honor of General Andrew Jackson. His royal trouncing of the British during the Battle of New Orleans brought about a unified city that in turn created a newly energized seaport and helped mush-room New Orleans into the fourth-largest city of that era.

Today, Jackson Square, normally a placid, elegant square filled with sightseers, was crammed with food booths, artists' displays, jugglers, clowns, mimes, and music stages. Over one hundred hours of music that included jazz, zydeco, gospel, Cajun, swamp rock, and even classical would spill out from these stages as well as additional stages set up on Bourbon Street and Royal Street. Several of the Mardi Gras krewes would be parading their floats past here and through the French Quarter. The Pirate's Alley art show was attracting more crowds just a block away. And a massive fireworks display was planned for tonight.

Though it lasted only a weekend, this French Quarter Festival, set among a maze of narrow streets, brick buildings with cast-iron balcony railings, and elegant shops and restaurants, usually drew more than a quarter million people.

By the time Carmela and Ava arrived at the Gumbo to Geaux booth, it was completely up and running. Kettles filled with gumbo sputtered and steamed. Cold beer lay atop sparkling clear ice cubes. A deep fat fryer cranked out golden-brown hush puppies. Another volunteer, a woman named Lindsey LaBranche, was already working the booth and seemingly doing a fairly brisk business.

"Carmela!" Lindsey exclaimed, looking more than a little frazzled, even though it was only four o'clock, and they had the whole night ahead of them. "Thank goodness you're here."

Carmela stashed her handbag and the scrap book basket Ava had assembled under the counter. Then she quickly set to work, handing out menu flyers, cajoling folks to give their gumbo a try. Her pitch worked, and in a matter of minutes she and Lindsey were swamped with customers. They dished up gumbo and hush puppies, handed out cold beers, and took in money like crazy. Through all of this, Carmela briefly wondered where Shamus was. This morning he had been so eager to get together and talk. Now, there was no sign of him.

When Carmela finally had a moment to breathe, she looked around and discovered Ava lounging at the back of the booth, munching away.

Ava noticed Carmela watching her and held up a little yellow-and-red-striped paper cup filled with grilled chicken livers. "You want some?" she asked. "These are topped with hot pepper jelly, so they're extra tasty."

"What?" laughed Carmela, "you're eating again? You downed two pralines on the way over here."

"I know that," Ava said with resignation as she patted her absolutely flat stomach. "And I know I'm gettin' really fat and bloated. But, honey, there are something like sixty different food booths here, all selling things like soft-shell crab, boudin sausage, blackened fish, and bread pudding. A girl's gotta indulge once in a while. I'll cut back next week. You know, skip the sauce on my bread pudding or something."

"Well, taste this gumbo then," said Carmela, ladling the rich brew into one of the plastic cups, then handing it to Ava. "Tell me what you think. And don't hold back."

Ava took a sip of gumbo. Almost immediately her eyes widened in surprise, and she made a quick fanning motion at her mouth. "Mmn, that's spunky gumbo, *cher.*"

"You like it?" asked Carmela, worried that the gumbo might be a little *too* spicy.

255

"Hell yes I like it," enthused Ava. "It's terrific."

"Good," said Carmela, satisfied that everything was, indeed, perfect. In this case, the familiar Creole saying, *"Jadin loin, gombo gâté,"* which translated to "when the garden is far, the gumbo is spoiled," did not apply. This gumbo was indeed spicy, the vegetables fresh, the seasonings serious, and the after burn savage.

"You want me to help?" asked Ava, finishing up her chicken livers and licking her fingers.

"Grab some more paper napkins will you?" asked Carmela. "I think there's a whole case of them stuffed in back."

Ava dragged out a paper carton, slid her fingernails under the plastic strapping tape that held it closed, said "Ouch!"

"What?" asked Carmela as she handed over four orders of hush puppies to an eager family.

"Can't get it open," muttered Ava, who favored long, high-gloss nails and lived in constant fear of breaking one.

Carmela bent down, stuck out her leg, and toed the basket filled with scrapbook goodies toward her. "Use the X-Acto," she told Ava.

"Good idea," said Ava. Removing the knife from its blister pack, she sliced open the box and handed a giant flutter of paper napkins to Carmela. "What about the knife? Stick it back in the basket?"

"Nah," said Carmela. "Tuck it in my handbag. But carefully, okay?"

"No problem," said Ava. "Say, you want me to deliver this basket to the silent auction people?"

"Please," said Carmela, as more people pressed toward their booth. "That would be a great help."

AN HOUR LATER, CARMELA WAS A LITTLE FRAZZLED herself as the influx of customers at Gumbo to Geaux showed no sign of letting up. To make matters worse, they were raking in money like crazy. Carmela was stuffing five dollar bills in her jeans pockets, down her bra, and wherever she could find a place for them. Typical of the Pluvius krewe, no one had made any sort of provision to bring a money box along, so they were forced to do whatever they could as they careened along.

And Shamus's family owns a chain of banks, Carmela thought to herself. *You'd think they'd have an old strongbox or something equally secure just laying around. And just where is that Shamus Allan Meechum, anyway?*

Two hours later, Tandy Bliss arrived to spell Carmela. Tandy, skinny as a rail and a perennial volunteer, thrived on chaos and disorder. In other words, Tandy was the perfect embodiment of relief troops.

Offering up a silent prayer of thanks to Tandy, Carmela popped the top off a beer, poured the tawny liquid into one of the plastic geaux cups, and stepped out from behind the booth.

Walking down the street, crowds jostling her on

either side, the French Quarter felt like a different scene entirely. Lively, visceral, with a throbbing pulse of excitement. Feeling suddenly free, refreshed by the malty taste of the beer, Carmela sauntered toward the music venues, happily carried along by the flow of the crowd.

At least a dozen stages were set up on the far edge of Jackson Square, and hordes of people were clustered there. Carmela stopped to revel in the music as trumpets wailed, keyboards flung out soaring notes, rhythm sections thumped compelling backbeats.

Carmela continued to wander, her eyes darting from food booths to music stages. She figured Shamus had to be around here somewhere. Unless, of course, he was over on Marais Street near Louis Armstrong Park. That's where the evening parade would be queuing up.

"Carmela," called a man's voice.

She whirled about, expecting Shamus. But it was Jekyl Hardy, with the remains of a fast-disappearing mufuletta sandwich clutched in his hands. Two French baguettes stuck out the top of a white bakery bag he had tucked under his arm.

"Jekyl," she said, hoping she didn't sound disappointed.

"What are you up to?" he asked. And then, without waiting for an answer, said, "Come on along, I'm having a party."

"In case you hadn't noticed, Jekyl, this is a party," said Carmela.

Jekyl leaned in closer, a conspiratorial gesture. "An *impromptu* party."

Carmela nodded, knowing Jekyl didn't do anything impromptu. Jekyl Hardy was a major planner. Case in point: about one week after Mardi Gras ended, Jekyl started working on designs for *next* year's floats.

"Tell me you haven't been noodling this around," she joked.

"All right, smarty," he replied. "So I've been thinking about a bottle of Vouvray, French baguettes, and crawfish étouffée for a couple days now. And so what if I'm not the most spontaneous fellow in the world. Don't hold it against me; come on up anyway. There'll be lots of wicked people and decadent things to drink." Jekyl glanced around sharply and dropped his voice. "I have a friend who just returned from the Czech Republic and smuggled in a tiny bit of authentic absinthe." He held his thumb and index finger close together. "Just enough for a teensy little taste."

The whole scene was slightly tempting, but Carmela decided she'd better keep looking for Shamus. She'd continue searching around here, and if she couldn't find him amid all these people, she'd go back to the booth and wait. He'd have to show up there, wouldn't he?

Chapter 24

As Carmela shuffled past the Louisiana Philharmonic Orchestra, her eyes scanning what seemed like more of a highbrow crowd, she suddenly met up with Ava again.

"I was lookin' for you," Ava told Carmela breathlessly. "The stud muffin wants me to have dinner with him at Antoine's."

Carmela raised an eyebrow. "Ooh. Fancy." Antoine's was one of the premier old-line French Quarter restaurants. White linen tablecloths, crystal chandeliers, and a who's who of past patrons that included Mark Twain, five U.S. presidents, and the Duke and Duchess of Windsor. Among Antoine's specialties were Oysters Rockefeller, *pompano en papillote,* and *filet de truite à la Marguery.* The latter being a fillet of speckled trout poached in white wine sauce with shrimp, mushrooms, and herbs.

"You come, too, okay?" said Ava. Her face was flushed, and she looked as deliriously happy as Carmela had ever seen her.

This invitation was also rather tempting, but Carmela shook her head. "I'm still working," she told Ava. "In fact, once I find Shamus and we have our little tête-à-tête, I'm probably going to go back to the gumbo booth and spell Tandy."

"You haven't found Shamus yet?" asked Ava. Small lines appeared in the middle of her normally flawless forehead. "I thought he was hot to have this big confab with you."

Carmela shrugged. "Yeah. This morning he was all primed for talking, and now he's nowhere to be found." She shrugged again, hating the fact that she sounded a little down, a trifle needy.

Ava caught Carmela's hand in hers. "Come along with me, honey. You look so damned cute, and Ryder's got some really nice friends."

Carmela stared at Ava. "You mean gentlemen friends." It wasn't a question.

"Sure," grinned Ava. "Them's the best kind."

"You're trying to set me up," accused Carmela. It was a nice gesture on Ava's part, but . . . she was still married, such as it was.

"Naw," said Ava. "I'd never do a slimy thing like that. You're a smart girl, you can set yourself up if you feel like it."

"Ava . . ." said Carmela.

"Just have one drink with us, okay? C'mon, it'll be fun." Ava eyed Carmela carefully, noting the look of distraction on her friend's face. "Take your mind off that old poo, Shamus," Ava added for good measure.

"Maybe one drink," said Carmela, weakening. Antoine's was one of her absolute favorite places, and they boasted a killer wine list. Correction, killer wine collection. With hundreds, maybe thousands, of hard-to-come-by French estate wines.

"Say," said Ava, suddenly casting an appraising eye at the front of Carmela's T-shirt. "Did you start wearing a padded bra? Or one of those uplift num-bers? 'Cause you suddenly look extra bootiful, not that you need to enhance your God-given gifts."

"What?" said Carmela. "Oh . . . hey." Her puzzled expression shifted to a grin as she plunged a hand down the front of her shirt and pulled out a wad of five dollar bills."

"Cher," said Ava. "You made really good tips, huh?"

"No," said Carmela, "this is part of the take. We didn't have anyplace to stash the cash. It all goes back to the Pluvius krewe."

"Too bad," said Ava.

CARMELA WAS INTRODUCED AROUND RYDER BOW-man's table at Antoine's and graciously welcomed. Ryder stood at attention, pulled out her chair, and immediately launched into an animated story about how Carmela was a natural-born craps player who'd almost single-handedly cleaned out the casino last night.

Ryder's two friends listened carefully, grinned enthusiastically, and had the waiter hustle a bottle of Haut-Brion to the table for Carmela. Both Ryder's friends were attractive, well-to-do-looking men. Gary did something in oil. The other one, Leonard, was a partner at one of the big downtown law firms. Both were single, Ava had been quick to point out in a whispered confidence. And Carmela figured they must have money, since they'd ordered her a three hundred dollar bottle of wine.

Ryder and his friends were into grazing, so they'd ordered single orders of escargot, boiled Louisiana shrimp, crawfish tails smothered with onions and peppers, steamed artichokes, and soft-shell crab to share.

After two glasses of robust Bordeaux and nibbles of crab and crawfish, Carmela was beginning to think she'd made a pretty good decision to tag along with Ava. The food was decadently delicious, the buzz of conversation vaguely pleasant, and they had a catbird seat right in the middle of Antoine's elegant cream-colored main dining room.

As Ryder and his friends engaged in a heated argument about a rebuilding project in the Storyville area, Carmela and Ava quietly chatted with each other. About Shamus, about Ava's hiring a new assistant, about what happened last night.

Picking up a plate of perfectly golden battered soft-shell crabs, Ava passed it to Carmela. "Have another—" she began, and then suddenly muttered, "Shit."

"What?" asked Carmela. She was relaxed and enjoying herself. They both were. So she wondered what exactly had prompted Ava's sudden unhappy outburst.

"Nothing," said Ava, looking nervous.

"Something," said Carmela, peering at her.

Ava's face took on a look of supreme unhappiness. "Uh, I don't know exactly how to tell you this," she said. "But, uh, Shamus is sittin' back there." She lifted a delicate forefinger and pointed surreptitiously toward the back of the main dining room.

Startled by this sudden revelation, Carmela peered through the crowd, saw the very recognizable top of Shamus's head. And instantly saw that he was sitting with someone. A woman. A very pretty blond woman.

This was almost too much for Carmela to handle. "Shamus," she stuttered out to Ava. "That *is* Shamus over there." Surprise mingled with shock.

Is this the same Shamus who'd promised to come find me tonight? Carmela wondered. *Who wanted to talk and work things out?*

"Do you know who, um, that girl is?" asked Ava, trying to be delicate. "I mean, she looks awfully cheap to me."

"Is that Zoe?" murmured Carmela. "You remember. From the—"

"Yeah, yeah," Ava cut in. "From the infamous Monsters and Old Masters Ball. I remember Zoe Carvelle. She was Shamus's date."

And he was supposedly talking to her last night, too, thought Carmela. *While I was struggling for my life.*

Ava leaned back, craning her neck to study the girl. Finally she said, "I'm not sure it's the same girl. I can really only see part of her. Seems like this girl's boobs are bigger. Course, Miss Zoe could have had them worked on since we last saw her. Seems like everybody's gettin' bigger boobs these days." Ava peered through the crowd again. "How big you think she is, anyway? A thirty-six E?"

264

"I gotta get outa here," said Carmela, glancing around frantically for her handbag.

"Whoa, whoa," said Ava. "Slow down, take it easy." She gripped Carmela's arm, pulled her back down. "Don't be so hasty."

"Are you crazy?" said Carmela. "Could this be any more *embarrassing?*"

Ryder suddenly pulled his attention from his friends to focus on Carmela and Ava. "You ladies okay?" he asked.

"We're just debating over the dessert list," said Ava smoothly. "Trying to decide which has a higher caloric count, the peach melba or the crêpes Suzette."

"Ah, then you'd want the baked Alaska," Ryder told them with a grin, then turned back to rejoin his discussion.

"I can't sit here pretending this isn't happening," hissed Carmela. "I have to get out of here."

Ava's face assumed a tough, hard-boiled expression. "Maybe you should just walk over there and calmly pour a drink on top of his fat head," she suggested.

"That seems a little . . . ah . . . melodramatic," said Carmela, who was of a mind to handle this little situation privately. After all, this was only between her and the rat.

"Oh really?" said Ava. "The man cheats on you in front of all the swells seated in this fine establishment, and you think dousing him with wine is too melodramatic? Let's think about this for a moment." Ava reached for her bronze leather clutch on the table,

265

pulled out a pack of cigarettes. She tapped one, lifted an eyebrow, and gave Carmela a challenging look. A look that clearly said, *The man is a putz and does not deserve you.*

Carmela took a deep breath, considered that her friend might certainly have a valid point.

As though reading Carmela's mind, Ava gave an encouraging nod, then selected a single cigarette. As if on cue, Ryder Bowman swiped a match, lit Ava's cigarette, then tossed the matchbook on the table.

"You're thinkin' about it, aren't you?" asked Ava, her eyes glittering.

"You've got demonic eyes," Carmela told her. "Along with a very demonic brain."

"Shamus deserves to be humiliated," said Ava. "He's been a very bad boy."

Very bad boy.

Those words suddenly rang familiar to Carmela. *Isn't that what the kidnapper said when he called about Shamus?* she wondered. *Yeah, it was something like that.* Her mind struggled to dredge up the exact words. *Oh yeah, they said he hasn't always been such a good boy. And were they ever right.*

Knowing she had to do something but embarrassed and overwhelmed by the situation, Carmela stared down at her wedding ring, a three-carat cushion cut diamond that sparkled on her left hand. It was a deceptive sparkle, she decided, more ice than fire. She drummed her fingers idly on the table, picked up the book of matches Ryder had tossed down, and suddenly stared at it.

Like underwater sonar, something pinged in the deep, limbic part of Carmela's brain.

She continued to stare at the colorful matchbook, her mind suddenly shifting into hyperdrive. The matches were for Napoleon's Parlour, one of Ryder Bowman's restaurants, and the type under the fancy French-motif logo said Baton Rouge.

Baton Rouge, Carmela thought, feeling an uneasy surge of energy course through her. *Why is that suddenly wigging me out?*

Finally, slowly, Carmela made a tentative connection. Baton Rouge was marked on the map in her altered book. The book that was sitting in the front window of her store.

Oh shit, thought Carmela. *Is there something really important about Baton Rouge? Is Ava's stud muffin the one who tried to break into my shop and steal the altered book? Is he the murderer? Are his friends, these friends, the kidnappers?*

"Carmela?" cried Ava as Carmela pushed back her chair and beat a hasty retreat from the restaurant. "Now what's wrong?"

Chapter 25

CARMELA elbowed her way through throngs of people. The sun was just going down, a spatter of orange in a purple sky, and the French Quarter was crackling with activity. Music boomed, and neon signs

267

glowed, gaudily touting their respective bars and music clubs. A loudspeaker blared, announcing the always-popular bartender's competition.

Ava dashed after Carmela, following her down Royal Street. "What's wrong?" she cried. "It isn't just Shamus, is it?"

Carmela stopped in her tracks, allowing Ava to catch up with her.

Ava fumbled a hand to her chest. "*Cher,* I've been eating and drinking for three solid hours, and if I have to run one more step I swear I'm going to either burp, belch, or hurl! And you don't want to be in the line of fire for any of them."

That brought a flickering smile to Carmela's face.

"See," said Ava, "things aren't that bad, are they?"

Carmela was sober once again. "They're not good."

"What?" asked Ava, as Carmela resumed walking. "Tell me." She caught her friend's arm, gently pulled her to a stop again.

"Okay," said Carmela, looking slightly grim. "This is going to sound weird . . ."

Ava nodded. "I understand weird. I own a voodoo shop, remember? I spent my formative teenage years competing in beauty pageants."

"You remember the altered book I made for Uncle Henry?" asked Carmela.

"Sure," said Ava. "The one you put on his coffin. With the little poem in it."

"I also included a little map among the collaged bits," said Carmela. "A map that Uncle Henry had

268

drawn a little circle on."

"Circle on what?" asked Ava, looking skeptical.

"A small area to the northwest of Baton Rouge. I thought it was the place where Uncle Henry grew up, but now I'm not so sure."

"Okay," Ava said slowly as she peered expectantly at Carmela.

"And just before," continued Carmela, "when I picked up that matchbook from the table . . . I noticed that Ryder owns a restaurant in Baton Rouge."

"Napoleon's Parlour," filled in Ava.

Carmela stared at her friend. "I think that area to the northwest of Baton Rouge has something to do with Uncle Henry."

"You mean with his *death?*" asked Ava.

"Maybe," said Carmela. Then conceded, "Yeah, probably."

"Holy smokes," breathed Ava. "You don't really think Ryder had anything to do with murdering Uncle Henry, do you? Or kidnapping Shamus?" Ava looked stunned. She also looked like she was about ready to cry.

Carmela tried to soften her next words. "I don't know," she told her friend. "But I think the key to this whole mess might rest in figuring out that map."

"Wow," said Ava, obviously shaken. "So now you want to . . . what? Hotfoot it up to Baton Rouge?"

Carmela thought for a moment. "Or, better yet, look at a map. Probably one that's topographical, if possible."

"What if we dropped by Biblios Booksellers?" suggested Ava. "Biblios carries all sort of old maps and charts, and they're just a couple blocks away." She was trying to digest Carmela's words, obviously nervous that Ryder Bowman might get pulled into Carmela's investigation. An investigation that seemed to be picking up speed faster than a runaway freight train.

"Good thinking," said Carmela.

"Hey," added Ava. "You think Wren's shop is even open today?"

"Only one way to find out," replied Carmela.

BUT PUSHING THEIR WAY THROUGH THE CROWDS WAS proving to be difficult. It felt like they were two neophyte salmon trying to swim their way upstream, a very crowded upstream.

"This is miserable," complained Ava. "We're not making any headway in these crowds. And my feet are killing me."

"That's because you're wearing four-inch heels," said Carmela. "Come on, let's cut over here." Carmela stepped into the narrow street, began to dodge her way through slow-moving traffic.

Ava teetered nervously in Carmela's wake, glancing about to make sure she wasn't going to get run over. "Whoa!" she called out suddenly, her face going pale.

"What's wrong?" asked Carmela. She paused between two cars, praying the light at the far end of the block didn't change in the next couple seconds.

"You look like you just saw a ghost."

Ava's nervous eyes searched out Carmela's. "I just saw a black Cadillac Eldorado."

Carmela stared at her. "You mean like . . . oh, holy shit!" screeched Carmela. "You mean like the car the kidnappers drove?"

Was I right about the guys from the restaurant? Are they following us?

"Where?" Carmela asked, whirling about frantically. Searching the crowded street, she stepped out of the way of a line of cars just as the stoplight at the end of the block finally did change.

"Just crept past us," murmured Ava.

Carmela caught sight of an Eldorado as it disappeared down the block. Late model, a little banged up. It looked a *lot* like the car Shamus had been tossed into. A lot like the car that had charged after her. She didn't spend a lot of time contemplating their next move. "We better get the hell out of here," said Carmela. "Now!"

They wove their way past a row of food booths and then ducked behind a large temporary wooden stage where the bartender's competition was taking place.

"You think we're safe here?" asked Ava.

"Doubtful," said Carmela, as cosmopolitans were being shaken, daiquiris and Ramos Fizzes whipped and whirled just a few feet from where they hid. "If these are the same Eldorado guys, they'll probably zip around the block and try to head us off."

They stepped out from behind the stage just as a

smiling competitor in a bow tie and long black apron stepped off the stage with a tray full of drinks for the crowd.

"Thank you," said Ava, grabbing two frothy pink drinks and handing one to Carmela. "But we have to be going now."

The two women worked their way down the block, crossed St. Peter Street, then ducked down Pirate's Alley through the art fair.

They paused at a booth featuring handcrafted silver jewelry set with freshwater pearls.

"You see anything?" asked Ava, sipping her drink.

Carmela peered in the direction they'd just come and shook her head vigorously. "Nope."

"There's nothing you like?" asked the dismayed jeweler.

"Oh no," said Ava, "we like your jewelry just fine. In fact, it's gorgeous, but there are a couple guys that—"

"Say no more," said the jeweler, nodding. He could tell when a sale wasn't about to happen.

Carmela and Ava abandoned their drinks, then continued to wind their way through the art fair. They ducked into booths filled with photography, metal sculpture, and oil paintings. Trying to use as many booths as possible for cover, they emerged again back at Jackson Square.

"Now what?" asked Ava.

"Let's just walk this way and try to be a little nonchalant," said Carmela. Now they were heading up

Chartres Street. "What we should probably do is call Lieutenant Babcock. Pronto."

"You're gonna sic him after my stud muffin?" asked Ava. "I can't believe you still suspect Ryder."

"I'm going to sic him after those guys in the car," answered Carmela. "Whoever the hell they are."

The two women crossed Madison Street, still didn't see any sign of the suspicious Cadillac.

"Maybe we were wrong about that car," ventured Ava finally. "Maybe it was just some good old boys out cruising. We never did see if it had a bashed-in taillight."

"Maybe," said Carmela. But she'd seen the car and it sure *felt* like the kidnapper's car. Same bad vibes.

They stopped near a booth selling seafood chowder, then gazed up and down the street, studying the traffic.

"Don't see anything at all," said Ava. The street was packed with cars, but no black Cadillac Eldorados loomed anywhere near them.

"You ladies want some nice hot chowder?" asked the man in the booth. He had a round, friendly face and had already dipped his ladle into a steaming vat in anticipation of a sale.

"We already ate," said Ava. As she continued to scan the street, she'd backed cautiously into the man's booth, was really only a foot or so from the counter.

"Have one on me, then," said the man, a little flirtatious now as he held out a cup of chowder for Ava.

"Thanks," said Ava, "but—"

273

Carmela cut her off. "Take the cup," she muttered between clenched teeth.

Ava grabbed the cup of steaming seafood chowder as she suddenly focused on Carmela. Her friend had assumed an unnatural, ramrod position. Plus Carmela's eyes seemed to be blinking and moving rapidly, like a cornered animal. Ava shifted her gaze slightly, suddenly took in the man standing directly behind Carmela. A man with a drooping mustache, sallow face, and denim jacket whose hand was jammed firmly into the middle of Carmela's lower back. Ava tipped her head to the side and caught a glint of dull metal. A gun!

"Walk," a rough voice instructed them. "Both of you."

Frightened, bewildered, Carmela turned to her left, and the man put his left hand on her shoulder and squeezed hard. "No. Into the street." He cast a menacing glance at Ava, who stood two feet away. "You, too."

Carmela and Ava marched woodenly toward an idling black Cadillac. A black Cadillac they hadn't seen slide up to the curb.

"Damn," muttered Ava.

"Shut up," ordered the man with the mustache. He pulled open the car's rear door. "Get in," he told Carmela.

When Carmela was halfway in, Mustache planted a hand in the middle of her back and pushed her roughly, causing Carmela to lose her balance and tumble in hard. Angered, trying to strike back, Ava tossed her cup of piping-hot chowder directly into the man's face. "Take that, asshole!" she yelled.

The steaming-hot liquid found its mark square in the man's eyes, and bits of seafood slithered down the front of his face.

Howling in pain, the gunman fumbled, clawing at the burning liquid. And his weapon clattered to the street.

Thinking fast, Ava kicked out a long leg and sent the gun spinning under the car.

"You bitch," howled Mustache. He made a grab for Ava, wrenched her arm cruelly, and tried to force her into the car, too.

Carmela, meanwhile, had landed hard but sprung back like an agile, angry cat. Fighting hard to get on top of a situation that seemed to be going from bad to worse, she flung herself forward and dug her fingernails into the sides of the driver's neck. Screaming in pain, the driver's foot trounced down hard on the gas and sent the Eldorado lurching forward. And directly over Mustache's foot. Ava hopped in, grabbed for the car door, and pulled it closed. There was a telltale *click* of the door locks as the car picked up speed.

"Buford, you asshole," screamed the mustached man, who was still clawing hot chowder from his face. His hand swatted the trunk of the caddy as it roared forward.

Inside the car, Carmela kept the pressure on. "Pull over!" she screamed as she continued to claw at the driver's neck. "Stop this fricking car right now!"

The driver, panicked, angry, fighting off Carmela's flailing hands, leaned to his right, and pawed frantically to open the glove box.

"No you don't!" screamed Ava. She reached forward and pummeled him about the head with clenched fists.

But the driver, not to be outdone, smashed his foot hard on the brake, sending the two women flying forward against the front seat, then immediately rocking backward into the backseat. In the split second it took for them to recover, the driver grabbed the gun and now had it securely clutched in his hand.

"Sit down and shut up!" he ordered.

"Let us out!" screamed Ava. It was an agonized shriek, filled with anger and hysteria.

"Shut up!" screamed the driver. He waved the gun wildly, screamed again. "Shut up and sit back!"

Fearful of the gun, they settled back. But it didn't stop them from continuing their angry tirade.

"You asshole," taunted Ava. "Such a big man. Let's see how tough you are without that gun. I bet I could drop-kick you from here to Metairie." She turned to an angry Carmela. "He thinks he can bully us just because we're women. What a jerk."

"Is your name Buford?" asked Carmela. "Buford Gallier? Did you kidnap my husband? Did you kill Henry Meechum?"

"It's polite to answer a lady's questions, asshole," chimed in Ava.

"He's a flunkie," snorted Carmela. "A goon. He didn't even set this thing up, somebody else did. Somebody smarter."

"That's right," said Ava, slamming a foot into the back of the front seat. "You're just the hired help. A lousy thug."

"Shut up," said the driver again, but this time it sounded like the battery was beginning to wear down.

Chapter 26

LIGHTS faded away, the hurly-burly atmosphere of the French Quarter dropped behind them as the Eldorado slid along the dark banks of the Mississippi. They passed dilapidated homes, an auto junkyard, a cement-block mini storage facility. After a couple miles, they finally pulled up in front of a large warehouse. Covered in corrugated tin, the place looked deserted. Like it had been damaged in the hurricane and hadn't been fixed up or used since.

The driver hit a mechanism on the car's visor, and a large garage door rattled up. Slowly, he aimed the Eldorado into the yawning darkness of the building. The door continued to creak loudly, rattled to a stop, then the creaking began again as the door descended behind them. The Eldorado crept forward into what seemed like the center of the huge, dark warehouse. And lurched to a stop.

The driver turned his head and snarled at them. "Get

out." He lifted the gun in a threatening gesture.

"*You* get out," snarled Carmela. Just moments earlier, she'd pushed the car's cigarette lighter down until the tip glowed red-hot. Now she thrust that hot tip against the back of the driver's stubbly neck and held it fast like a branding iron.

The driver responded with an ungodly banshee-like scream and a diatribe of nasty curses. Though he still held tight to his gun, he pawed wildly for the door handle.

"Big man screams like a little girl," taunted Ava as the driver kicked open the front door, then frantically dove out, grabbing for his wounded neck. They could hear the echo of his footsteps as he stumbled away from them.

"C'mon," yelled Carmela, pulling at Ava. "We have to get out of here!"

At which point a dazzling array of overhead lights suddenly snapped on.

"Damn," said Ava, blinking and holding up a hand to shield her eyes from the barrage of light, while still trying to gaze out the car windows to see what was going on. "This is like one of those movies where the good guys stumble into the drug cartel's warehouse."

"Don't say that," warned Carmela.

But Ava was not to be deterred. "A warehouse filled with AK-47s, or stolen Porsches, or little plastic dolls stuffed with hashish."

"You have a very vivid imagination," muttered

Carmela as she cracked the back door open and eased one leg out.

"Probably read too many comic books when I was a kid," explained Ava.

"Ladies," boomed a man's voice.

"Uh-oh," said Ava as footsteps approached. Confident, purposeful footsteps.

They both slid out of the car and stood bathed in spotlights as they watched a shadowy figure approach.

"Now who's *this* asshole," murmured Carmela.

"Hello, Carmela," said the man. "We meet again."

The man's voice sounded vaguely familiar to Carmela, but with all the bright lights she still couldn't see who it was. Then he stepped a few feet closer, and Carmela was able to make out his face. As well as the gun that was pointed directly at her heart.

"Landry Douglas?" said Carmela in a small voice.

There was a rich chuckle. "At your service," he said. "And how nice to meet your friend, too. Ava, is it?"

"Screw you," snapped Ava.

Landry Douglas rocked back on his heels. "Yes," he said in a mocking tone, "I see exactly why Glory disapproves of you. Both of you, really. I understand you gave my man and his accomplice a good deal of trouble." His smarmy smile changed to a tight-lipped sneer. "I don't much care for troublesome girls."

"Hey, asshole," said Ava. "Better make that troublesome *women*."

"You think this is a joke?" barked Landry Douglas, his face suddenly hard and filled with anger. "A game?" He shifted his gaze to Carmela. "Tell her what happens when you don't play by the rules."

"Whose rules?" asked Carmela, her voice dripping with scorn. "*Your* rules? What a sicko." She shook her head as if to indicate that Landry Douglas, even in his power position, didn't mean a whit to her. "Jeez, why is it every peckerwood with a gun in his hand thinks he's the next crime kingpin?"

Ava shrugged. "Search me, but it's the darn truth."

Carmela's words may have been casually sarcastic, but her mind was working overtime, trying to put together the pieces.

Landry Douglas? she thought. *What's Landry Douglas got to do with all this?* Then she remembered. He was the CEO of Terrapro Oil. Which meant he was probably the guy selling those oil leases that Shamus was so hot for. And just maybe his oil fields were . . . What? Located northwest of Baton Rouge? Just like on Uncle Henry's map?

"Skyline," said Carmela, dredging up the single word she remembered hearing from a very quick exchange between Shamus and Glory. "Oil leases." She suddenly recalled the shirt she'd found in her wicker hamper this morning. The one with the gas or oil smell on it. Or had it been crude oil?

Landry Douglas's hard eyes fixed on Carmela. "You had to go and make that stupid little book, didn't you? Had to add in Henry Meechum's little map and then display the damn thing all over town. At the funeral, in your shop window. Sooner or later, someone was going to put two and two together. That old man's murder and his little map pinpointing what's going on up in Pointe Coupee Parish."

"You were drilling for oil and came up with . . ." began Carmela.

"Dry holes," hissed Landry Douglas. "Every damn one we drilled in the Skyline field came up dry."

"So . . . what?" asked Carmela. "The bank was going to call in your loan?"

"Henry Meechum wanted to. But I'd already launched my oil lease scheme. Unfortunately, that wily old man started figuring things out. That's why I had to get rid of him."

"And then you kidnapped Shamus," said Carmela.

"I needed more financing," shrugged Landry Douglas. He said it in a matter-of-fact tone, as if kidnapping people were a part of everyday business. "I thought I'd pull my hair out for sure when you two girls showed up like the proverbial cavalry. But then Glory Meechum, bless her silly soul, came to my rescue." Now Landry Douglas was almost chortling. "She was delighted to buy into my offering of oil leases and receive a generous return on investment. And poor unsuspecting Shamus thought my oil deal was so sweet he agreed to tell all his friends and banking clients about it, too."

"Do you know what he's talking about?" Ava muttered to Carmela.

"Oil futures," said Carmela. "Some kind of Ponzi scheme where you pay off the initial investors with

281

money you receive from the next tier of investors. And so on."

"Oh man," said Ava. "Kind of like a chain letter. Only with money."

Landry Douglas continued to stare at Carmela with his mirthless, murderous smile. "You know what's really funny? I probably didn't have to kidnap that worthless husband of yours, after all." He leered at Carmela. "Although, if you'd kept your nose out of things I probably could have done you a real favor. Garden District widows usually get awfully fine settlements. To say nothing of that lovely family tomb that's just sitting there waiting for the next Meechum to roll in." He barked a harsh laugh. "Whoever that may be."

Carmela stared at Landry Douglas, and a white-hot fury burned inside her brain. She fervently wished for a weapon, any weapon. This murderer, this cold-blooded killer, wasn't even remotely sorry about Uncle Henry. In fact, Landry Douglas was probably a borderline sociopath. And under the guise of a business deal was now going to bilk hundreds of innocent people out of their money. People who had already tapped deeply into their life savings to help rebuild New Orleans.

"Now we're all going to shut up and take a little drive," announced Landry Douglas. He made a half turn, glanced toward the back of the open warehouse. "Buford," he called, "get out here with some handcuffs."

Buford came limping out of the darkness. An angry red welt puckered at the back of his neck, and Carmela took some satisfaction in that. Buford, much to his credit, seemed genuinely wary of Carmela. He handed a set of handcuffs to Landry Douglas, then stepped back, as though Carmela might come spinning toward him like a crazed ninja and attack him again.

"Buford, you imbecile," bellowed Landry Douglas. "*Two* sets of handcuffs."

Buford loped off as Landry Douglas held the cuffs out toward Ava. "You." He waved the gun at her. "Come here."

A weapon, thought Carmela. *If only I had* . . .

She suddenly remembered the X-Acto blade. The stainless steel cutting tool that Ava had stashed in her handbag earlier.

I do have a weapon. In my handbag. Do I dare?

Carmela's handbag dangled from her arm. A little leather bag stamped to look like snakeskin. Innocent-looking, yes, but if she could get it open and wield the X-Acto blade . . .

As Ava stepped resentfully toward Landry Douglas, Carmela carefully snicked open the bag's catch, dug her hand in and felt around. Her fingers touched lip gloss, comb, a tin of mints, and then . . . *Ouch.*

"You don't have to do this," Ava was telling Landry Douglas. "Believe me, this is a really bad idea. You're probably going to end up going to prison for a long time. And I think living conditions inside Angola are awfully dreary."

Landry Douglas barked a harsh laugh. "Shut up and hold out your hands. That's it, put them together!" He held the gun loosely as he fumbled with the handcuffs.

That was the tiny break Carmela needed. She wrapped her fingers around the cold, metal handle of the X-Acto, then whipped the knife from her handbag. Slashing violently at Landry Douglas's gun hand, she came down hard across the back of it, putting as much force into her effort as she could muster.

Caught completely unprepared by Carmela's deft and daring attack, Landry Douglas watched in horror as a viscous line of blood bubbled up from a cut that ran almost to the bone. Then he let loose a bloodcurdling scream and doubled over in pain.

"Jump in the car!" yelled Carmela as Landry Douglas stumbled away, still howling, cradling his wounded hand.

"What?" shrilled Ava, still caught in major panic mode. "The car?"

"I think the keys are still in the car!" screamed Carmela. She dove for the driver's side, found the keys dangling from the ignition. "Yeah, they're here. Come on, let's move!" Jumping into the Eldorado, Carmela hastily pulled the door shut and cranked the engine hard as Ava ran around to the other side and flung herself into the passenger seat.

Just as Carmela jammed the Eldorado into gear, the overhead lights blinked out, plunging them into total darkness.

"Now what?" panted Ava beside her.

Carmela's fingertips skittered across the dashboard, hitting switches, turning on the radio and the windshield wipers until she finally located the lights. "Buckle your seat belt and hang on," yelled Carmela as she gunned the engine, spinning the wheels on slick cement. Then the car lunged forward.

Maneuvering the Eldorado in looping circles inside the giant warehouse, Carmela searched frantically for a way out.

"How do we get out of here?" she yelled.

"I don't know, I don't know," Ava yelled back.

They made a giant oval, running fast as though they were on a tight Indy track.

"Push that little button thing on the visor!" yelled Ava.

"I'm trying, I'm trying," Carmela yelled back. "But nothing's happening!"

"Watch out!" warned Ava, as Buford Gallier suddenly appeared before them, his angry, tight face illuminated in the high beams. As they flew by, he swung something at them that looked like it could be an ax. "Lordy, what on earth . . . ?" cried Ava.

But Buford had found his mark and a resounding *crash* echoed from the front of the car, followed by the *tinkle* of breaking glass. Then the right front headlight went dark.

"Damn!" said Carmela. "Jerk smashed a headlight." She muscled the wheel to the left, and the car lurched in the opposite direction. Which caused Ava to slide across the wide front seat, slamming directly into Carmela's right shoulder.

"Uh, in case you didn't notice," gasped Ava, pulling herself back to her side of the car, "you're driving in circles."

"Gotta find a way out," said Carmela, trying to fight a rising sense of panic.

"Oh man!" moaned Ava. "This is like being on a Tilt-A-Whirl and I always barf on Tilt-A-Whirls!"

"Then kindly aim the other way," Carmela told her. They could hardly hear themselves over the roar of the motor, the squeal of the tires, and the shouting of what had to be Buford the driver come back to haunt them.

Suddenly, Landry Douglas popped up in front of the single headlight, looking all the world like an angry rabbit in a shooting gallery! Carmela veered around him but not before she caught sight of his bloody hand waving at them, saw his anger-crazed eyes. He looked like some horrible Halloween apparition stumbling after them.

"Aaaaargh!" screamed Ava. "Gotta get out of here!"

"I'm trying!" yelled Carmela as she cranked the wheel again, took the car around in yet another fruitless oval.

"Good lord, there he is again!" yelled Ava as Landry Douglas, the angry specter, rose up in front of them once more.

Carmela swerved to avoid him, but a loud, hollow *thunk* sounded against the front fender. Then a few drops of red spattered the windshield.

"Cripes!" screamed Ava. "I think you just killed him!"

Bang! The retort of a gun boomed loudly inside the warehouse.

"He's not dead!" yelled Carmela. "If he's shooting at us, he'd not dead!"

"Damn," said Ava, "he's like a zombie. Just won't lay down and quit!"

"Enough is enough!" yelled Carmela as she suddenly spun the car in the direction of the oversized garage door. "Seat belt!" she cried to Ava. "Put your seat belt on! Buckle in!"

"What are you gonna do?" screamed Ava as another burst of surround-sound gunfire filled the air.

"The exit!" Carmela screamed back. "Gonna aim for the exit!"

"That door's shut tight as a drum!" shrilled Ava as she pulled herself into a tight crouch and threw her hands over her head to protect herself. "There is no exit!"

There was a fierce rending of metal against metal as the hurtling Cadillac struck the garage door dead-on. A loud whine filled the air as Carmela kept pumping down on the gas pedal. And as the Cadillac shuddered madly, the door began to crumple like a cheap accordion.

They crunched their way past metal splinters that threatened to shear off the top of the car. And then, wonder of wonders, were outside. The engine coughing, internal mechanisms grinding like gears filled with sand.

Moonlight streamed down, illuminating the weedy parking lot in front of them.

Glancing over her shoulder, Carmela stared at the gaping hole in the door and heaved a giant sigh of relief as the Cadillac limped forward.

"Guess what," she said to a still-panting Ava. "There's an exit now."

Chapter 27

As a result of Carmela's rather distressed and disjointed phone call, Detective Edgar Babcock had swooped in to take charge. Now everyone sat huddled around a large round table in the recently commandeered Rex Room at Antoine's. Everyone being Edgar Babcock, District Attorney Stanley Thyson, Carmela, Shamus, Ava, and Ryder.

There was no sign of Zoe Carvelle.

"I'm sorry to tell you this, Shamus," began Edgar Babcock, "but Glory and your Uncle Henry were underwriting Terrapro Oil."

Carmela cast a hard sideways glance at Shamus. "That's your buddy, Landry Douglas," she told him. "The same asshole who *kidnapped* you. Who *murdered* Uncle Henry." She fairly spat the words at him. Earlier, she'd told the group about how she'd been attacked last night and ended up in the river.

"This is all so hard to digest," muttered Shamus. He looked crestfallen and ashamed, like a kid who'd been called to the principal's office.

District Attorney Stanley Thyson cleared his throat. He was a small, thin man with wire-rimmed glasses who looked like he meant business. "First thing tomorrow we'll have forensic accountants in place at Crescent City Bank. They'll tear through all the records."

"*Forensic* accountants?" asked Ava. "There really are forensic accountants?"

"Absolutely," said Edgar Babcock.

"Tearing through records," Carmela said to Shamus. "Glory's going to love that."

Shamus hunched forward and dropped his head in his hands. "This is like a bad dream," he murmured.

"Hey pal," said Ava, gazing across the table at him. "You shoulda been there to experience the knives, handcuffs, flying bullets, and smashing axes. What your wife and I just experienced was the *real* nightmare."

"I'm still not clear on why Landry Douglas was after Carmela," Shamus said to Edgar Babcock. He cleared his throat nervously, avoided meeting Carmela's eyes.

Edgar Babcock allowed himself the luxury of a faint chuckle. "I'd imagine Landry Douglas must have been awfully jittery to find that a book made to celebrate the man he'd murdered also pinpointed the exact locale of his phony oil wells."

Ryder Bowman was gripping Ava's hand, looking very supportive, taking it all in. Now he spoke up.

"Douglas was afraid that map in the reconstructed book might be a major tip-off."

"Exactly," said Babcock. "Which is why Landry Douglas went after Carmela. Get rid of her, get rid of the book. That was his primary motive."

The motif was the motive, Carmela thought to herself. *Weird.*

"How long could this Ponzi scheme have gone on?" asked Ryder. "I mean, don't these perpetrators generally get found out?"

"Depending on how good their sales pitch is," said Babcock, "and how gullible or greedy the investors are, these schemes can sometimes stretch on for years. With nobody the wiser."

Shamus's shoes clunked against his wooden chair as he stumbled to his feet. "Are we finished here?" he asked in a too-loud voice. "Because I really need to speak to Carmela privately."

Babcock nodded pleasantly. "We can take this up again in the morning."

"Agreed," said the district attorney. "There'll be lots to do."

Carmela, Shamus, Ava, and Ryder trooped through Antoine's main dining room and outside onto St. Louis Street. No one spoke until they got outside, and Ava put an arm around Carmela, gave her a kiss on the cheek. "See you later, *cher.* Go home, get some sleep."

Ryder also gave Carmela a gentle peck. "Take care, call us if you need anything."

Neither one said a word to Shamus, and he glared

resentfully as they wandered off.

But Carmela wasn't paying any attention to Shamus. Above the Mississippi River, the blue-black night sky was suddenly alive with fireworks. *Pops* and *snaps* rang out as streams of red, gold, and blue burst in starlike clusters and seemed to hang there forever. Then, as if traveling in slow motion, the fragmented sparkles slid downward into the dark river and disappeared.

Strains of Aaron Copland's "*Fanfare for the Common Man*" drifted up from Jackson Square where the New Orleans Symphony Orchestra had begun a concert that was carefully choreographed with the bursts of fireworks.

Shamus tugged lightly at Carmela's sleeve. "It's been a long day," he said. "Let's go home."

"You were sitting with Zoe Carvelle," said Carmela, still gazing at the night sky. "I saw you."

Shamus's words were even and measured. "Zoe doesn't mean a thing to me. Truly. I ran into her, and we decided to have a quick drink. It was a casual thing, really."

Decided to have a drink, thought Carmela.

She wondered how many other women Shamus would run into and decide to have a casual drink with. Five? Ten? More than that? Did the number, whether it was one or one hundred, even matter?

Like a warm light snapping on in a front window to welcome someone home, Carmela suddenly realized that any future decisions she made really wouldn't have much to do with Shamus. They'd be about her.

What kind of life she wanted. What kind of trust level she was comfortable with. What actions she herself chose to take.

Carmela tilted her head back as a silver-bright burst of fireworks did a slow dance in the sky, illuminating the brick buildings of the French Quarter in pure, white light. She let the moment wash over her, savoring the beauty and the throbbing pulse of this crazy yet courageous 200-year-old neighborhood. *The French Quarter has a way of getting in your blood,* she thought. *Of insinuating itself in your viscera.*

"Come on," said Shamus, a bit more impatiently this time. "Time to go home."

Carmela turned and smiled at Shamus. It was a smile tinged with sadness, for she would always love him, would always be charmed by his boyish exuberance. "I don't think so," she told him gently.

"What are you . . . ?" stammered Shamus. Fear and frustration suddenly flooded his face. Shamus wasn't a good loser, but he could tell when a situation was hopeless.

"The French Quarter," Carmela whispered. "This is where I belong." Her eyes again sought the outline of the venerable old buildings as they shimmered against the night sky. "This is my home."

Scrapbook, Stamping, and
Craft Tips from Laura Childs

ADD PHOTO WINDOWS
TO YOUR SCRAPBOOKS AND CARDS

Cut out three sides of a window using an X-Acto knife, then fold open the fourth side and make a solid crease. Place this sheet on top of another sheet of paper or your scrapbook page. Lightly mark the boundaries of the window area with a pencil. Adhere your photo in place, replace the top sheet, and fix together.

PAPER SCRAPBOOK JACKET

You put book jackets on books, so why not dress up your favorite scrapbook albums or journals? Start by cutting a piece of paper to the exact height of your album and three times the width of the album plus the width of the spine. Lay your album in the middle of the paper and fold in the back fold to one-half the width of the album. Now wrap the rest of the paper around the spine and front cover. Pull tight, then fold the remaining paper inside the front cover.

ALTERED BOOKS

Creating an altered book is one of the hottest projects

going today. Start with a book that's ready to be retired but still has a fairly sturdy binding. Then think of that book as a blank canvas, something that you will turn into a one-of-a-kind piece of art. Pick a theme—mystery, family tree, memorabilia, reliquary, etc.—and work from there. Sometimes the subject of the book itself can spark a theme. For example, an old cookbook from the thirties or forties could inspire you to carve out niches for antique spice tins or bottle caps, or add old family recipes, baking visuals, and antique advertising. Old church hymnals are perfect if you want to pursue a religious theme.

CD BOOKS

Take two old CDs and use them to trace four rounds of your favorite paper. Now rough up the sides of the CDs so your glue will adhere. Glue on a two-inch hinge of yarn or fiber to bind the CDs together like a book, then glue on your four paper rounds. Now decorate the cover, insides, and back cover with photos, bits of map, or elegant paper—whatever you want to turn your CD book into an invitation, a piece of art, or a little round book that holds a picture or poem. Don't forget to add beads, ribbons, or embellishments to the front cover. Hint: Create a CD book using leather-look paper and use a piece of leather as the hinge. Inside might be an image of a horse or photos of a western vacation.

WATERCOLOR IMPRESSIONS WITH RUBBER STAMPS

Rubber stamps aren't just for traditional stamping. You can use them to create shimmering, almost ethereal images on cards and tags. Here's how: Select one of your favorite rubber stamps, perhaps one with a floral motif. Then take a couple watercolor pencils, dip them in water, and apply color generously to your rubber stamp. Now simply press your stamp to a piece of paper. With a little experimenting you can create elegant art pieces.

FAST TRACK ALBUMS

Want to make a special album but you're pressed for time? Buy one of the preprinted accordion albums that are readily available and use that as your starting point. Add photos and extra embellishments and in no time at all you'll have a piece that's perfect as a gift or keepsake.

SCRAPBOOKED GIFT BAGS

Instead of using traditional gift wrap for gifts, why not buy plain white or kraft paper bags and scrapbook them? Create a collage with scraps of paper or select of theme. A baby shower gift tucked in a white bag that's been decorated with baby motifs, ribbon, and embellishments becomes extra special.

Chicken Gumbo Ya-Ya

1 tsp. oil
¼ cup flour
3 cups chicken broth
1½ lbs. chicken breasts, diced
1 cup potatoes, cubed
1 cup onions, chopped
¼ cup celery, chopped
1 small carrot, grated
4 cloves garlic, finely minced
1 bay leaf
½ tsp. thyme
½ tsp. black pepper

Pour oil into good-sized pan and heat on medium. Stir in flour and allow to cook, stirring constantly, until flour begins to turn golden brown. Slowly stir in chicken broth and cook for about 2 minutes, making sure there are no lumps. Add the rest of the ingredients. Bring to a boil, cover, then reduce heat and let simmer for 30 minutes. Serve in bowls or over rice.

Carmela's Beer and Brown Sugar Sauce

¼ cup dark beer
¼ cup brown sugar
¼ cup light soy sauce
¼ cup Worcestershire sauce
½ cup ketchup or barbecue sauce
1 Tbsp. minced onion

Mix all ingredients together in a saucepan and simmer over low to medium heat for 25 minutes. Serve warm over broiled or grilled steak.

Hot and Cheesy Breakfast Casserole

1 lb. ground sausage
¼ cup chopped onions
2 cups milk
1 cup shredded cheddar cheese
1 dash hot sauce
6 slices white bread, trimmed and cubed
1 tsp. salt
8 eggs

In large pan, brown sausage and onions together until cooked. Add milk, cheese, hot sauce, bread, and salt. Gently beat eggs and add to mixture. Pour into a greased 9"x13" baking dish and bake at 350° for 40 minutes or until set. Yields 4–6 servings.

Ava's Dixie Julep

2 oz. bourbon
1 tsp. powdered sugar
3 sprigs mint

Combine bourbon and powdered sugar in a tall collins glass. Fill with ice and stir gently until glass is frosted. Add the three sprigs of mint and serve with a straw.

Roast Beef Po'boy

12" French baguette
Sliced roast beef
Chopped lettuce
Sliced tomato
Grilled onions
Creole mustard
Remoulade or aioli sauce
Pickles

Cut the roll lengthwise and hollow out the bottom half. Toast or grill, then add roast beef, fixin's, and condiments. You really can't go wrong here. In fact, po'boys come in an endless variety of ingredients. You can create roast chicken breast po'boys, grilled shrimp po'boys, ham po'boys, grilled salmon po'boys, shredded barbecue po'boys, sausage po'boys, and even hamburger po'boys. Just get creative with the condiments and pile them on until your po'boy is good and dressed!

Chicken Salad Eulalie

4 chicken breasts, cooked
1½ cups mayonnaise
2 Tbsp. curry powder
1 Tbsp. olive oil
1 Tbsp. orange juice
3 cups red seedless grapes
1 cup chopped walnuts
1 tsp. black pepper

Dice chicken into a bowl. Mix mayo, curry powder, olive oil, and orange juice in a separate bowl, then add to chicken. Toss in grapes and walnuts, add pepper. Cover and refrigerate for at least 3 hours.

Spicy Sausage Balls

2 lbs. spicy hot ground sausage
½ cup brown sugar
½ cup wine vinegar
1 cup catsup
1 Tbsp. soy sauce
1 Tbsp. Worchestershire sauce
½ tsp. garlic powder

Roll sausage into small balls, then place under broiler for ten minutes until light brown. Drain carefully on paper towels. Combine remaining ingredients in medium-sized saucepan and heat until bubbly. Add broiled sausage balls to sauce and simmer for 2 to 3 minutes. Serve hot.

Baby Boo's Baby Food Cookies
(For dogs only!)

2 jars beef baby food (2.5 oz. each)
¼ cup dry milk powder
¼ cup Cream of Wheat

Combine all 3 ingredients in a bowl and mix well. Roll mixture into balls and place on well-greased cookie sheet. Flatten slightly with fork, then bake in a

350° oven for 15 minutes or until brown. Cool on a wire rack (while dogs watch eagerly), then store in refrigerator or freezer, or feed to waiting dogs. They surely do love 'em!

Chicken and Broccoli Divan

2 cups broccoli, cooked and cut up
1½ cups cubed chicken, cooked
1 can cream of broccoli soup
⅓ cup milk
½ cup cheddar cheese, shredded
1 Tbsp. melted butter
¼ cup dry bread or cracker crumbs

Arrange broccoli in a shallow casserole dish, top with chicken. Combine soup and milk and pour over chicken, then sprinkle with cheese. Combine butter and bread crumbs, then sprinkle on top. Bake for 15 minutes at 425°.

Bayou Buttermilk Biscuits

2 cups flour
1 Tbsp. baking powder
¼ tsp. salt
1 tsp. sugar
¼ tsp. baking soda
3 Tbsp. shortening
1 cup buttermilk

Mix all dry ingredients together, then cut in shortening until it resembles a coarse meal. Add the buttermilk and mix to form dough. Turn out on a lightly floured surface and knead for one minute. Pat or roll out gently to ½" thick, then cut out approximately 12 rounds, using a glass or biscuit cutter. Place rounds on an ungreased baking sheet and bake in a 400° oven for 12 to 14 minutes or until golden.

Center Point Publishing
600 Brooks Road ● PO Box 1
Thorndike ME 04986-0001 USA

(207) 568-3717

US & Canada:
1 800 929-9108